AXEL

DIABLO DISCIPLES
ONE PERCENTER MC

By **V. THEIA**

AXEL

This is a work of fiction. Names, characters, places, and events are the products of the author's
imagination or are used fictitiously. Any resemblance to persons, living or dead, is coincidental.

Names and characters are the property of the author and may not be duplicated. The use of any real company and/or product names is for literary effect only. All other trademarks and copyrights are the property of their respective owners.

Axel

Cover photo: Depositphotos.com
Cover Design: V. Theia. ©2022
Published by V. Theia 2022
All Rights Reserved

DEDICATION

To my gals who have found their tribe in our book community. This one is for you!

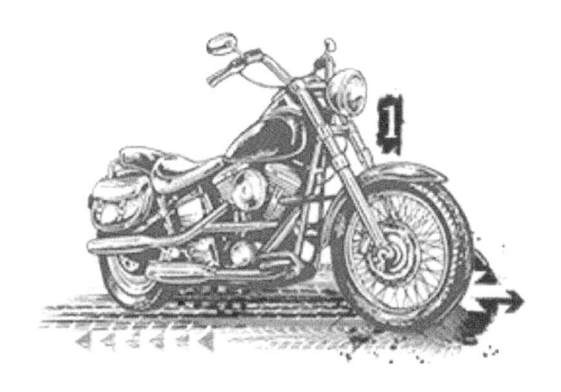

Axel
BEFORE

Brutality came with the job description of being an MC president.

Mark 'Axel' Tucker wasn't a violent man by nature.

He didn't get off on bones breaking, and blood splattered over his clothes. But he knew how to handle himself and his business when people stepped out of line or tried to get one over him. He had zero tolerance for bullshit and backstabbers.

"Clean this garbage up," he spat, looking down at the wasted pile of shit that was once one of his dealers who'd thought it was clever to skim off the top and no one would notice. He'd worked the piece of shit over with his fists, preferring teaching a lesson the old-fashioned way.

Until he'd turned twenty, Axel had been dirt poor. A kid who didn't know where his next meal was coming from. His teen years were spent permanently hungry, never having good sneakers or new clothes. So for some piece of shit to assume Axel didn't know, down to the last cent, how much money his club was bringing in was a bad mistake.

The guy was bleeding and bruised, hanging onto life by the plaque of his teeth. He'd begged for his life like the rat he was. Axel didn't feel gleeful for putting the hurt on someone; he didn't have Ruin's constitution for torture. But examples had to be made of traitors, and he was bitterly disgusted that he had discovered someone untrustworthy in his employ.

Little maggot got off lightly because he was still being sent home to his family alive and not dumped in the river. Moreover, he had enough on his plate already dealing with a serial maniac who'd been dropping dead bodies on their doorsteps for weeks to frame the Diablos.

One day, Axel would catch a break. But today wasn't that day.

Two of his prospects rushed forward and dragged the guy to his feet. Blood dripped out of him like a faucet.

"Get your family packed up and fuck off out of my town, Will. If we see your face, it won't go as nicely as now. You understand?"

"Yeah, yeah, Axel, I'm sorry, man." He dripped blood from his lips. Excuses and apologies were ignored.

"Get him out of my sight." He issued with authority, and the prospects dragged the guy over to the rig to drop him off.

"What happened to honor among criminals?" asked Chains. Axel's VP was just as disgusted.

"Fucking Gen Z."

Behind them, Reno chuffed a laugh. "Thank fuck I scraped in as a millennial. What are you, Chains, a boomer?"

"Fuck you, kid." Laughed Chains. "Now, we heading back to the clubhouse? Because I have business with my future Mrs."

Axel smirked, leaving the scene behind Chains' strip club, The Den, and got into step with his friend and VP as they headed toward their bikes. "Is Monroe giving you trouble?"

"She's as ornery as that cat that wandered into the club last winter and scratched everyone up when we tried to feed it."

Axel smirked. He wished his friend luck with his future wife. He still didn't know why Chains had put his neck into the noose and volunteered for a marriage of convenience with a business associate's daughter.

It sure as hell was not something Axel would sign up for.

His one turn at domestic bliss was more like a Freddie nightmare.

His daughter, Roux, was the only good thing from his short-lived relationship with Selena.

No seventeen-year-old kid wanted to be a father, but Roux was the best accident of his life. And now he had two hellions to call him Grampy.

A grandfather at forty-two. No wonder his bones creaked when he got out of bed each morning. Those kids were aging him before his time, but he wouldn't have it any other way.

Family and love were Axel's driving forces.

Everything he's ever done was for the good of those he cared for.

Roux might now be under the care of her husband, The Butcher, a member of the Renegade Souls MC, and Axel knew that the man had already been through hell for Roux and would go through more. But that didn't mean Axel took his foot off the father pedal. He'd untangled himself from a disastrous deal with the Mexicans when they firebombed his house a few years back. And now he was about to cut free from Donahue's agreement just as soon as the ink dried on Chains' marriage license and the Irish got their criminal asses across the ocean to set a new, more lucrative deal in stone.

Axel was sick to death of trading with boys pretending to be entrepreneurs. But, at least, he knew the Irish had their code of honor, much like himself.

He wasn't looking for a quiet life, that was for the average Joe. He enjoyed gaining money by any means necessary. Besides, he'd be bored in a day if his job comprised of clocking in and out.

His outfit might not be as big as some MCs around the country, and he was okay with that. He liked his finger on the pulse. But, the bigger they expanded by adding new chapters, he would lose some of that control.

The prospects went to do their job dropping off the thieving scum. Chains climbed on his bike. Axel got into his RAM and told Chains he'd see him later. He wanted to pick up food before he headed back to the club. Being away for a few days in Colorado to celebrate his birthday with his girl and her family meant he was behind on shit.

Axel Tucker hated desk work more than anything; he'd rather have his eyelids stapled to a table most days than sit behind a desk and deal with the bland side of owning numerous enterprises. Only a carton of noodles would appease him and his hungry belly. While waiting for his order, something outside the Chinese restaurant caught his attention.

At first, he thought he was seeing things.

Had to be, because no dummy in this town would ever attempt to break into his truck.

They'd have to have a screw loose to even think about fucking with anything Axel owned. He was well known. Not only because of his MC status, but he was also a landlord to many of the Laketon's townsfolk, both domestically and privately.

It was said people feared him, but he'd always taken care of the town and plowed enough money to subsidize when the economy tanked.

He'd stopped hard drugs; he never shook down businesses for a cut of their profits, and the club was sometimes hired as muscle to resolve trouble for those who couldn't give their own beat downs.

As he stared out the restaurant window at the bundle of clothing attempting to break into his truck, his feet rooted to the floor. Stunned for a second.

They were checking all the RAM doors. It was the colder months, and Utah got hit hard with the icy fronts during the fall, but the person was dressed like they were going on a six-month expedition to Iceland. The hooded overcoat looked four sizes too big, and the wool skull cap was pulled down on their forehead. Most likely, it was a teen trying their luck.

"Un-fucking-believable," he murmured as he watched them take a tool out of their coat and fiddle with the door until it popped open. He didn't think they'd continue to break in. It was obvious his RAM was the new model and, therefore, worth a fucking ton. Any thief, even not knowing whose truck it belonged to, would be stupid to go for something new. But there Axel stood as he watched the baggage of clothing climb onto the tall step and haul themselves into his truck.

Axel turned to the counter and rapped his ringed fingers to gain the server's attention. "I'll be back in a minute."

"Sure thing, Axel. Carl is wrapping it up to go now."

He strode out of the restaurant, standing by the opened truck door while the body sprawled over the passenger seat, rooting through the glove compartment. He watched them palm something and wiggle backward.

That was when they encountered the bulk of Axel.

"Finished robbing me, have you?" he growled.

Anger and disbelief bubbled inside of him.

The body froze like a deer caught in a hunter's trap.

When he got his hands on them, he realized they weighed next to nothing, just a bag of bones in oversized clothes.

"Get your goddamn hands off me before I kill you." the person threatened, and Axel realized the voice was feminine as he thought, a teenager.

"I'd like to see you try, you thieving shit. Get the hell out right now." He helped by dragging the body down the steep height, catching them before they landed in a heap.

They went wild in Axel's hands, trying to fight themselves free. He caught elbows in his ribs and jaw before stopping the flailing by crowding the body against the truck. He blocked the legs with his knees and shackled both arms with a hand, and with his free one, he yanked down the face scarf.

She looked too young to be on the streets.

Axel saw peeks of colorful red hair. Her skin was too pale, and when he grasped her chin to hold her head still, she was icy cold as she bared even white teeth at him like an animal.

"Don't touch me," she hissed. "I didn't take anything."

"Is that so?" He asked. Some anger disappeared because what kind of fucking parent let their kid roam the streets like this bag of bones? "Open your hand. Let me see what you're holding."

Guilt entered her green eyes, and Axel freed her arms but kept her barricaded so she couldn't run off. He saw how they darted left and right, gauging if she could push him out of the way and make her escape.

He weighed two-thirty pounds of lean muscle and also towered over her by at least a foot. She was small and too thin. If she could push him down, that meant Axel was already dead.

Axel waited until she unlocked her fingers and opened the palm, showing a tightly scrunched five dollars.

Now he was surprised.

He took it from her, smoothed it, and held it between two fingers.

"This is it?"

"Yes." she snapped, "you have it back now, so can I go?"

It didn't make sense. "You break into my forty grand truck to steal five dollars? Empty your pockets."

She bristled, and if looks could kill, Axel would be a corpse in biker boots. He wasn't playing around with this thief; he had a belly to fill and a night of paperwork.

"Either empty your fucking pockets, or I do it for you."

"You dare touch me, and I'll scream so fucking loud your ears will bleed while they drag your ass off to a cop car."

Axel chuckled. The balls on this one, she kept surprising him.

"I would only have to hold you upside down and let everything fall out. Now show me your goddamn pockets."

"That's all I took, you giant idiot man."

With the passenger door still wide open, he pinned the thief to the side of the truck and leaned in to yank the glove compartment open with the other hand. He always kept a roll of money, probably around six hundred, give or take.

Color him surprised it was still there.

"All you took was five bucks?"

"Yes."

"For what?"

"To get a sandwich."

Fuck's sake. Something gnarly twisted in his gut at the challenging way she held her chin high, like she was embarrassed by the admission.

"Why didn't you take the entire roll?"

"I wanted food, not to buy a yacht on the gold coast."

Funny little shit.

Without thinking, he grabbed her to throw her into the passenger seat.

Panic covered the waif's face even as the gloved hand tried to shove by him. It was a wasted effort because Axel pushed harder and kept the woman in the seat.

"This is kidnapping!"

"Hardly. Stay the fuck there, don't dare try to move."

"You're not taking me to the cops. I'll say you kidnapped me."

The cops. Now that was hilarious.

Axel wouldn't voluntarily go to the law. Ever since he became the President of the Diablo Disciples MC and walked his own lawful path, the badge holders had made it their mission to pin any crimes on the club they could.

It had worked in the past. Not so much in recent years, and not now he had a crooked cop in his pocket to keep him abreast of the shit the law was doing.

"You try to move, and you'll see what happens, and it won't be the cops." He warned. Axel watched those green eyes flair with temper, but she had some control over her tongue because she clamped her mouth shut and pulled the scarf back around her face, masking most of her features again.

Axel let off a shrill whistle and gained the attention of the restaurant hostess. He motioned with two fingers, and she came to the door carrying a white takeout bag. He fished in his pocket to pay, but the woman smiled. "It's on the house, Axel."

"Tell Carl thanks." A few months back, he'd made a problem right for the chef when he encountered a wannabe gangster trying to shake him down for protection. That guy didn't like the talk Axel had with him, so Ruin, his club enforcer, got to play for a while until the guy was no longer a problem. He handed the hostess a tip for bringing the food out. She gave him sex eyes, but he had a bigger issue to deal with than thinking about his dick. He slung the food into the back seat and slipped behind the wheel.

"Where are you taking me?" she asked finally, after he'd been driving for a minute.

"Home with me," he told her through his clenched teeth, surprising himself. Because the intelligent thing would be to leave her on the sidewalk, let the waif have the five bucks, and leave the problem behind. "You stole from me. So now you owe me, do yourself a favor and shut up."

He was going to blame the lack of thought on his fucking hunger.

Scarlett
BEFORE

Leaving behind a home life immersed in coercive control wasn't as easy as it looked on TV.

Escaping was closer to the truth.

Scarlett Bass had finally reached her limit. Oppressive rules, forcing obedience, and so much more. She was glad to be leaving it behind.

Running away meant planning for a long time.

Weighing up the logistics. Things like what to pack and only to take essentials she could carry in a shoulder backpack. It meant squirreling away any money she could.

And though Scarlett held down a 9-5 job in the local market, she rarely saw any of that money. Her family were big believers in *sharing* as part of controlling her.

Not that it applied to her five older brothers.

Rules were different for men.

They wielded power and control. The women in her community were told what to do, where to go, and what not to do. It had taken her a long time to realize it, but Scarlett had grown up in a modern-day cult.

Oh, no one ever mentioned it like that.

But it amounted to the same.

She wasn't so dumb that she couldn't recognize the glaring warning when she finally realized her family was despicable.

It might not have religion as its driving factor, as most cults do, but her father's word with everyone was as strong as God's. So when rumblings had started about her being married, she'd accelerated her escape plans. She'd stolen and plotted like she was part of Tom Cruise's team on Mission Impossible.

And she only knew about that movie franchise because she'd sneak out sometimes to go to the local theater. God forbid she be allowed to do anything normal, like have friends outside their community, or see a crappy movie without it influencing her.

She only knew of any movie because each one she'd seen over the years was seen by deception. There was no way a woman her age should have a list of rules of do's and don'ts as long as her leg.

To be fair, she was only five-foot-three on a good day, but her legs were still in proportion for her height, so it was still a sizeable list she'd had to adhere to her whole life. And she'd run out of patience.

Stupidly, Scarlett had watched her mom follow her father's lead but had thought when she'd grown, it wouldn't be the same for her. She'd be allowed to be her own woman, go out into the world, move to an unfamiliar state, to date men of her choosing.

Ha. How wrong she'd been.

The Bass' were emotionally void, who wouldn't know love if it bit them on the ankles. Family loyalty came not from love and affection, but from fear of stepping out of line.

But in their community, they were classed as a hierarchy.

They not only had a ton of money but clout, too.

People came to her father for financial advice and marriage arrangements for their daughters. It was so archaic that it made Scarlett sick to know those regressive people existed in a modern era.

Not being permitted to go to college was her first clue into how her life would be. Being home-schooled hadn't been awful, though she missed out on friends who didn't live in their twelve-block radius community. The day her father arranged a minimum wage job behind her back killed a little something inside her. She knew then her life wasn't her own. All her hopes and dreams were dead.

Prearranged marriages were a big thing in her world. Money was the primary factor.

Having your father tell you who you would marry was archaic and beyond logic.

Only the girls. Of course. Her brothers had more freedom than Scarlett.

They could fuck around with the outside girls and then choose a neighborhood girl to marry and pop out their babies.

She'd never met a rule she couldn't break and do it slyly. So, while her family thought she was a good girl, Scarlett started sneaking out of the house at a young age, just for the fun of it. But then her teens hit, and she'd wanted boyfriends like every other ordinary girl. But that was out of the question under her father's regime. So she took it upon herself to experience everything. That meant stealing kisses from eager boys in the neighborhood. And then, when she'd wanted to experience more, she'd slipped out at nighttime and had wonderful flings.

Oh, sure, none of those boys had been suitable for her long-term, but she hadn't wanted perfect, she'd wanted an exciting adventure. Anything to make her forget the monotony of her existence.

And the best part was, she'd never been caught.

The day her father told Scarlett she was to marry a man she'd thought of as her uncle, a man in his freaking late sixties, she'd laughed in his face. So sure he was joking.

He couldn't even choose a guy in her age range. 'Uncle' Marcus was not even on the list of likely men she'd consider. She'd nearly thrown up in her mouth when she was informed it was no laughing matter, and she better adjust quickly.

There was no reasoning with her mother. She was too far under her father's thumb to speak out in her daughter's defense. So instead, she acted like it was a joyous occasion.

Like hell it was.

Money.

Two changes of clothes.

And a time to go.

It was all set.

She'd thought slipping away when everyone was busy would be a breeze.

But her first attempt failed because her lunkhead of a brother came home early.

The next time, her mom had friends over.

The third time she tried to leave, her other brother was sick and needed someone to look after him.

Scarlett believed she was trapped in a life that wasn't meant to be hers.

She had food in her belly and clothes on her back. So what did she have to complain about? But as time went by, the walls closed in, stifling her and removing what little personality she had held onto.

Life was unfair for millions of people, and Scarlett decided one rainy Thursday she'd had enough, and it was like all the stars and planets were aligned because when she left, there were no obstacles in her way.

Someone was on her side that early morning because she easily found her brother's car keys and got out of town without detection. She couldn't keep the car, of course, not once her brother found it missing and reported it. But she drove for hours, feeling the stress drift away the more distance she put between her and them.

She wasn't world-savvy yet, but she vowed she would be.

She'd soak up the world like a sponge and stick it to her family every day for stealing all this time away from her.

One thing Scarlett knew for sure; she wanted nothing to do with men. *Ever.*

It was men who brought trouble, irritation, and downright annoyance. It was men who thought they could push her around and expect her to follow their orders.

She'd rather have a million dogs for companions than trust her heart to a man.

This, she vowed.

Scarlett
BEFORE

The overbearing neanderthal used minimal effort to shove her into the high-raised truck, and Scarlett's limbs had to scramble to catch up.

She knew she was in big trouble from the dark scowl on his face.

When he'd told her, "You stole from me, now you owe me, do yourself a favor and shut up." It was delivered in a deep baritone. Scarlett was in no doubt he meant it as a threat, so she shut up. All the while, her heart thumped with fear.

She'd been hungry and desperate.

God, how long had it been since she wasn't hungry?

It had been six months and five days since leaving Idaho to venture alone. Finally, after moving around regions for a few weeks, she landed in Utah, enjoying the clean air. Though she'd planned to go as far as Maine to put as much distance between her family as possible, Utah felt homely. Well, that was looking like a dreadful mistake.

Scarlett had been riotous with freedom in those first few weeks, living in the cheapest motels she could find.

Getting drunk on only three cocktails.

Eating every junk food she could find from the 7-Eleven until she was sick of looking at hot dogs and slices of pizza. She'd even gotten tattoos because she'd always been forbidden to mar her skin. Now she was inked along her left ribs and all down her outer thigh. She freaking loved her tattoos and wanted to get more. But regrettably, because she'd gone so hard those first few weeks, she'd soon run out of money.

That's when the motel rooms had to stop. Eating every day became a luxury. But, if she ate once every three days, she considered herself blessed. And then everything became real because Scarlett found herself homeless, unable to find work without a stable address.

Not knowing where she'd sleep put fear into Scarlett she'd never felt before.

Some nights, if the local shelters were full, she could sleep at the bus station. It was cold, but at least it was light and relatively safe.

On other nights, she found abandoned buildings to bunker down in.

Raiding trash cans behind stores became a daily occurrence if she wanted to eat. Thankfully, they tossed away a lot of good, unopened food.

It was hard. Demoralizing, shameful. Undeniably appalling when she got to the point of hunger that she'd eat discarded trash food and had to wash up in public bathrooms.

But never once did she consider calling her family.

Anything was better than being back there, deprived of her own choices.

Scarlett made the best of her situation. And finally, when she arrived in Laketon in the last few days, she'd decided to see if she could get an under-the-table cash job to afford a motel room. The colder months were upon them, and sleeping in damp buildings meant she'd suffered with more flu in the last month than she had all her life.

Because she'd been in some dicey situations, thankfully nothing life-threatening, but still scary for a woman alone on the streets, she knew not to panic until it was necessary as she surveyed the man sitting at her side.

He had a tight jaw, dusted with fine stubble, and looked pissed off. Probably because she'd attempted to steal money from his truck, had she gotten away with taking the five-dollar bill, she would have left a note to say she was sorry and hoped to pay him back one day. She had a tally in her little notebook of everything she'd stolen, with intentions to make amends for all of it.

But she hadn't stepped from the truck before the big bastard grabbed her. Now Scarlett was all but a hostage.

Don't panic.

Breathe.

Figure it out.

"You don't need to do this, mister." She started. "Roughing someone up or even murder is not worth five bucks. I don't think you want to go to jail."

Oh, God, please let him have a sense of right and wrong and not want to mess his day up by hiding a corpse. It would seriously ruin her day if that happened.

She didn't have much, but Scarlett enjoyed being alive.

When he didn't speak, she swallowed her rising fear and looked closer at him as he maneuvered the streets.

He was driving too fast for Scarlett to hurl herself out without breaking all her bones. And she'd considered it more than once in the last two minutes.

What else could she do but sit there and wait to see what the strange man would do?

"Are you a serial killer? A one-time-only killer?"

Would murderers advertise the fact?

She hoped so, because she needed an answer. And right then, the dark-haired man switched his gaze to her, and Scarlett inhaled swiftly.

He had the bluest eyes she'd ever seen.

"You want to hope and pray I'm not."

Her blood ran cold, and though her life was pretty shitty, she suddenly felt hopeless more than ever. Struck with the insane need to cry and beg for her life, but where had tears ever gotten her?

With that ominous statement, Scarlett stayed quiet, oblivious about where he was taking her. She was new to town and had seen only the homeless shelters and resource center. Those places had been lifesavers for her.

Okay, think. *Think.* She told herself. *Breathe.*

Now was not the time to detach and lose focus; she had to escape this.

What did she know about him?

Information could be used as a weapon. Her father did it all the time. How hard could it be?

First, the guy was huge with big, heavy-looking arms. When he'd been standing over her, she felt overshadowed by his size. And he looked lean with muscle. Scarlett didn't hold back on the staring. If this guy would do something heinous, she wanted a full description in her brain.

He was big. She'd established that.

He had a flat stomach and tattoos peeking out from under the cuffs of his shirt. He wore casual clothes: jeans that looked too faded, black boots, and a gray t-shirt underneath a button-down shirt. His belt buckle was thick leather and silver, and he wore one of those chains wrapped around his waist attached to a wallet.

Scarlett put to memory the two rings. One on his thumb, the other on his pinky finger, both silver.

It was his hair, she noticed, though.

It was thick, shoulder-length, glossy brown, and caught in a half ponytail. With his blue eyes and days' worth of stubble, the guy resembled a contemporary pirate minus the ship.

Now that his features were pressed to her memory if she needed to talk to the cops, she faced forward again and realized they were far out of town. Hardly any buildings lined the roadside now, and her panic intensified.

"You can drop me off here, dump me in the middle of nowhere. That's a fitting revenge for what I did." Her voice turned high and squeaky.

What if she punched him in the side of the head when he slowed the truck? Would that give her the precious seconds she'd need to jump out?

Or would it just enrage him into violence?

Kidnapped at twenty-five. Holy shit, she'd become a statistic. This was not the way she wanted to become famous.

"Seriously. You've scared me spitless and taught me a lesson. I won't steal from anyone again. So please drop me off here."

He ignored her, but she watched the muscle in his jawline tighten and tick incessantly.

Then they were driving through gateways that opened into a sizeable fenced-off compound with a massive brick building that looked like an old fire station. There were several other buildings, one of which was a working garage, and thank God, she saw people and many other vehicles.

Surely she wasn't getting murdered with witnesses around?

Scarlett exhaled and readied her frozen limbs for the fight of her life. If he thought she'd go along like a docile lamb, he had another thing coming. She'd watched every Karate Kid movie, she'd sweep his leg so damn fast.

The guy pulled into a parking bay and stopped the engine, pocketing the key. He turned to her then and growled. "Don't dare move."

Move? What was that? Her body was paralyzed.

But when he stepped down and walked around the hood to her door, pulling it open, she came back online with a jolt when he tried to reach in and grab her. She'd already unbuckled herself and started flailing.

No way was he taking her to a second location. That's where murders happened, and Scarlett refused to get killed today wearing yesterday's underwear. It was so inconvenient.

The realization that she held no power was staggering when she was easily lifted down. The guy didn't need to use violence. His build was enough to overpower her, so Scarlett went limp and heavy as her next survival option, and he ended up half-dragging her behind him with ease.

That's when she heard a chuckle. "What's going on?"

"Caught this little shit trying to steal out of the rig."

It was five freaking dollars, she wanted to scream! Not worth all this drama.

He was marching her toward the tall building. She only caught a fast glimpse of the other man before they swept by.

"Need a hand?"

"No, brother, I got this," her captor said, and as he was telling the other man, he gave Scarlett a shake by her coat to stop her from struggling. "Keep working my last nerve, and I'll string your thieving ass up."

She heard music from around the side of the brick building, and the food smells were enough to make her stomach ache.

All this had started because she was desperately hungry, which hadn't changed.

There was no time for her to look around as he pulled her inside, but her understanding became crystal clear, this man was in charge of everything when eyes, primarily males, darted their way, and no one looked shocked that he was dragging her behind him.

The marching continued, and Scarlett had to pony-trot to keep up, or she feared she'd fall flat on her face. They turned corners a few times, went down hallways, and then she was in a square office.

And he closed the door behind them.

"Sit." He issued in a rough, smoke-filled voice.

Scarlett was panting, half from having to jog like an athlete when she felt so weak, to begin with. And half from fear.

What was this place?

"Sit down," he rumbled with force, pointing to the chair in front of an old desk. Scarlett's ass cheeks met the chair automatically, and she watched him dump the paper sack of takeout food on top. Fear made her lip wobble, but stubbornness meant her chin was pushed high, daring him to kill her.

The scent of good-smelling hot food assaulted her nose, and she had to keep a groan of need at bay as her stomach bubbled loudly.

Her stomach noise was no match, though, for the man's angry growl as his stare bore into her soul.

And now she was terrified.

Axel
BEFORE

He couldn't say why he was so pissed off as he stood behind the desk, staring.

It was no secret around here that Axel hated being inconvenienced. If people did as they were meant to do without fucking whining and complaining, he wouldn't have to step in as much as he did.

Yeah, that could be it. The inconvenience of dragging this waif back to the clubhouse to what? Dole out punishment? String up the kid in Ruin's play shed?

Not likely.

He wasn't into killing teens. And from her size, she was high school age.

But the sound of her belly growling with hunger, loud enough to make Axel think the kid hadn't eaten in days, made his fury burst from his skin.

When she finally listened, eyes firing like she wanted to put his blood all over the walls, he placed a carton of noodles, beef, and broccoli in front of her, along with a set of chopsticks.

"Eat." He issued, and she blinked at him like he'd spoken in a foreign tongue.

"What? You're feeding me before killing me?"

The waif had an overactive imagination, but he didn't discourage her thought process. Axel rolled up his eyebrow. "You broke into my truck and stole money to get food. When was the last time you ate anything?"

She shrugged a shoulder under the dark green army jacket six sizes too big for her. It looked like it needed a decent wash. The same went for the skullcap and wide-brimmed hoodie she kept pulled down, almost masking her entire face. He was about to demand she tell him when she answered, "a few days ago, but it's no big deal. I got places to go, so can I leave now?"

"You can take off the fucking hood and eat the goddamn food."

He sat finally and realized his looming bulk was freaking her out. He watched her shoulders lower some of her tension as she gazed again at the steamy cartons of food. Her belly groaned again.

She wanted it, but was too damn stubborn to take it.

"I can't eat under the threat of being killed at any moment. I'm not a lunatic."

Christ, the theatrics on the street urchins these days.

Why did he care if she got food in her empty belly? He shouldn't. But she must be ninety pounds underneath her garbage clothing. And guessing she lived on the streets from the state of her. But she had a fire in her soul, which meant she wasn't completely torn down by circumstances yet. And she reminded Axel of the day he met Reno and Ruin. The twins had strode into his club and boldly asked to join. Reno did all the talking, with Ruin hanging back, but even back then, Axel remembered how hungry his eyes looked. Maybe not physical hunger, but the hunger to belong somewhere. He'd taken a chance on those two idiots and never regretted a day of it.

Now he considered the pair part of his extended family.

Another loud sound from her empty stomach, and he'd had enough. He slapped a hand on the desk, making her flinch and dart her eyes from the food to him. What he could see of her face looked ashen. "No one is killing you, so fucking eat before you pass out in my place, and I have to deal with your dead body."

"Nice," she huffed, but suddenly the hood was whooshed off her head, and she leaned forward to grab the broccoli and beef container and the set of chopsticks. She used them like she'd never learned how, but got delicate bites of food into her mouth, spilling nothing. Slower than he expected her to wolf it down if she was hungry as her body sounded.

"Thank you," she murmured with the sticks in her mouth, chewing, avoiding his eyes.

It meant Axel could stare at her.

And stare he did.

Fuck, she looked young.

Too young to be fending for herself on the streets.

How was she looking after herself? Besides stealing? Was she selling the only thing she could? There were no pimps in Laketon. He'd made sure of it. Axel had never wanted to deal in skin, using women for their bodies, even if they wanted to sell it. The heaviest the MC got involved in was Chains' strip club, which they bought for a song and refurbished into something classier. It was easy, clean money to funnel through their less-than-legal endeavors. Axel was a bastard but hadn't stooped so low to sell women. And now his jaw ticked as he stared at the waif, speculating how she was surviving.

"Where do you live?"

"Here and there."

"Where are you from?"

She switched cartons and slurped noodles into her mouth. "Nowhere you'd know."

Sneaky little urchin. But he couldn't blame her for not offering any information.

While she ate, he stood and walked across the room to the mini fridge, pulling out a soda can. Eyes on him the entire time, like a wary cat. He handed it over silently and was met with another quiet thank you. Axel retook his seat. Really looking at her this time while the girl gave all her attention to the food. She enjoyed eating, he noted. And had manners when she reached into the bag to pull out a napkin to wipe her mouth before resuming eating.

Her hair was almost boyishly short, angled around her too-thin face. It was red, too red to be anything but from a bottle. She had sunken cheeks, with a smattering of freckles over her pert nose, and her lips were chapped as hell.

Was she sleeping rough or holed up in one of those hostel places for the homeless?

"How old are you?"

She stopped chewing and glanced at him; then, he saw the moment sass entered her eyes and wasn't surprised when she replied, "how old do you want me to be, daddy?"

Axel felt anger ready to explode out of his veins at her flippant tone, like she'd replied the same thing to creepy men who tried to use her.

He couldn't explain why it angered him other than she looked like a kid with no one to watch out for her wellbeing.

"How long have you been on the streets?"

"Who said I am?" she snapped back.

Axel only needed to look her up and down at the clothes she was wearing or those wearing her. He observed her colorless face flame with pink embarrassment.

"These could be Paris chic. You don't know anything. How old are you, anyway? Ninety-four? Where are you from?"

"I'm forty-two."

"As I thought, boomer."

Food had obviously filled her belly and her bratty confidence.

"And this is my place."

"What *is* this place? Are you running a criminal organization for senior citizens? I noticed all the other golden oldies when you dragged me through. The one with the mohawk looks old as Medusa and prefers crocheting over gin rummy."

Chains would be thrilled to hear that appraisal, smirked Axel, thinking of how he would share that with his buddy.

"It's the base for my MC."

"MC? Like motorcycle club? Like the tv show Sons—"

"Stop right there," he growled. Offended by the comparison. Fucking Hollywood for putting rose-tinted glasses on his lifestyle.

"I asked you questions. I want answers." He issued. Fear flashed on her face again, and Axel relaxed his clenched jaw.

"What's it to you?"

"If I'm gonna offer you a job, I wanna know who the fuck is working for me."

Axel watched the girl blink, confused. And he could have easily matched her because he didn't know where that came from until hearing it as it came out of his mouth.

What the hell?

He was no humanitarian.

He didn't take in street orphans, not those who tried stealing from him. He despised thieves. They couldn't be trusted as far as he could spit. He'd severed business transactions for less than the girl had done to him, so why was he offering the pathetic creature a helping hand?

What he didn't expect was to see her burst into tears.

"Fuck you," she spat out between choking sobs, jumping to her feet as though attached to springs.

Scarlett
BEFORE

Jokes were only funny if two people laughed.

Scarlett found nothing funny about what the guy said. Tears leaked out of her eyes against her will, hating to cry, especially in front of anyone.

She was not weak, so she dashed them away with her hand.

"Fuck you," she said, almost under her breath. Then louder, glaring at him, "I don't need charity. Not from you or anyone."

"You'd prefer to steal? You wanna go to jail, is that it? 'cause you're a piss-poor thief, girlie."

Emotions weighed her down, feeling more sluggish and worn out.

She could see no way out of this life, which only worsened by the day.

Her plans had been so unrealistic, she realized now. How stupid she'd been to run away with nothing to run toward.

"I do alright," she lied.

"Do you? What's your name?"

"Scarlett," she said before she could bite her tongue. "What's yours?"

"Axel Tucker. We need a bartender, cleaner, whatever, around here."

"And you're going to give me a job just like that? After I took your money and you dragged me back here?" call her suspicious, but she didn't believe this guy had an altruistic bone in his looming body. He looked too cunning to be the *do-a-good-deed* guy.

"You'll pay me back for your crime."

Scarlett blinked. Shocked. "How… how will I do that? You got your five dollars back already."

"I can read people, girlie, and you look torn up about having to steal. I need a position filled. You'll fill that position and make good on what you did."

Her head whirled.

Was he for real?

Could she have a job and possibly save money to get a place one day?

"Is it legal?"

He half smirked, and she thought she saw the real him for a second. A cunning man. "Can you afford to care if it is or not?"

He had a point. She shrugged, unbothered by the legality of his business. She couldn't be so picky about where she found her first job post-breakout.

Something he said a moment ago came back around her mind, and she swallowed. "You said bartender, cleaner, whatever. What is the *whatever*? Because I won't do anything hinky. I'm not for sale."

A smile appeared on his face, and warmth hit Scarlett's belly, seeing those full lips, surrounded by facial hair, stretch to showcase perfectly straight teeth. He sat back in the leather chair, a finger up by his lips. Rubbing.

She bet this Axel guy had women falling at his feet if he wasn't already married. No, not falling, crawling to get to him. He'd have his choice, and here she was, letting him know he couldn't have her. She looked terrible and probably smelled worse. Even though she tried to keep clean, her clothes were very damp and smelled it.

"If I meant you'd have to repay me on your back, I would have said so. You'll learn in time I don't say shit and not mean it. So you want the job?"

She wanted any job so badly, but she hadn't decided if she could trust him yet.

"How much is it?"

He mentioned a sum, and her mouth dropped open. "Monthly?"

"A week."

"No fucking way. You're pulling my leg."

"You'll earn every penny."

Her mind went nuts with the amount. She could stay in a shitty motel and save as much as possible to afford a small apartment.

There was no actual decision to make. But something had to change, and was this it?

"I'll take it."

"I thought you might. Now the ground rules," Axel started in his no-nonsense tone that compelled her to listen. "You'll learn fast, Scarlett. I don't give second chances; consider yourself lucky that you have one. That means rule one is never steal from me and mine again. You won't go hungry, meals are included."

Shame washed over her once more, and she lowered her eyes until she heard him knock on the table to gain her attention, and her head snapped up. Finding him watching her.

"Now answer, how long have you lived on the streets?"

"Not long. My money ran out, and I couldn't get a job. Is Axel your government name?"

"Mark is. No one uses it. You didn't try hooking?"

She jumped to her feet again, fucking offended. "No, I did not!"

"Calm down; it's a legit question. I don't want a disgruntled pimp looking for you."

There was no pimp, but probably her deranged family. She kept that to herself.

"I'd rather die in a ditch than sell my body."

He chuckled. "Got it. Next thing, you need to clean up. We don't stand on ceremony here, but you look like shit."

Color ran across her face, but she kept her chin pointed high. She'd survived and had done it all by herself. She was proud of that. "This shit kept me warm."

"I get that. Your room upstairs has its own bathroom."

"Wait, what do you mean, my room?"

"The job is live in."

"Are you joking with me? Is this funny to you to fuck with a homeless person?"

He sighed like her dramatics were giving him a headache. Well, tough shit, she had her own headache, which was much worse than his.

"Okay, rule change. Rule one is now to believe whatever the fuck I say, yeah? Repeat the rules, so I know you're listening."

Rolling her eyes. Was this guy for real?

But that rough quality in his voice almost made Scarlett snap to attention. With her back straightened, she answered. "Believe whatever the fuck you say. And no stealing." That meant… "you're offering me a job and a place to stay? There are apartments here?"

"It's rooms, some better than others. My men mostly have their own off-compound homes but keep a bedroom here to sleep off hangovers. It'll be your room, your key. Come on. I'll give you the two-bit tour."

Scarlett stood and followed behind like she was attached to him by an invisible string, clutching her one meager bag crossed over her chest under the coat. It held everything she owned, and she felt tiny and empty at that moment.

But hope flared in her chest.

Was this her chance to make things better?

For the next ten minutes, she barely took a breath.

Taking in every nook and cranny, Axel showed her.

It comprised three floors, with twenty or so rooms on each floor. But she could tell they used the bottom floor most of all. It had a huge gathering area with couches, a large TV area, games, a long bar with stools in front of it, and a wall of alcohol bottles displayed behind.

She felt self-conscious as she gained attention but held her chin high and her stare pointed, daring them to judge her.

They didn't know her. Didn't know what she'd been through to look the way she did.

The room Axel offered her was perfect, and her jaw dropped open. Though it was sparse, just a bed, drawers, and a chair, with a separate bathroom attached, it was bigger than some motels she'd stayed in early on her journey.

She almost ran into Axel's back when he stopped at the top of the stairs.

"Well?"

There was no hesitation. "Yes, I would like the job. Thank you."

Could he hear how her heart wanted to escape from her chest?

She was afraid.

Afraid to believe in hope.

Afraid he was joking with her as a cruel punishment, and then he'd toss her back onto the street.

On frosty nights, when she'd been huddled in the corner of a vacant office block, terrified other homeless people would find her, she'd fantasized about being rescued.

Nothing fancy.

She'd never dreamed about a prince or castles or even having riches beyond her means. No, she'd dreamed of simple things. A roof over her head, food in her belly, hot showers, and reliable days.

Was this her rescue?

Could she hope for a miracle?

There was only one way to find out.

And like before, Scarlett padded behind Axel, following him down the stairs and through hallways, jogging a little to keep up with his long stride. Her eyes were glued to his broad back and commanding gait.

She wished she was a stronger person who didn't feel relief sluice through her veins at the prospect of a helping hand.

She'd been alone so long, even with her family, that she longed for someone to say *I see you, Scarlett*.

It was humbling and brought her down to earth with a slam for how people ignored homelessness like it didn't exist in their privileged world. Now she knew how easy it was to lose everything. She'd never take help for granted again.

An invisible line connected her to this man.

A man who could have been cruel and handed her over to the police.

Whatever his reasons for extending her a chance at a better life, she would never squander it or take it for granted. She'd be the best damn employee he'd ever had and would never give Axel an inch of trouble or an excuse to get rid of her.

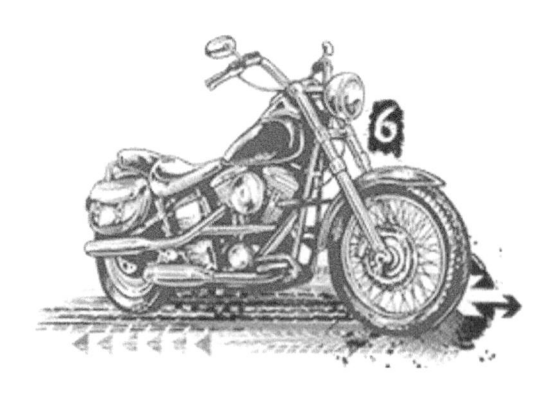

Axel
PRESENT DAY

"I will smother you when you're asleep!"

"You've used that one before, wildcat. You need a better script if you're trying to threaten me."

The red-headed woman who was his club bartender and resident pain in his ass glared at him, the green flashing in shades of her temper, which she didn't hide very well. Oh, she'd tried those first few weeks of working for him. She'd sneaked around the club like a mouse, hardly saying shit to anyone, bothering no one, doing her work, and then slipping off to her room.

Axel had watched her too closely.

Not sure why he was observing her weeks later when he'd known already she wouldn't steal from him again. But he'd gotten to know her schedule better than his own. She exited her room around seven a.m., ate breakfast in the kitchen, and started working behind the bar, clearing the mess from the night before and restocking. She was an efficient worker. All the boys noticed and started gathering around the bar like groupies at a gig.

He didn't like it, but didn't know why.

So he ignored the feeling churning up his guts.

It took less than no time for her mouthy behavior to make itself known.

All these months later, she was only bratty with him.

It was like Axel brought the fire out in her simply because he existed.

How the fuck was that for gratefulness?

That first week he'd given her a job, a roof over her head, and free food in her belly, he also discovered she had only two shitty outfits. So without patience, he'd frog-marched her to his truck again and taken her shopping, forcing her to choose clothes. That started a ten-minute back-and-forth argument in the store, giving him a fucking headache. What woman didn't want clothes?

She'd paid him back with her first paycheck.

Offended, he'd tossed the money into her room and threatened that she wouldn't like the consequences if she tried to return it.

Axel ruminated. Maybe it was his fault she became hostile. He was not the friendliest guy, as Chains liked to remind him.

When he discovered she didn't have a cell phone, he'd bought her one, putting her on his data plan. That had pissed her off, too. There was no reason he did it; he needed to have contact with his employees. Chains was practically giddy when he pointed out to Axel he'd bought no one else a cell phone, apart from Roux, but that was his daughter. Until she got married, he'd bought her anything she wanted. Still did if she asked for it. He'd spoiled his wild girl rotten and wasn't ashamed.

But to hear Chains compare Scarlett to his kid made rocks sit heavily in his stomach, because Axel did not look at the waif like a daughter.

Not at all.

He didn't understand the curiosity.

She irritated him on a molecular level, an illogical irritation that made no fucking sense, but did it stop him from seeking Scarlett out to annoy her in the same way? No.

She wandered off, holding empty beer bottles in both hands. Their current spat over until the next one rolled in. It happened frequently and needed little provocation.

Axel smirked, watching her swishing ass for a second before he ripped his eyes away. *Fucking hell*. What was he doing? He had no business checking out her goodies like that, and instantly a boil of guilt hit him in the solar plexus.

Helping the stray to get off the street meant nothing to him. On the contrary, it was a good move for the club. She was helpful, and everyone liked her around; she'd become a right hand for the house mouse, so he had zero fucking rights by looking at her longer than was necessary.

He groaned and scraped a hand down his bearded face.

"Trouble in paradise?" he heard and saw Chains, the VP of their contrasting crowd and longest friend, standing in the doorway. Smirking like he had all the answers to what forbidden and uncalled for shit was going on in Axel's head.

That would make one of them.

"DeCastro left another dead gift at the car wash last night. You see paradise 'round here?"

"Just left my smiling wife in bed, so yeah." He boasted like an asshole. Now he was happily married, so he strutted like a bull in mating season. Advancing into the office, he straddled a chair opposite the desk.

"You know what they say about men who brag about getting laid, don't you? They're probably not getting any at all."

Chains chuckled. "It's a marvel how I'm still walking, Axe."

Axel cracked a half grin. "Shut the fuck up. What brings you in so early?"

"Besides cleaning up DeCastro's gifts, I got father-in-law problems." He grated.

Months back, when they'd been in business with Donahue, they'd wanted collateral for his debts. As luck would have it, his daughter Monroe was that collateral and was now happily married to Chains. That side of the deal worked out better than expected, and Axel was pleased for his VP. The Donahue side of the business was severed, thank fuck. The guy didn't know his ass from his elbow, but he'd been causing issues for Chains in the background, mostly because he continued to force a relationship with his remaining daughters, which they refused.

"I wanna make the problem go away."

"Kill him?"

Chains grimaced.

That kind of wet work ordinarily would go through their enforcer. Ruin was the best in the business. With a cast iron stomach, he could torture, maim, or even murder and did it with a sinister grin. But Ruin was taking care of another matter.

"As much as she hates her dad, I doubt Monroe would forgive me for taking him out. Nah, I want the guy to suffer. Death is too good for him. If I put the wheels in motion, can you get your cop friend to do the rest?"

"You know she'll do anything for the right price. I'll see that it's done. But you're sure about this?"

"I want the man gone from Monroe's life, her sister's, too, so they can have peace while they grieve. And I want him to suffer in a jail cell, penniless, without a pot to piss in. If he's being ass-fucked every day, even better."

Axel spat out a laugh. "You sadistic bastard." With what trouble they were dealing with from DeCastro, they could treat finishing Donahue as a rainbow over their storm.

They talked about other club matters over a coffee, discussing how they could invest this quarter's profits into one of their other ventures. As the MC president, Axel was forever concerned with shifting clean money into dirty projects, recycling for the greater good. Their most significant investment was with the Murphy's from Dublin, and there'd been no hiccups with their importing business, which was fewer headaches for Axel. He'd soon be meeting with Redd Murphy, the head of their firm, to discuss furthering ties. For once, his cash flow was more than reasonable, and he wasn't constantly looking over his shoulder for the next enemy out to double-cross him.

His dealers had been reporting how they were getting more and more inquiries and not enough stuff to push. Funny how they were dealers for prescription drugs, not the hard, illegal kind. If Axel had figured out years back, there was a gap in the market for health medicine that people's insurance wouldn't cover; he would have been rich much sooner.

He parted from Chains soon after, grabbing the keys to the RAM. The worst torture for a biker was to make him drive a cage, but the roads were still like black ice. He'd learned to compromise since his grandbabies came along, but he hated getting in the truck when his gleaming Harley Davidson was under a protective tarp, just waiting to be ridden.

Halfway through the common area, he'd intended to ignore Scarlett, forcing his eyes forward on the exit. But what do you know, the second he clocked Splice sitting his single ass at the bar, making Scarlett belly laugh, his feet had other ideas and rooted him to the floor.

It wasn't a rage exactly seeing one of his men flirting with her, making her pale cheeks all flushed and flattered by the attention.

But it was close to it as it flashed through his belly.

What the fuck did he care if Splice flirted? He seduced anything with a pulse and usually got them into his bed. And he was closer to Scarlett's twenty-five.

His feet moved across the bar like they were attached to magnets. Splice catching his arrival, he offered a grin. "Yo, Prez. I told Scar about when I had to outrun that tiger at a rally."

"You're pulling my leg. No one has a pet tiger." Scarlett grinned at Splice, and Axel felt that rage bubble up again.

"Honest to God, right, Prez? Some yokel thought bringing it to a biker rally would be cool. Nearly scared ten years off my life when the thing started chasing me."

"Yeah, it's true," he answered, trying not to bite off the words. Irritation stung his throat as he watched Scarlett light up for Splice.

"That's hilarious and crazy."

Before Splice could roll into another impressive story, Axel said, "you're needed at the carwash today."

"Yeah, Prez, I know. I was heading there now." He rose from the stool and winked at Scarlett. "You still owe me that game of cards."

"I know, but I stink. You'll beat the pants off me."

"That's the plan, Scar baby."

She giggled and turned red.

Motherfucking player, Axel nearly put his brother and friend through the wall.

"That was subtle as a tap dancing rhino, boss," laughed his SAA once outside and in step with Axel. Axel only curled his lip and kept right on marching to his truck. "You were about to drag me away by my ear like my Ma used to do when I'd chase all the pretty girls in the street to kiss them."

"Already warned everyone when she got the job, she wasn't to be bothered."

"I don't bother Scar baby. She likes me."

"*Scarlett.*" He grated through his teeth, whipping a stare at Splice, who, once again, said the right thing to push Axel's buttons.

"Look at you. You're ready to throw down. Why don't you stake a claim then, huh? We all got eyes. We see how you look. We hear the spats you two have, like an old married couple bickering all day long but without the makeup fuck."

He enjoyed debating with her, not that he'd told anyone. It put color in her cheeks; she'd been deathly pale and too thin for those first few weeks. So he'd seen it like medicine for her, bullying her into eating, having her snap at him until she was full and didn't need more. It escalated from there until now. It felt like a *good morning* when she hissed insults at him.

Axel hadn't been aware that people around the club also noticed it.

Standing at the side of his black truck, Splice rested a hand on the hood and met Axel's eyes. "Gonna be straight up with you, Prez. If you're not feeling her like that, then I wanna get to know her. Unclaimed chicks are fair game in the club. That's always been the rule."

"She's not a fucking sweet bottom you can tap." He growled low and warningly.

"I haven't treated her like that either. She's fun and funny. Besides, she's too ripe for the picking. It would be a shame to waste all that sweetness."

Pushing.

His.

Fucking.

Buttons.

And Axel reacted like he'd been kicked in the balls.

It was a nuclear reactor going off in his head. For a second, he pictured Splice with Scarlett and didn't like what he imagined.

Splice was a decent enough guy; he didn't beat or verbally abuse women. He just liked to sleep with many and would probably not settle down with an old lady and a couple of kids one day. It ripped Axel to pieces inside because he'd put himself in protector mode for some fucking unexplainable reason. Now he was acting like an overly possessive asshole when someone he trusted showed sexual interest in his employee.

He should mind his own goddamn business, but his feet moved, and he went toe-to-toe with Splice. "She is my employee, and you'll keep your sticky mitts off her. You got it?"

Splice smirked like the devil and then chuckled, unfazed by a threat. "Aw, damn, Prez, why you gotta warn me off? You know what that does to me. I gave you a chance, didn't I? I said you should put a stake in the game, and you didn't. So, should I say game on now?"

Axel knew his motives and wouldn't play more of this fucking game than he had already. *Asshole.* He turned to climb into his truck. "Fuck off, Splice."

The guy belly laughed like he'd won that round.

Had he?

Did Axel want to put a claim on her? The thought of it scorched his gut.

Too fucking young for him.

Too innocent.

Too everything else he could think of that meant it was bad news even to have it roaming around in his head for a minute.

He'd seen up close the fear and mistrust she'd carried, which played a part in how he felt now.

Axel had placed a tape of protection around his newest employee, even without acknowledging it to himself, because that would mean he'd have to delve into the reasons behind it. After all, he hired many of the sweet bottoms, too, and he wasn't going caveman for their protection, was he? He'd never warned his boys off from fucking one or more of the sweet bottoms.

What made Scarlett Bass different?

Women came to the club for a reason, most of it pleasure based. Scarlett was brought to the club against her will and forced to stay, even if he'd prettied the package with a job and a roof over her head.

It amounted to the same thing. He'd given her no way out.

Why didn't he feel guilty about that?

She could walk out—Scarlett liked to talk, and he'd already heard how much money she'd saved, so she wasn't down on her luck anymore. She'd have enough for the first and last month's rent on an apartment. That didn't sit well with Axel, but because he'd gotten proficient at suppressing his reactions, he didn't dig into why he didn't like that.

Instead, he got on with his day, phoning a few contacts and checking on his numerous businesses around town. He touched base with his cop informant to stay abreast of anything that might come the club's way.

Things kept him busy for most of that day and away from the club, but it didn't stop Axel from checking in several times with phone calls.

To his bartender only.

Scarlett

It was odd that she now had genuine friends who cared about her.

No way had Scarlett thought working for an MC would alter her life for the better all those months back when she was dragged here.

It sounded ridiculous, but she felt she was meant to be at the MC. Why else did she fit in as she did? Why was she comfortable around all those sailor-mouthed men?

She loved working for the Diablo Disciples MC. Now she had money in her pocket and a clean room that was all hers. It wasn't laborious work and hardly stretched her brain, but it was fun, and she enjoyed talking to everyone who sat at the bar, even if they were uncouth and sexist.

Here she could be outspoken with her own opinions, even if she was wrong. She could have lively debates, laugh, joke around, tease people, and not be chastised for being unladylike.

She'd said *fuck* more these past months than she had her whole life, and she loved it. Her days had a routine, and for that, she was grateful. When she woke and dressed, she headed down to the first floor, where Stella was usually cooking, plus a few skeleton crew around until the rest arrived. Stella was the house mouse, as the guys called her. It meant she cooked, cleaned, and kept the MC domestic side running smoothly. Scarlett made friends with Stella right away. She was a motherly woman in her fifties who was married with two grown kids and, like Scarlett, enjoyed working for the MC.

Scarlett would help in the kitchen if Stella needed a hand. Usually, the guys weren't in the mood to drink first thing on a morning unless one had an attitude or they'd had a lovers' spat. Then she'd pour the drinks and let them talk or brood silently. Her days weren't exciting by someone else's standards, but she appreciated being busy.

During the day, the club was approachable; it looked like any other company. And no one should ever assume it was just a hobby club for motorcycle enthusiasts. It was the center of operations for all their businesses.

At night, the clubhouse came alive and appeared dangerous to those unfamiliar with how things were.

Droves of bikers dressed in leather cuts with their women came for the long-spoken-about parties.

Some outsiders, too, were sometimes invited. Usually, it was because of business connections. Other times it was men who were interested in joining the MC.

The music was ear-shattering, and she'd learned to pour the drinks fast, catering to demanding thirst and men with no filters or manners.

Weeks and weeks had drifted by since that first night at the clubhouse, and she was no longer timid and unsure. So much so that she felt acceptable shouting across the space to gain a prospect's attention. He came trotting over to the bar.

"You called, beautiful?" Mouse smirked. Such a flirt. But she definitely would not go there even if she was interested because this one had a wife at home. As rumors suggested, he was taken even if it wasn't a happy home. So she turned a blind eye to what he did within the club walls with other women. It wasn't her business. But as a buddy, Mouse was cool.

"Do you and your big, strong muscles wanna cart in those beer crates for me? They're out by the back door."

"Ah, man. You appealed to my guns." He flashed a pretty boy grin, holding up both arms, making his forearms and triceps pop. Scarlett chuckled, men and their egos. "You're a sly one, Scar. I'll lug them in now. You need 'em back here behind the bar?"

"Not right now. The storage room will do. Thank you, you're the best."

"Bet you say that to all the guys."

She did. And meant it because she wasn't used to men doing things for her. Chores were women's work, according to her father and brothers. Those lazy jerks wouldn't know how to run a washing machine if their lives depended on it. So, to have men around who would assist when asked for it was still something she was getting used to.

While she cleaned down the bar top until it gleamed, she listened to Mouse talking about one of his kids. It wasn't much later that Monroe came through the entryway, and Scarlett waved her over.

She'd bonded with Monroe first. She was gorgeous and intelligent and so fun to talk to. Then, because Scarlett had been at the club only a few weeks before Monroe, she'd taken the other woman under her wing when she married Chains.

"Hey, Scar. I have some time to kill. Do you want to grab a coffee? My treat."

"Sure, would love to." She tossed the dish rag behind the bar and made her way around.

"What about my invite?" scoffed Mouse.

"Sorry, girls only."

"Fine. I better shoot off before you two start plotting whatever chicks plot."

"That's sexist, Mouse," Scarlett told him, and the man grinned in return.

"Yup." He was so unrepentant he made both women chuckle.

She found out quickly that the Diablo men said everything without a filter.

Monroe drove them to a coffee shop in town, and they sat in the window with lattes and a plate of cookies to share while it snowed outside.

It was picturesque, and yet another day she was grateful for.

Those days were coming thick and fast now.

In part for Monroe's friendship.

"How's married bliss treating you?"

Monroe beamed a smile as she sipped foam from her coffee cup. "It's perfect. Am I sickening if I say Chains is perfect?"

"No, you're not. I think it's lovely."

"Do you want to get married one day?"

Scarlett nearly choked. She couldn't think of anything worse. Or that's how she'd once thought when being pushed into it. But it had worked out for Monroe and her arranged marriage. Although, it was a different circumstance. Plus, Chains had been crazy for Monroe all along.

"I can't think of marriage if I'm not dating."

"There was that one guy, wasn't there? Months back."

"Todd. Ugh. Don't remind me."

Monroe giggled and bit into a crumbly cookie. "I heard alllll about it from Roux. How she and Axel had gone to the same diner as you and Todd. Didn't Axel punch him?"

Scarlett's cheeks turned beet red. "He was an ass, and he embarrassed me."

"Yeah, but he had a reason."

"So he says. I didn't even get a kiss."

Not that she'd been attracted to Todd, but he'd seemed a sweet guy, and she'd wanted to date anyone to stop the beat of lust for her stupid boss. How was she to know he'd turn up to the same diner and glare at them like they'd stolen his prized stallion?

"The way Chains told me, while you were in the bathroom, Axel heard the guy on the phone bragging to his buddy that it would be an easy lay with his date. Axel protected your honor."

Hmph. Maybe she'd felt a type of way after she'd let him explain once her temper had simmered down. Perhaps she'd loved seeing him drag Todd by the collar of his shirt and growl in his face.

"Yeah, well. Let's say I don't think me and dating are suited."

"That's because you're hung up on Axel, Scar."

Her head whipped up like it was on a spring, eyes open wide with shock.

"You don't think all that arguing you guys do fool anyone, do you? It's like a long version of tantric foreplay. Some guys even have bets on when you'll sleep with him."

"No way! Are you kidding? I'm mortified."

She loved arguing with Axel about anything and everything. Usually silly, inconsequential things because it was just nice to bicker and not have someone tell her to be quiet or her opinions didn't matter. Axel gave as good as he got; his growls and scowls were hot, making her lungs clench with need each time he rolled out that sexy noise from his throat.

God, his voice was campfire rough, like crackling sparks going directly to all her hot spots.

The thing was, Axel became her foundation stone for everything after she'd moved into his clubhouse and after she'd relaxed and stopped being fearful of everyone. Happy, sad, mad, and horny, he was the hot button to it all.

She hadn't given it a thought that those around them might see their squabbling as verbal foreplay.

"Aww, sweetheart, don't be. You know I'm teasing you. Not about the bets. That's all real. But I think it's cute you like Axel."

"It's not cute. Not at all." She groaned, rubbing the embarrassment from her burning cheeks. God, she'd thought she'd been stealthy, hiding her feelings. Now she found out everyone in the clubhouse knew and was probably laughing at her. It wasn't hard to feel something for Axel, all those thoughts of wanting to be filled and fucked and screams torn out of her. It was natural because he was sexy personified. She bet even the grocery clerk lady had those feelings about Axel when he stopped in to buy cigars and milk.

No way Axel would go for her. He showed his irritation with her at every opportunity.

"It's just a stupid crush for someone who helped me. It doesn't mean anything."

But she knew it did.

At least to her.

It wasn't a crush, and it hadn't gone away.

But it was all one-sided, so she had to ignore it.

The attraction and need to be near him, even if they started biting each other's heads off, was the highlight of her day. Stupid. *Stupid.* But it never stopped Scarlett from going back for more. One more fix from his fired-up eyes or hearing that sexy slick growl of his. She might live with drenched panties daily because of it, and she was fine with that.

Axel had become a constant in her life, and she couldn't claim it was an accident because Scarlett herself put him there.

She made him *necessary*.

"Ugh." She groaned to herself, but Monroe reached across the table and covered her hand. "You know it's okay to like him, yeah? Axel is a good guy."

"An off-limits good guy, maybe. I should have nipped it in the bud when I started to feel something. He's my boss."

"Take it from someone who knows. It's difficult to stop that train once it leaves the station. I wanted to punch Chains almost every day, but I also wanted to jump his bones. Have you thought about doing that?"

"Punching him? Oh, yeah. So many times, he irritates me like no one else."

Monroe laughed. "No, well, unless that's foreplay. I meant going for it. Seeing how he feels."

"God, no. Never. He doesn't feel anything for me. You've seen Axel; he isn't shy. If he wanted a woman, that woman wouldn't be left wondering about his feelings. Her panties would already be around her ankles."

Monroe choked on a sip of coffee as she laughed. Then, smiling, Scarlett passed her a napkin to slop up the spillage.

"I don't want to make it awkward, you know? Or put all my girlie feelings on the floor, and Axel has no choice but to fire me for harassing him with my boobs."

"You're sexy. No man would say no to your boobs, Scar."

She flashed a smile. "Thanks. But yeah, no, my crush will fade, and he'll be the annoying boss I bicker with."

Axel Tucker, with his devastating scowl and amazingly hard butt that looked phenomenal in jeans, was so off-limits to her he wasn't even in the friend zone. More like the *don't even look at me* zone.

Like she needed a glaring reminder, not even twenty minutes had passed, and they were on their second coffee when a familiar beast of a truck parked across the street. It was Monroe who spotted Axel climbing out.

"Speak of the gorgeous devil, and he shall appear."

Scarlett's heart whipped up like a tornado, thinking impossible thoughts, like he might be looking for her.

Of course not.

He entered the diner opposite, and her eyes ate him up as he threaded his massive body through the tables to sit at a booth against the wall.

Only he wasn't alone.

Her rampant heart sank seeing a blonde woman smiling at him and moving closer as he settled into his seat.

"Oh, shit," Monroe murmured. Scarlett watched the woman and Axel like they were close.

She'd heard nothing around the clubhouse about him having a woman. The sweet bottoms were notorious for gossiping about the bikers, like it was a badge of honor how many they'd screwed or wanted to screw.

Damn, this sucked, and her stomach hurt to watch the scene, so she tore her gaze away, only to face Monroe's sympathetic eyes, which was worse.

"There we go, all cured." She tried to smile.

"Scar…"

"It's fine. I should have known someone like Axel would have a woman."

"Someone as awesome as you should have a man. Let me set you up with someone."

"Maybe another time."

Sneaking another glance across the street, her heart plummeted, watching Axel's lips moving, engaging in conversation. He wasn't smiling, but she didn't see him often smiling unless his daughter and grandkids were in town.

She couldn't believe she crushed on a guy who was old enough to have grandkids.

He made forty-two look *good*.

Her life was stable now.

She didn't fear seeing her family around every corner, not months later. They've probably forgotten all about her now, thank God.

But she was terrified of the feelings she had for Axel. Even off limits to her, they felt monstrously overwhelming. She oscillated between snapping his head off and wanting to smash a kiss to his full lips, to feel what his beard did to her softer skin. Would it leave marks?

And now she'd seen him with a woman; she'd have to get over it. She couldn't keep slipping her hand into her panties each night.

Imagining him prowling into her bedroom to tell her what a mouthy brat she was and to shut her up the way he knew best. Fucking her brains out or making her choke on his cock.

Even now, as those thoughts flooded her brain, she covered her hot cheeks. Yeah, it was time to get over it and move on.

No more daydreaming about banging the boss on his big, old desk.

Scarlett

Scarlett couldn't get the woman out of her head as she flittered around the clubhouse that afternoon.

Who was she?

Date?

Lover?

Something more?

Did the other bikers know Axel had a woman, or was she a secret from everyone?

The more she thought about it—obsessed over it—the worse she felt.

Her stomach was in a constant tight knot.

Hating herself for the strangling emotions swirling through her.

It had to stop.

Axel was her boss only. Nothing more. And before that, he was nobody, just a man she tried to steal from.

Who he fucked or dated was nothing to do with her.

She'd read too much into what Axel had done to her date that night. He probably protected all women the same way. She was nothing special. He unquestionably had a hero complex. That's why he'd stuck his neck out to help Scarlett the way he had.

Just when she'd talked herself into forgetting the whole thing, ignoring her feelings and not acknowledging Axel, she heard his raspy voice, and her instinct was to duck down behind the bar. Breathing like she was hiding from a serial killer.

Shit. What was her plan here? To stay on her knees, hiding out of sight forever?

She didn't want to leave her job. She loved being at the clubhouse. So her only option was to get over her one-sided crush.

She could do that, Scarlett determined, while being a chickenshit as she listened to Axel's heavy footsteps going by, holding her breath.

Dodging him seemed like a good idea; if there were any problems or questions, she could take them to Chains. He'd always been kind to her in the past.

Yeah, good idea, Scarlett, she told herself, popping up from behind the bar.

Only it wasn't safe.

She'd come out of hiding too soon because a pair of blue eyes drilled down to her soul from the other side of the bar, and everything in Scarlett came to a screaming halt under Axel's scrutiny.

His eyes glittered as his eyebrows popped high on his forehead.

She hated how she documented each tanned line on his face, the tight shave of his beard, and how his lips were open only an inch. His frame came naturally. He wasn't overly pumped up like a gym rat would be. And any clothes he wore hung powerfully on that body like they'd been made to emphasize every muscle. *Damn*, she could have died on the spot when he wore his shirt sleeves pushed back. Such pretty arms. The masculinity rolled off Axel like ocean foam. Never-ending and all-consuming.

"Why were you hiding back there?"

Ten snappy retorts were lingering on her tongue, and she wanted to fire them all at Axel for making her jumpy in his presence, but she said none of them, not when he had her so flustered.

"I thought I saw an elephant."

His snort felt like a passionate caress between her thighs, and she unconsciously pressed her legs together. Thank God the bar separated them so he wouldn't see the shuddering reaction.

Scarlett could only reason it was her agitated state, which made her do what she did next because no rational woman would ever put herself in that position.

And not with her employer.

She knew she'd overstepped when she blurted, "Why does no one know you have a girlfriend?"

Rather than display surprise, as a normal person would, she should have figured Axel wasn't ordinary, not at all, because his thick, brown eyebrows folded over his suspicious eyes and his lips flattened into thin lines. "What?"

Her verbal diarrhea persisted, and she wanted to slap a hand over her fugitive mouth, to hold the words at bay and not leak her jealous curiosity all over the floor in front of Axel. "I saw you earlier with a blonde woman. How come she's never been to the clubhouse if she's your woman?"

She'd seen a lot of rage in men's eyes.

It wasn't precisely that as Axel strode to the end of the bar, and she wasn't exactly scared as he stepped behind, but her heart did clatter in rapid taps when he lassoed her wrist with his fingers and pulled her out, walking her behind him at a fast pace.

"Hey, now." She complained, and he ignored her. Pulling on his arm was as useful as flying to the moon with only a balloon. He was solid and immovable, so Scarlett ended up trotting behind him.

When Axel dropped her arm once inside his office with the door closed, he was standing so close, her lungs forgot how they functioned.

Lethal in every bone, yet gorgeous enough to make a woman forget she could be in danger. He appeared to expand before her very eyes. Filling up the space surrounding them.

Good lord, the man was attractive.

He made her brain stutter.

It was insanity, high on crack.

Catching sexual feelings for the boss was every Hallmark movie ever made.

The amount of fucked up layers to her feelings would embarrass a nun. They mortified her regularly when she let herself feel anything but sarcasm and irritation for Axel.

How Stockholm syndrome of her to fall for the one guy who offered her a helping hand. Thank God she snarked at him more often than not and did not batter her lashes and offer her pussy on a platter. Her only saving grace was that he wouldn't know the depth of her secret passion.

"You're too accustomed to frog-marching me places," she criticized, rubbing her fingers over her wrist. She saw him glance and scowl, and then he picked up her arm, inspecting it before letting it go again.

"Repeat what you said," he growled. His words were hefty with command.

Jeez. Someone needed a chill pill or a decent back rub to untie all those knots.

"You're too accustomed—"

"Not that," Axel interrupted. "What you said out there."

Oh. The girlfriend thing. He was pissed, she supposed.

Lifting her chin, she did what she did best with this biker, putting on a hard front for fear of him seeing her true self and then laughing at her. "Jeez, Axel, if you didn't want people to know you had a woman, don't moon over her in a public restaurant. But don't worry. Your secret is safe with me. Consider me Switzerland. They couldn't drag it out of me even if they waterboarded me with a milkshake."

Did her voice warble with jealousy?

Could he see it breathing fire out of her eyes?

Was he aware of the funny feeling he made swirl in her stomach?

She didn't even know the blonde woman, yet she hated her. She hated Axel for wanting her and allowing the woman to get close to him.

If she didn't need her job, she would pack her things, leave, and never think of him again, but that was too dramatic.

While in her screwed-up thoughts, she didn't know Axel had moved again, closer by inches, until his woodsy soap filled her nose, and his shirt almost brushed against her cheek. She looked up and found his eyes so dark and spitting fire embers.

She wasn't proud of letting an unknown woman get under her skin, but to feel fury radiating out of Axel might make it worth it because she got goosebumps all over.

"Who she is, is none of your business."

"Fine," she snapped, trying not to let the hurt burn through her blood.

"Were you spying on me?"

"Spying?" she choked, blinking. "Ha! You wish. I was having coffee with a friend and saw you. It's no big deal to me who you cozy up to."

"I was not cozy with any-fucking-one." He grated through his teeth, bristling like a giant grizzly bear. He paced away, hands on his lean hips. She loved his hands. It was one of her secrets, how she watched him sometimes handling things. A pen, his phone, or a power tool. He had perfectly long fingers and nicely cut nails. When he worked in the garage, those nails would get pitted with oil, and she imagined him running his dirty hands all over her clean skin. So when his hands dropped to his hips, her eyes followed. Thank the baby

Jesus; his sleeves covered his veiny forearms, or she might have whimpered.

One pace away, and he took two back, putting him further in her space, so she had to crane her neck to meet him eye-to-eye, and what she saw… what she saw made Scarlett's mouth flood with longing.

"You are fucking frustrating," he rasped like he was talking to himself. "I want to wring your neck every single day."

She didn't take it as a threat, not while her stomach bloomed warmly.

This was their thing.

They snapped at each other, but neither meant what they said. She wasn't afraid of Axel, however much he scowled and hissed at her. She'd never felt safer with anyone. That could be why she stepped forward, bumping into his chest as she took two fistfuls of his shirt front and told him. "Go ahead then, boss. Get rid of me for good."

It was a risky move and one she might regret later when she was back in her logical mind. But, compared to the life she'd escaped from, living in a motorcycle clubhouse was a charmed existence, and she didn't want to lose it.

But in those few seconds, she felt unmoored as Axel dropped his head.

Trepidation and tingling exhilaration tangled in her chest as the seconds ticked by, Axel's stare unwavering as his hand came up and curled around the front of her throat. Shock zapped Scarlett. Apart from that first day he'd pulled her out of the truck, they hadn't touched each other much. For Scarlett, it was deliberate. She couldn't be that close to Axel and not show how she felt. Now, with his hand spanning her hammering pulse, it was as though their energy danced together in a way she'd never felt before. She felt alive with blistering energy pouring from her skin, agitated with the need to push at the growling biker until he snapped, so she gripped his shirt tighter.

Provoking him.

The perverse side of her needed to see what he'd do next.

Would he thaw and show her who he really was?

Probably banish her to the cellar to count pieces of coal like Cinderella.

But that didn't happen.

All Scarlett saw next was his brown head lowering, then her mouth was smashed underneath his, and Axel was walking her backward until her spine hit the far wall.

She didn't have Axel kissing her wildly on her yearly bingo card.

His lips were incredible. *Indescribably good.*

Firm and insistent, his tongue prodded hers, and they sprang open to let him inside; that first taste was heaven itself. He tasted of smoke and rich coffee. She knew how dark and strong he liked his brews, and she moaned as that rich coffee bean flavor wrapped around her senses, as he lavished her with what she could only presume was a punishment kiss.

He wasn't seducing her.

Though she was wholly seduced, clinging to him like a maiden on her wedding night.

His lips were rough and then soft. She listened to his grunts as though warring with himself, but for what felt like minutes, he barely gave her a second to breathe.

And then the epic kiss ended abruptly, leaving Scarlett shaken to her core.

Did that happen? There was no way she had control of her belly flutters, not now.

Had Axel Tucker kissed the ever-loving hell out of her like he hated her guts but couldn't get inside her mouth deep enough?

Yes, I'll take 900 for what in the fantasy is this, Alex?

Scarlett would have loved ten minutes' grace to roll around the pounding lust and to overanalyze what just happened, but she wasn't afforded even a millisecond before Axel detangled her clutching hands from his shirt and marched away.

"For fuck's sake," he growled.

And then he pierced her with his stare, and Scarlett's rapid breath got trapped in her throat because she realized one thing really fast.

While she was wet between her legs with swirling lust for this man, he was angry.

Angry with her.

How could two people share the same experience and have opposite reactions?

"That did not happen," he grated, his jaw manically ticking with regret.

She was hurt.

It stung her all over.

But she was also pissed.

How dare he!

He'd been the one doing the kissing.

"It happened," she spat back, not letting him bury his head in the sand, however much he regretted kissing her. "*You* were the one who put your hand around my throat." She'd think about it later, how good it felt, and why she'd loved it. "*You* pinned me to the wall. It was *you* who kissed me, Axel. So if you're angry at anyone, maybe look at the idiot in a mirror."

He blinked like he wasn't used to someone putting him in his place.

In any other instance, Scarlett would have bitten her tongue and said nothing. She couldn't afford to get fired, and he could kick her out if she crossed a line.

Being kissed like all her dirty dreams and then told to forget it occurred put a flare of rage in her blood, so she'd deal with the fallout, whatever it may be, but she wasn't bowing down to a fragile male ego.

She tipped her chin back. Defying his stare.

"Forget it happened. And forget what you saw earlier."

Of all the nights and days she'd had silly fantasies about this man and how it would feel if she could ever kiss him, being this rejected never factored in.

Pulling in a breath, Scarlett pushed herself off the wall, moving her feet toward the door. "Forget you mauled me like an animal? And you loved it even if you deny it. Because we can't have the little girlfriend finding out you cheated, can you? I bet you'd love me to get amnesia right now."

His dark, gorgeous eyes flared to life, and she would swear to Jesus and his pet lambs she saw desire as he balled up both fists hanging by his sides. "Get out, Scarlett."

As a parting shot, he'd won because she had to swallow down her hurt feelings, but she glared at Axel before she slammed the door behind her hard enough that she heard him say "fuck" again.

If nothing else, at least Axel fucking Tucker had cured her of all feelings she once had for him.

"Stupid man," she muttered, her feet carrying her further away from his office. She didn't see the biker until she almost collided with him. "You talking to me, babe?" he grinned.

Scarlett shot him a glare. "All men are stupid idiots and need castrating."

"Ouch, what did I do?" he laughed, but she was in too much of a furious funk to entertain a foolish man with a conversation he wouldn't understand with his two floundering brain cells.

Ignoring the opening for a conversation, she stole through the clubhouse and up two floors to her room, where she locked the door and leaned back against it. Her hands cupped her flaming cheeks.

Axel Tucker had given her the kind of kiss she'd waited all her life for, believing it didn't exist. He'd kissed her with passion and dominance, almost like he was kissing her without permission, taking what he wanted, regardless.

And she'd loved every biting second for the short time it had lasted before stupidity stepped into the room and made Axel act like a jerk.

Axel

Since early that morning, Axel had been putting out fucking fires, not of his making but which affected his club and members if he didn't do shit about it.

It meant he had to contact Sofia Fielding again.

Meeting the shady cop he paid to deliver information was not his favorite thing because it gave the delusional woman the idea that he *wanted* to see her personally.

"Make the investigation go away, Sofia." He issued into the phone as he strode back to his Harley after spending time at one of his front businesses. Although it was just a hardware store to the outsider townsfolk, one of his unpatched senior members ran it and made a decent yearly profit. But in the back, it was used for his security boys, who were paid to protect and be heavies when the price was right.

"You realize I can't just miraculously make shit disappear once it's in the system, yeah? I'm good, but I'm not that good."

"I handed over five grand only days back. You better be able to piss rainbows if I tell you to. Get it fucking done. Throw something else in the way. I'm sure you can find a crooked politician doing dirty shit in a motel room without even trying."

He heard the feminine huff on the other end. The corruptible cop was a lot of negative things, but remarkably, she didn't whine.

She got back to him three hours later and said she'd made the assault charges disappear. He didn't need the details of how. Now he could tell the good news to his boy, who had been arrested by an off-duty cop who saw Diamond roughing up someone they were paid to put the heavy on.

Now that all fires were out, he headed back to the club, starving.

He was tired as his solid, well-worn leather boots crossed over the entryway of the clubhouse once he'd punched in the code at the door, but the moment he was inside, he felt a sizzling heat down his spine.

She was in here somewhere, and his body knew it.

Too fucking young for you, asshole.

His body didn't listen.

She hadn't tasted too young for him. She'd tasted of spice and fury.

After that kiss the other day, they'd unanimously avoided each other. Not that it mattered, because he still saw her everywhere. Making coffee in the kitchen and delivering clean towels to the gym shower area. Laughing with Splice. Playing cards with Splice. Each time, he turned around and headed in another direction, knowing it was for the best he forgot how goddamn delicious she tasted and how her tongue had submitted under his. But with each quick step, he grew angry and wanted to put Splice's head through a wall to stay away from her.

Whatever Scarlett had been running from, what put her on the streets, she seemed happy within the MC, and Axel realized he'd give anything to keep that girl happy.

Did that mean making room for Splice to put the moves on her?

Even thinking it made his bones tight, he had to banish the thoughts because the truth was he was fucking jealous. *So possessive.* Off his rocker to have an imaginary claim on the woman when he had no rights to it.

If she wanted to spend time with Splice or any other man, that was up to her. However, a phone call with his daughter changed the trajectory of Axel's thoughts when he was grabbing food from the kitchen.

"Anything going on?" he asked, and Roux laughed.

"I can call my dad without needing a reason."

Old habits die hard. Roux had been an undisciplined, potty-mouthed child because he'd given her a long leash. If there'd been trouble to get into, his Roux was head of the line, asking for seconds. He'd lost count of the jobs she quit because she disliked the work or the people hiring her.

She was strong-headed, wilful, a card shark, talked like any of his bikers and had all his heart. Axel would have bet his life on being a shit father, but somehow, between them, he'd given her the best life he could.

She was now married with two kids, but he'd always worry about her safety. It was instinctual.

"The Souls not getting into shit, are they?"

"You know I can't talk about what the Renegade Souls are up to, Dad. I married one of them, which means I took the secret handshake."

"It's not too late to come home," he half-joked. She might have a Souls old man now, but his Roux bled Diablo Disciples. They'd all learned to compromise to keep the peace among the clubs. If nothing else, it gave him and Rider Marinos, the Souls leader, a reason not to clash heads.

His unbridled daughter laughed. "This again? And what do I do with Butcher? Build him a doggie house outside for him to live in?"

Axel smirked, biting into the sandwich. "Sounds fine to me."

He liked his son-in-law. *Now.*

Not so much in the start when the older guy snuck around with Roux, and Axel put Butcher in the hospital. Not that it stopped them from seeing each other, which he later found out. They just got better at hiding it. He learned to accept some things he couldn't control, and who his Roux fell in love with was one of those things. Butcher was the best man because he'd walk into an apocalypse for her.

"When are you bringing my grandbabies to visit?"

"Soon. I need the break. They're gremlins."

Chuckling, Axel took a slurp of soda before answering. "Payback is so sweet, kiddo." He'd seen the kids in action and had to agree with Roux. Not that he didn't spoil and encourage them. It was a grandfather's privilege to hand them back to their parents.

They spoke a while longer, and he was relaxed as his boots carried him down to his office to finish some work before getting some sleep. Maybe tonight, he'd make it home to his house. How long had it been now? Weeks. Maybe more.

He didn't dig into why he was now sleeping at the club when he had a spacious house.

The peeling scream from the floor above robbed Axel of his next steps, and before he could think about it, he sprinted to the stairs, taking them three at a time.

It could only be one person, and Axel double-timed it down the hallway, assuming he was about to witness Scarlett in the middle of a murder scene.

Delivering a kick to the door, it split along the lock, and another scream ripped through the air. This time, he suspected, because of his entry.

There was a murder.

But it was only on TV.

Scarlett was sitting on the floor, her face ashen, lips hanging open.

"Oh, my God, Axel. Are you nuts? You scared me to death."

"*Scared you*? You fucking screamed like you were being massacred."

"And you broke my door!"

Heaving in a relieved breath, he looked to the ceiling and asked a God he didn't believe in for patience not to drag her over his lap and lay punishing swats to her ass for making him react like a fucking idiot.

When he was finally ready to speak, he did it in a low tone, staring at the more petite woman sitting on a pile of pillows. A throw blanket around her lap. "You can't yell like you're in trouble, not in a place like this, Scarlett."

Had he been carrying his 9mm gun, she would have pissed herself with fright if he'd come through the door ready to lay waste to an enemy.

It was selfish of him to imagine her being in danger and how she'd cling to him for protection. He shook that feral thought away and concentrated on the moment. He glanced at the TV to see a familiar movie.

"You were screaming at Final Destination?"

She scrunched up her nose at the paused scene. "It was gruesome. I've never seen these movies before. It might be the most horrific thing I've ever watched."

Huh. On the scale of horror movies, they were pretty tame. She must not be a horror movie fan. She answered his thought when she said, "I'm trying to catch up on the big movies I've missed."

"Why are you only seeing them now?"

As always, when he tried to get any info from Scarlett about her past and how she got to the place she had, she dipped her head, avoiding.

"Probably busy. Anyway, you broke my door. I can't believe you did that."

Neither could Axel.

His only thought had been reaching Scarlett to fix whatever made her scream, and the door had been in his way. He turned to look at the damage. It wasn't too bad.

"I'll see to it." He left without another word, returning minutes later with the tools and a new door lock. Scarlett was now sitting on her twin bed, looking at him.

"You're not usually here this late." She observed.

If only she knew.

He hadn't wanted her to sleep alone at the clubhouse.

It was safe as he could get it, protected by security and outside cameras. And sometimes, his brothers were around, choosing to sleep off a hangover in one of their rooms, but seeing how scared she'd been that first night, he'd stayed in his room one floor away.

And then he'd stayed the night after that.

It had continued now for months.

And on the rare nights when he forced himself to go home, he couldn't sleep over worrying if she was okay, so usually, he dragged his insane ass back to the club at insane hours to be closer in case she needed anything.

Because of the pattern of bickering they'd found themselves in. Axel suspected she'd choose to ask a mangy dog for help before she asked him. It never stopped him from being close by.

Kneeling on the carpet, he changed the broken lock, aware of a pair of green eyes boring into the back of his head.

No matter how wrong he felt about it, how much of a dirty old pervert he was, he couldn't keep that kiss out of his gray matter for long.

It danced and seduced along his memories, making a hot boil of steam gather at the base of his spine. He'd wanted to fucking devour her, swallow her whole, taking her whimpers into his lungs.

Never had a simple kiss gotten to him before.

He'd steered clear of Scarlett for days, only seeing her in the peripheral, unable to stay away for good. Now he was in her orbit, inside her room, which smelled like her. Coconut and spring. He didn't even know what that fucking meant, but she smelled of springtime, and he inhaled long and hard as he finished and rose to his feet. He tested the door by locking and unlocking it a few times.

"All fixed."

"Do I say thanks for breaking it?"

He arched an eyebrow. "Don't be a brat. It would have been a different story had someone been climbing in your window." He instantly regretted frightening her. "Don't worry, that wouldn't happen. It was hypothetical and a warning for you not to scream your head off."

Unless I'm buried balls deep, giving it to you in the way I need to.

The thought came unbidden, unleashing like a great horny beast, and Axel swallowed a rush of arousal, angling his hips so she wouldn't see the growing bulge in his jeans.

He was a pervert thinking of her that way.

Too young for him.

Or he was too old.

Either way, it was a bad idea to let thoughts like that break free and make him reckless to fuck her down on the floor like a rutting animal.

However much Axel attempted to ignore it happened, to forget the taste of her or how her fingers had gripped tightly on his shirt, pulling him closer. He couldn't.

Somewhere between dragging her into his clubhouse and now, he'd written an invisible contract with himself to look out for this woman. Like he thought he was a good man.

His debauched thoughts proved he wasn't.

Sighing, he went to turn to leave when she said, "if you can stand to be around me for a while, do you want to finish watching this with me?"

Fuck. Stand to be around her?

If only she knew.

After that kiss, maybe she did.

Axel closed the door and retraced his steps. It was madness to be in her bedroom. Not that he needed a bed to take her. He could sink his cock into her in the middle of the forecourt and not care who saw them.

"There's drinks and snacks in the mini-fridge, although it's pretty sparse. I need to go shopping tomorrow and restock my goodies."

He eyed the fridge, pulling it open to see two bottles of beer and a package of green grapes.

"Scarlett, the kitchen is fully stocked, so is the bar, and you know what's in the stockrooms because you help keep them that way. You don't need to buy your own food. Take whatever you want."

"I don't feel right helping myself to more than my meals."

Christ, this woman was so prideful.

Turning, he went out the door without a word, returning five minutes later with his arms full. A six-pack of the beers she liked, crackers, chocolate, cheese, and nuts. He rammed them all into the mini-fridge. Then, when he crouched down to the floor, beer in hand, and sat with inches separating them, he said. "When it's empty, get whatever you need from downstairs."

"Is that part of my salary package, too, boss?"

"Yes." He grated through his teeth. It was *now*. "Press play on this thing. Let me see if it's worth your screams."

She sniffed and let the movie start again. "From the beginning or here?"

"Here is fine."

"Just wait. It'll scare the pants off you, too."

"My pants are staying where they are."

Goddamn him. Now he was flirting. He took a long pull of the bottled beer and forced his eyes on the screen. "This TV is shit, Scarlett. It's too small."

"Hey, it's fine. Chains told me it was in the basement, and I could use it. It doesn't get cable or anything, so I bought a refurbished DVD player on eBay, and every week I treat myself to discounted DVDs to watch."

He'd noticed the towering pile of DVD cases in the corner. "You watched all of 'em?"

"I'm making my way through. Comedies are my favorite. Kevin Hart is so funny. Do you know him?"

Didn't everyone? How she said it confused Axel again. It was as though she saw things for the first time.

"Yeah, I know him. You should watch his stand-up comedy specials on Netflix."

She grinned, and his stomach muscles flexed. He'd become greedy for her smiles. "I'm gonna write it on my to-do list." And didn't she just pull out her phone to type something? He couldn't read her list, but it was pretty long.

"What else is on that thing?"

She slipped it under her pillow. "Oh, you know, just silly things I want to do. Go places, see the sights."

"And catch up on old 90s movies?"

Another grin. "Yep."

"Didn't you watch much TV growing up?"

She looked agitated, glued to the screen as two women climbed into tanning machines. Axel had seen this one and knew how Scarlett would react when she saw them both burned alive.

"My parents didn't allow it. They said it rotted the mind."

He didn't push for more info, but it was the first time in all the months he'd known her she'd mentioned any family.

As predicted, a minute later, she shrieked when the women died horrifically.

Axel laughed at her shock, and she scowled at him. "You knew that would happen."

"I don't think these movies are for you, Scarlett. They get progressively worse."

She shuddered, and he had to stop pulling her onto his lap to soothe her.

It didn't make a damn bit of sense.

If he fucked a woman, it was sex. He never got the urge to fill up her fridge, kick down doors, and hover like a demented pervert to ensure she was okay. He sure as hell didn't think about holding her on his lap.

The movie continued; he finished his beer, and so did Scarlett. With every passing minute, he told himself he needed to leave. And each minute, he ignored his fucking self.

"If death was coming after you, what would you want to do first?" she asked suddenly. Scarlett laid her head on the edge of the bed as the movie progressed. Axel felt the burn of the few inches separating them.

Why was he torturing himself?

He could easily find a willing body downstairs with any sweet bottoms to settle the fire within caused by the waif innocently looking at him through slow blinking eyes.

"I'd see my kid and grandbabies."

"Aww." She beamed a smile.

"And then get drunk for the rest of the time. What would you do.?"

The way she streaked her gaze over him and the blush filled her cheeks. He knew her answer, and his dick loved it even as Axel rubbed his teeth together behind his closed lips. Frustrated. Willing her to choose a different, safer answer.

"If death knocked at my door, I'd crawl into your lap and kiss you with my last breath."

Fuck.

Fuck.

It had been a hypothetical question, and yet still, Axel knew with the oath of his entire rotten soul that if death chased Scarlett, he'd move mountains to save her.

If she wanted to kiss him afterward, he wouldn't say no.

There was a strong possibility he'd never say no to this woman.

And Axel knew he was truly fucked.

Axel

Her words rattled around his skull in a loop. It felt like he'd been punched in the throat.

Feeling weakened was a sobering thought as Axel shot to his feet.

With the last shred of decency in his free-from-morals body, he knew he needed to put space between them before he did something he'd regret.

Would he?

Or would he roll around in her taste like a junkie on a line of coke?

The phantom taste of Scarlett, even now, drove him mad, needing more of it in his mouth.

"I'm worse than death after you, Scarlett," he rasped.

"Sorry. *Shit*. I shouldn't have said it. I've had two beers. Ignore me. I didn't mean to disrespect your girlfriend like that. That isn't who I am."

His girlfriend?

Fuck. He'd forgotten she'd spied on him when he'd been meeting Fielding, put two and two, and came up with him being a happily ever after. He should allow her to keep thinking he was taken. It would undoubtedly put the brakes on her feelings. The feelings she couldn't hide because they shone out of her eyes. He'd never cared about sparing someone's feelings before her, and now he tread on unbroken ground to save her from being hurt by him.

But she looked so regretful that he confessed. "There's no woman, Scarlett. You saw me meeting a cop I pay."

She blinked. "You bribe a police officer?"

"I do a lot of bad things."

She appeared to digest that as she climbed to her feet. Axel nearly swallowed his tongue, seeing her in the tight-as-skin sleep shorts, leaving nothing to his perverted imagination when his gaze dropped to the imprint of her pussy through the cotton material.

"That means you didn't have a girlfriend when we kissed."

"No," he grated.

"Whew." She smiled at him. "I felt guilty about it."

That sweetness would kill him faster than diabetes. There was an ache in the center of his chest at the hopeful look on her face, and he hated himself because he knew he would crush her.

"That means…"

Shit. She looked so hopeful, and Axel wasn't a strong man. He wanted her, he fully admitted it, accepting the depravity that lived in his head now and made his cock act like a teen with its first taste of pussy.

But there was no way he could act on it.

He already felt like a lecher.

"No," he growled too harshly, watching her flinch as he dragged a hand over his head. "Listen, Scarlett."

"No, I got it."

"Do you?"

"Yes," she hissed. "I'm far from stupid, whatever you think about me."

"Scarlett. I've never thought of you that way."

"Could you please not say my name authoritatively like you're about to chastise me?"

"You're the same age as my kid, Scarlett. I saw your license, and your birthdays are two-fucking-days apart. Do you know what a sicko that makes me for kissing you? Wanting you? this can't happen. Whatever you think you feel, it'll pass."

"Oh, my God. Don't fucking condescend to me, Axel. Your *kid* is a grown woman with a husband and two children. I'm all grown up, if you haven't noticed. So maybe if you didn't think of her as a kid, you'd realize you and me are not the same as you and her."

He couldn't say anything because he knew logically she was right. It wasn't as though Scarlett was sixteen.

But she was innocent, especially in his lifestyle.

Fuck him for wanting to do the right thing by someone for the first time.

His back molars mashed together, and he headed for the door.

"After everything I've seen within these walls, everything you guys do, you're growing a conscience over my age?" he turned long enough to see Scarlett shake her head, disappointed, and he felt it in his stomach. "You're only my boss. Got it."

"Scarlett..."

"I got it, Axel. Now it's late, I'd like to go to bed."

Envy stirred around his chest, wondering how she'd feel laid on top of him, all drowsy and cuddly. She'd feel incredible, and he had to get the fuck out of there.

With regret, he closed the door.

It was the first night in months he had stayed at home, and he hated every second, but he knew it was necessary.

Axel had never been the dating kind of man.

After the disaster of Roux's mother, and he used that term loosely since she'd never been a mother to her, he'd played with women when he'd had the urge, but he'd put his kid and his club as priorities.

Dating was what other men did, not Axel.

He couldn't date Scarlett, and he couldn't be her boss *and* fuck her.

For once, he was doing the right thing by someone else.

She'd thank him one day.

Whatever lies he fed himself with a rusty spoon, he didn't sleep much that night thinking of the sweet, hopeful look on her face or tasting her mouth all over again.

Sweet and innocent couldn't be his flavor.

Not when he played rough.

Breaking Scarlett was something he wouldn't compromise on.

He'd protect her against anyone.

Him and his filthy ways most of all.

Axel

"Is there a reason we now have a home theater in the basement?" Chains asked, lounging against the office wall.

The mohawk VP should have better things to do with his time. Shit always needed doing around the club, but apparently, he'd chosen to poke at Axel instead.

"We needed one?"

"Did we?" he smirked.

So fucking what he'd spent all yesterday fixing up a large projector in one of the empty basement rooms, dragging in lazy boy chairs with the help of the prospects, and then getting a tech guy in to wire it up for all the streaming channels.

"Make your point, Chains. I'm busy."

Chains advanced into the office and threw himself down into the chair opposite.

Five years ago, he was a contained, angry man, living with the grief of losing his sister. Axel had thought Chains had always been like a live grenade, unsure of when he'd erupt. So, he spent months keeping Chains away from flames. Nowadays, he was a changed man. Finding love had healed the darkness within him, and Axel was happy for the guy. Though not so much when he walked in on him dry-humping Monroe or interrupted one of their many phone sex conversations. He could live ten lifetimes without hearing those ever again.

"I'm just saying it's a weird thing for you to do. You took prospects off jobs so they could lump furniture to the basement."

"Then fucking enjoy my weirdness when you wanna watch Rambo."

Chains burst out laughing and knocked his ringed fingers on the table before rising, a knowing smirk on his face. "Hope the girlie enjoys your gift."

Axel kept his mouth shut.

She'd stayed out of his way all day and most of yesterday, and he felt like shit about it. But he was filled with purpose when he left the office sometime later to find her. Burdened with the need to fix some of the hurt he was responsible for.

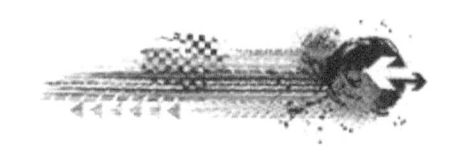

Scarlett

She hated how seeing Axel striding through the clubhouse became like a breath of fresh air in her lungs.

After the embarrassing rejection part two the other night, she'd sneaked around like a ninja, hoping not to bump into the big boss man. But what do you know? Her lungs inflated when she saw his long-legged gait bringing him forward. Scarlett went nuts cleaning the bar top, though it was pristine, and watched him from her peripheral.

"Scarlett, I need you a minute."

Oh, God. She *wished*.

"Sorry, boss. I have a million things I need to do here." She addressed Axel without looking his way and mentally high-fived herself for acting cool as a melon.

With her back to him now, pretending to count the bottles, she didn't hear him step behind the bar until her skin heated, feeling him along her spine. But it was too late to duck and run or try to throw herself across the bar. Maybe if she'd had long enough, she could have ninja jumped over it if she grabbed a step stool first.

She found her wrist lassoed and pulled behind Axel.

"Oh, my God. Here we go again!" she trotted to keep up.

"Your hostage giving you trouble, Prez? I can find a switch if you need to punish her." Called out Tomb, and she scowled his way. She'd always liked the guy standing well over 6 foot 5 with his juicy dad bod and millions of tattoos, but now she mentally put him on her enemy list. It was growing by the second. The man yanking her arm from its socket was the top-tier enemy.

"I'm not his hostage, you big bully." She yelled back, and Tomb belly laughed, winking at her.

"They'll rile you the more they see you react," Axel said calmly as he walked her through the hallways and started on the staircase leading down to the basement. Was he taking her to the torture room she'd heard about? She hoped not. She wasn't wearing the proper footwear.

"Then tell them I'm not your prisoner. Sheesh. A girl tries to steal a lousy five dollars for food, and she's been treated like the Artful Dodger ever since." Scarlett bumped into a solid chest when Axel stopped walking, and she didn't. He'd turned around and gazed down at her through those eyes she could drown in. Damn his gorgeous eyes to hell and back. She glowered, showing her disdain for being dragged everywhere.

"If you don't want to be a hostage, stop acting like one." Axel started walking again, keeping her wrist firmly in his grasp, giving Scarlett no choice but to follow behind. Her mouth opened and then closed.

"What the hell do you mean by that?"

"Figure it out, wildcat."

He marched her through the gymnasium. Splice gave her a wink. Devil looked on, amused. "Gonna tie up the hostage, Prez? Don't forget the gag. She's got a set of pipes on her."

"I'm going to tell Kelly, and I hope she makes you sleep in the rain!" the biker only laughed and carried on with his shadowboxing.

These bikers were despicable. She took silent vows of vengeance out against them all.

"You have a freaking fetish about dragging me around."

"Hardly dragging,"

It was true. And he was holding her wrist gently. If she tugged, she'd have it free, but the sick part of her enjoyed being touched by him, even in this way.

It didn't stop her from complaining, though. It wouldn't be their dynamic if she did.

"Is it because I've been a bad girl, boss?" she taunted. "Oh, Sir, I'm so, so sorry."

The way Axel whirled around nearly gave her a heart attack because the heat pounding out of his eyes made her breath hitch, and she wondered what she'd said to trigger those flickering flames.

The air was palpable as she watched him, almost seething air through his clenched teeth.

Whoa, boy. A nasty, hot shiver went down her back as his fingers flexed around her wrist.

Axel was gorgeous up close. Seriously panty wetting luscious. He was the man you'd want to make furious to see his desire roar out of control.

She had to know.

Curiosity would kill her if she didn't know.

"Okay, fine." She wheezed, "I wasn't a bad girl."

Not a flicker.

"Sorry, Sir."

His pupils dilated to two black disks.

Ding. Ding. Ding. We have a winner.

Whoa. He enjoyed being called Sir.

"Don't be a brat," he rasped, restarting their epic journey. Where the heck was he taking her, anyway? "Come on." He dragged, and Scarlett trotted like an obedient puppet because, of course, she'd follow Axel. She'd Stockholm imprinted on him like a baby duckling.

What he had to show her was not even on her list of guesses.

"Do you like it?"

"I… I don't get it."

"It's for you to watch TV or your movies." He told her it was set up for every streaming service she could ever want.

Her mouth went dry, and her heart triple-timed.

If she cried, she would kick him for making her emotions go nuts.

"You did this for me?"

"Your TV is shit, Scarlett."

"You made me a whole movie room with comfy chairs."

He rolled a shoulder like it was no big deal, but it was a massive deal. Colossal.

Why would he do something nice for her if he didn't want her to catch romantic feelings and kiss his face off? It made no sense.

But she thanked him for the incredible gift and smiled like a lunatic for the rest of the night, even when Axel disappeared, boasting to everyone that she'd charge them to watch movies in *her* special room.

Never once forgetting that heated look on Axel's face when she'd called him Sir.

Scarlett

"Why aren't you thrilled about this?"

"I am," Scarlett answered Monroe under her sharp gaze.

"You might want to tell your face that, babe."

"I've already watched eight movies and started two boxset shows."

"Axel Tucker made you a whole media room. I thought you'd be doing cartwheels."

"It's fantastic, and it was nice of him, Monroe. But I'm over that silly thing now."

"Silly thing?" smiled Monroe. "You no longer want to jump his bones, then?"

"Shush. And no, I don't, not anymore. I realized how pointless it was to attach feelings to someone who helped me. He's just my boss."

"Mmhm." Replied Monroe, as though not believing a word of Scarlett's bullshit.

And that's what it was.

But she was trying to fake it until she made it.

Axel had done a lovely thing for her. The least she could do was not have sexual fantasies about the man every time she laid eyes on him. It seemed only fair.

"Okay, then. I'm glad you said that because there's this guy I know who would be perfect for you, I want to set you guys up. He's an accountant."

Now it was Scarlett's brows turn to shoot up into her red hair. She looked at her friend agog. "You think an *accountant* is perfect for me?"

"Hey, now." Laughed Monroe. "I'm an accountant."

"Yeah, and I don't want to have sex with you. No offense, babe."

"None taken. Now let me fix you up, trust me. Dan's a hot geek." When Scarlett hesitated, Monroe reached across the bar and laid her hand on Scarlett's. "Sweetie, I won't push if you're not interested. It was just an idea to get you out of this place for the night."

"I like this place."

It was safe.

It felt like home, crazily enough.

But Scarlett spontaneously nodded, and before she could change her mind, she said. "Okay, set it up."

"Really? That's great. You'll love him."

"Not sure about love, but there's no reason I shouldn't date someone."

She wished there was.

She wished a tall hunk of a scowling biker would object and forbid her to date anyone because she belonged to him.

But pigs would fly in a rainbow tutu before that happened.

And as if she'd conjured him by magic, he walked into their conversation at the wrong time while Monroe called Scarlett's blind date.

Scarlett instantly fused with heat around her cheeks and neck, trying to look busy and avoid Axel's scrutiny as he strode by.

He made her nervous and excited. Though she knew she should, she couldn't tear her eyes away from him until he walked over to the prospects.

"Okay, it's set up. Dan is eager to meet you, Scar."

"Hm? Oh, yeah. That's good."

Monroe followed Scarlett's eyeline and then looked back at her. "Are you sure you want to go on a blind date?"

Scarlett almost snapped to attention, embarrassed she'd been caught mooning over her boss. "You're the one who wants me to do this."

"Because you seem lonely sometimes."

Who could she tell that she longed for companionship?

After leaving that mess back home, she thought she wouldn't want to date anyone or have a man in her life trying to run it.

But it turned out Scarlett's heart was like anyone else's, and it yearned for someone who was only hers. Someone to be there in the middle of the night when thunder shook her eardrums or to laugh with as she discovered new movies.

She wanted passion, desire, and so much sex she'd oversleep for work the next day.

If there was a complete package of lover and partner, Scarlett needed it.

And if she couldn't have it with the man she was infatuated with, she'd kiss many frogs instead. Hey, it worked for Disney princesses.

Axel turned then and headed back their way. Everything in Scarlett tightened, braced to be in his orbit again. But, anxiously, her greedy, traitorous eyes looked their fill.

"There's no reason I shouldn't go on a date," she answered Monroe, but directed her words toward Axel. Secretly pleading for him to intervene. Forbid her to dare even look at another man.

But he did nothing. And the only reaction she caught was a powerful jaw tick. And then he walked off.

This new rejection hit differently.

It was sore and open, salt pouring in.

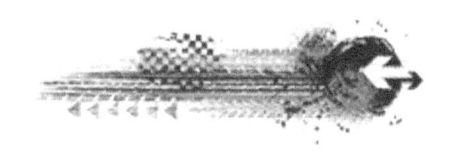

Axel

He wanted to lie and say it was fury driving him.

But Axel wasn't in the habit of lying to himself.

If a man couldn't be truthful, he had no business being a man.

And because Axel hated liars more than anything, he couldn't get into self-loathing, not at his age. He was too damn old to buy new habits.

It was *jealousy*.

He sat on it for more than an hour until his chest cavity felt as though it were filled with gasoline-guzzled flames.

Shooting to his feet, he quit pretending he was working and headed for the hallway, stopping a prospect who was mopping.

"Have you seen Chains?"

"Not in a while, Prez, but he was 'round back last I saw him."

That's where Axel headed, and Champ greeted him. The unofficial club dog. Champ had come around looking for scraps about a year ago. He looked to be a mix of English Alsatian and mongrel. He was friendly enough now after Axel worked to gain his trust, but he'd never become an inside dog.

Champ liked to roam wherever he wanted to go. He probably had bitches in every town and hands to feed him, too.

The bushy tail wagged, and Axel leaned down as Champ rested against Axel's leg, giving him a stroke. "Hey, boy. You were fed, huh?"

It was the prospect's job to always see to the dog. He'd even had them build Champ a kennel to keep the pup dry in cold and wet weather. It was a toss-up whether the dog used it but couldn't get that mutt inside, no matter what food he enticed him with. Axel reckoned he'd been abused, and being locked inside was a trigger to him.

"He just scarfed down the leftover steaks. That beast eats better than I do." Said Chains, and Axel followed the voice to see his VP hosing down the soles of his mud-caked boots.

Axel picked up one of the discarded rubber balls and threw it across their land as far as possible. Champ, liking a chase, ran at full speed after it. Bringing it back for the game to continue.

"How's it going with your father-in-law?"

"I ran into a hitch. Who knew the lazy fucker was paranoid, huh?" smirked Chains. "He's not letting any new bodies into his lair, so to speak. But I got around it. I paid one of the strippers to give him some special attention, and when he inevitably invited her back to his place, she planted the drugs and flash drives in his car."

Axel whistled through his teeth. Impressed. "She had to give it up to Donahue?" he pitied any woman climbing into bed with that sweaty sleaze.

"Nah, she pretended to get sick, and he tossed her out of the Merc."

Chains had played the long game in waiting for the perfect time to stick it to his father-in-law for being the one who made his wife grieve for her dead sister. Setting up a guy to go to prison for drugs and child pornography wasn't the worst thing either had done in their time. They did what they did for those they loved.

However morally gray it was.

Axel didn't know if he possessed a shred of decency, but he'd forged his world now and made it as strong and protected as he could for his family.

"The IT guy must have a cast iron stomach to look at that filth."

"He's been paid enough. I couldn't look at that shit." Chains said, finishing with the hose. He hooked it back onto the wall. Axel threw the ball again for Champ, who happily chased off into the wilderness to retrieve it. "I trusted he found enough on the dark web to incriminate Donahue without leeway for him to buy his way out of it."

"You want Fielding to move on him soon?"

"Yeah, set it up. I want it done, so my Monroe can forget that jerkoff ever gave her life."

A call with Sofia lasted less than a minute, giving her the heads up to pull Donahue over on a regular traffic stop. The shit they'd find was enough that he wouldn't even make bail. And after Axel made an anonymous tip-off to a cutthroat journalist to follow the story, he ensured Donahue couldn't line the pockets of corrupt judges to sweep it under the carpet.

Axel might not lean toward goodness, but it felt right to eliminate scum.

While looking at the dog sprinting after the ball, he threaded both hands down into the front pockets of his jeans. "I need a favor."

"Yeah? What's that? Are we digging a large grave?"

Nah. That shit was straightforward and didn't touch his conscience. What he wanted to do involved something else.

Fucking *emotions* that wouldn't be ignored any longer.

"Your wife has set Scarlett up on a blind date. I want a name and where it's happening."

Axel counted silently; he didn't reach three before Chains snickered.

Champ returned, dropped the ball at Axel's feet, and trotted to the water dish, panting. With the razzing he'd given Chains when he was trying to win his wife over, he figured it had come full circle, and Chains deserved the payback laugh.

"Get it the fuck out of your system, then make the call, hm."

"This is rich. Like fucking cake in my mouth, brother. I never thought I'd see the day you lost your marbles for a chick. So, Roux was right, you punched a guy because you were jealous."

Partly.

What the fuck ever.

Grinding his back teeth, he replied. "He was bragging to his buddies about using her. You want me to ignore that and let her go home with him, huh? Would you do that with some prick talking about Roux that way?"

"You know I wouldn't, but I love Roux like a daughter. Scar isn't your daughter, and this isn't fatherly protection. Just admit it, Axe, and I'll make the call and get all the saucy details for you." The fucker smirked, loving knowing he had Axel over a barrel.

"It's not fatherly fucking protection. Now make the call. Asshole."

The other man grinned ear to ear. "You got it, brother."

He stepped away to play catch and fetch with Champ while Chains talked to his wife. He didn't want to hear the inevitable snickering between them.

It was inexplicable why he was doing what he was going to do.

Not like his thoughts on the matter had changed.

He still felt like a lewd bastard for looking at Scarlett.

For dying to do the nastiest shit to her and hear her cries of pleasure ringing through his ears. He didn't even know if he would pursue anything, but overhearing Monroe set Scarlett up on a date with some jackass and how she'd looked directly at him, delivering the cutting words that there was no reason she shouldn't go on a date.

The re-surge of irritation made his Adam's apple bob.

He fucking *objected* to her even thinking about dating.

He had a big reason for the wildcat, and that was he *forbade it*.

And if she threw a hissy fit over his interference, he'd put her over his lap and teach her manners.

Fuck. His cock liked the idea and wouldn't calm down behind the zipper, demanding satisfaction from her. If Axel jerked off anymore in the shower, his wrist would need a brace.

Just because he didn't voice his wants didn't make them any less powerful. He'd stewed on it for months, trying to make it disappear with little success.

Axel wouldn't call running the MC a hobby. It was too damn stressful for that. Ordinary men had regular hobbies.

Axel had made Scarlett his hobby.

Watching her every move.

Eye-stalking her wherever she was in the clubhouse. He felt like the worst kind of depraved man for manifesting fantasies of her with every sway of her hips or tilt of a smile.

He wished he could pinpoint when it started.

Maybe in his office that day when he forced her out of that overcoat and finally got a look at the woman beneath.

Something had snapped inside of him.

Possibly his fucking sanity.

Champ sat patiently at his legs, looking up at Axel, waiting for the ball to be thrown again. He leaned down and grabbed the yellow ball as Chains walked over.

"Right, this guy is called Dan. Monroe's worked with him in the past."

"He's a number cruncher?" scowled Axel. That was all wrong for Scarlett. She was wild inside; he'd seen glimpses of it. An accountant would bore the life out of her after five minutes. She had a zest for life; he'd watched her soak everything up like a sponge and take delight in the dumbest shit. She was so goddamn pretty when she got excited about something.

"And get this. He's meeting her at Shay's."

Fucking Shay's. A number cruncher inside a biker bar. Now Axel was insulted and wanted to put the hurt on this guy.

"And she'll kill me if I don't repeat what she told me to tell you. Monroe said if you're not serious about Scar, leave her alone because Dan would be good for her, and Scar needs some good in her life."

Axel committed only a grunt. He couldn't tell Chains to control his woman because she was another outspoken one. Plus, Chains was under her thumb and would do anything she asked.

"What's the plan?" he asked, getting in step with Axel once he walked back inside.

"You're not coming."

"I abso-fucking-lutely am. You think I'd miss this?" the jackass clapped Axel on the back and followed him.

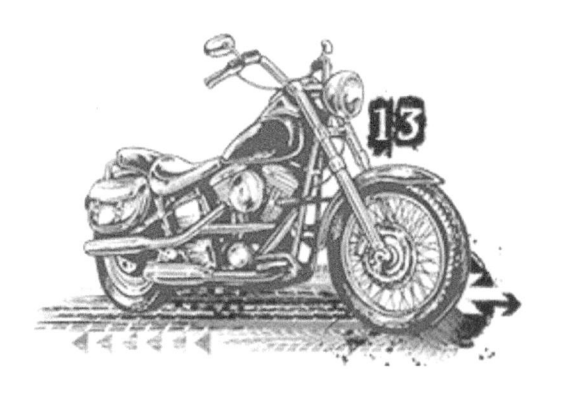

Axel

It was no effort to spot the bean counter in Shay's bar because he was the only one wearing a Wallstreet blazer.

"My dude looks like he's waiting for his Hollywood cue," clowned Chains. Both men stared at the blond guy sitting with his fingers laced in the corner booth. Axel didn't wait around. He took the steps and slid opposite Dan, who looked up and jolted with uncertainty.

"That seat is taken."

"Yeah, by us," added Chains, who followed suit and pushed in alongside Axel.

Axel didn't beat around the bush, not when his neck felt tight and his usual calm attitude had taken a coffee break, leaving him untethered and ready to fight.

"You're Dan. And you're meeting Scarlett tonight for a blind date, yeah?"

The guy blinked. "How did you—"

Axel interrupted. "You're gonna break the date."

"I'm what now? Who even are you?"

"You got cotton between your ears, guy?" asked Chains. "My friend here said you're gonna break the date."

Axel took over as he brought his locked fingers on top of the table, leaning in just a little. A nasty scowl etched around his lips. He wasn't fucking playing around. He'd let this polished dickhole date Scarlett over his dead, rotting body. And even then, he'd rise from the soil and choke him out for even thinking about half the things Axel was thinking about doing to Scarlett. Nah, this GQ wannabe had to go, and not a lick of guilt was felt about running him off.

He could chase off a thousand guys and make it into his new favorite sport.

"The date isn't gonna happen. It's your unlucky night, but there's still time for you to find a hookup elsewhere. So stand your fashion plate ass up and get out of here."

When the guy only stared, unblinking, across the scratched brown table, Axel growled low in his throat as a precursor to his first warning. He had no patience to pussyfoot around a fool who couldn't comprehend he was being given a get-out-of-death-free card here.

And then the accountant opened his big mouth.

"What the fuck are you talking about? Is Scarlett not coming? Who are you?"

"So many questions for a man who should be fucking off," smirked Axel amiably. "So, I'll explain in smaller words for you to understand. Your date is canceled. You don't contact Scarlett again, and if you're a good little boy, you'll walk out of here with all your bones intact. But if you wanna take your chances, here's what will happen in ten seconds. First, I'll drag your carcass out of this booth by your throat. Next, I'll start breaking your fingers, then move onto your kneecaps, and if you're still conscious, it's your ankles next. Think I'm joking?" he arched an eyebrow. "Test me out, Dan."

"Jesus, fucking Christ. You're insane," he huffed, looking around the bar with startled eyes. His skin had paled. And Axel felt nothing for scaring the blameless guy.

"No point looking for help. These are my people, Dan. Times ticking. Eight… seven… six…"

"Fuck it. This shit isn't worth it." He pushed himself out of the booth, and without a look backward, the mousy accountant, who didn't deserve to inhale the same air as Scarlett, scuttled off.

It was Chains who broke the tension by cackling. "We haven't done that in a long time. That was fun."

Axel had doled out many threats but never possessively over a woman. He rested back in the booth and checked out the door. It was almost time for Scarlett to turn up. He nudged Chains. "Okay, take off."

"For real? I can't stick around for the rest of the show?"

"No. Fuck off, and tell your woman not to do this again, or I'll take it out on your face."

Chains smirked. "Since you caught feelings, you're no fun anymore."

Axel stared at his VP. "Fine, if your hostage kills you for this, I'm burying you with the skunks." He climbed to his feet. "Good luck, brother. Don't fuck it up; she's the best bartender the club has ever had."

Axel wasn't thinking about losing an employee.

He didn't know if he was staking a claim on Scarlett.

But he sure as shit wasn't sitting back while someone else got his grubby mitts on her. Absolutely not. The rage still bubbled within at the thought.

Shifting seats so he could watch the door.

He waited for Scarlett to arrive for her blind date to break the bad… *good* news.

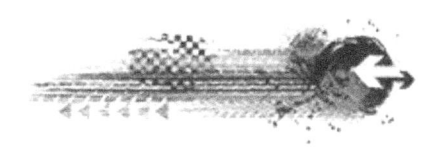

Scarlett

Nerves skittered over her skin as she stepped into the bar entryway once the prospect dropped her off. Axel had insisted, Mouse told her.

Okay then. That didn't hurt. Nope. He was so eager for her to date that he'd arranged transportation. Well, thanks, boss.

She'd waited outside for a few minutes, deciding if she wanted this, but she couldn't come up with a legitimate reason she shouldn't sit opposite a lovely man to have a drink and conversation with. Besides the fact, she had no desire to.

After a lengthy hyped talk, she squared her shoulders and made sure her skinny white jeans had no dirt on them after climbing down from the truck. Her B cups looked good in the casual t-shirt. Then, touching her hair a little, she headed inside the noisy bar.

It was her first time at Shay's, and the atmosphere swept over her.

Lots of leather and denim-clad bikers everywhere. She recognized a few out-of-towners who'd been to the clubhouse, but it wasn't a biker who she was looking for. Monroe gave her Dan's description. She said he looked like Liam Hemsworth.

Truth be told, the Hemsworth brothers didn't do anything for Scarlett, so she didn't expect much, certainly not to feel fireworks burst in her stomach as she met a pair of eyes.

Her feet came to a stop in the middle of the bar.

It wasn't her mystery Hemsworth lookalike date she saw staring at her.

Axel Tucker was here with his head slightly tilted and his eyes raking up and down her body in that way, women wouldn't be confused about what he was thinking.

He was checking her out. Depravity at its rawest, she experienced it rubbing over her skin, making Scarlett winded.

What was he doing here?

Oh, shit. She would die on the spot if he were on a date, too. There was no way she could sit in the same bar and watch a woman fawn over Axel. She couldn't trust herself not to army-pounce on the woman and smash her head into the table.

Forcing her feet to move, she figured it was impolite to ignore him, though that's what she wanted to do. Pulling her gaze from him, Scarlett searched the bar, hoping to see a man also looking at her. She'd told Dan she'd be wearing white.

"Axel. What are you doing here?"

"Take a seat." He issued, and her eyebrows folded in. He was alone, but it didn't mean a woman wasn't in the restroom and would be back any second.

"Thanks, but I'm meeting someone, so have a good night."

Pulling herself from his gravitational pull was all she could think about; she turned away, tempted to cancel the date, seeing as Dan wasn't here yet. But before she could take another step, Axel was out of his seat and towering over her. "Scarlett, sit down." He repeated. The quality in his tone sounded like smooth whiskey and bonfires. A sound she couldn't resist, and inexplicably, as it always did, she obeyed without question, sliding into the half-bucket booth.

She nearly died when Axel followed her on the same side, his more considerable body touching hers.

Oh, God. This was torture.

"I can't stay. I'm meeting someone, Axel. Who are you here with?"

"I'm here with you."

Oh. No woman, then?

She saw him motion with his head to someone across the bar, and then a server hurried over. "What can I get you, Axel?"

"I'll take a neat scotch. And a sour cherry rum." That was her drink of choice lately.

The drinks arrived, and because Scarlett's nerves had tripled and brought cousins along for the show, she downed half in one gulp. Regretting it when she had to hold a cough at bay. Good thing she wasn't trying to look sexy for Axel.

"Are you meeting someone?"

"Told you already. I'm here with you."

She frowned. "You're alone?"

He smirked, and her stomach butterflies went crazy. Why did he need to be the hottest man alive? His command over whatever room he was in was undeniably sexy.

Sometimes, she'd stealthily watch him when he was talking seriously with a group of his men. How his arms crossed and made his forearms bulge with muscle and sinew. His mouth worked words like a filthy spoken poet, just rich sounds stroking her erogenous zones expertly. He talked about things she didn't understand, people she'd never met, but how he did it showed Scarlett he was entirely in charge as people rushed to do his bidding.

It must be nice to be that effective.

For most of her life, she'd been powerless, following orders like a good obeying doll, worried about voicing her opinions because she knew they'd be ignored.

Being around the bikers had shown Scarlett her opinion was worth something, and she'd been opening up more in the last months.

Every person within the MC made her comfortable, except this man.

Axel got her nerves hyper-sensitive and her tongue tied, unless she was exchanging barbs with him. Only Axel could bring out a temper she never knew she had.

Did that mean something?

"You're thinking deeply, wildcat."

Wildcat. The first time he'd used the name was when they'd argued. Over something she couldn't recall now, but she'd thought it was an insult. Now the nickname felt special to her.

"Because I'm meeting a date here soon," he was late. "I don't know how it will look if I sit with you. You're intimidating."

Axel smirked, and she wanted to bask in his tanned face. She took another big drink instead.

"Do I intimidate you?"

"Hardly," she snapped. "You bore me most of the time," she lied. And Axel chuckled.

"It's not nice to lie."

"I bet you lie all the time."

"Not to you."

Five minutes.

And then ten minutes passed by.

Was Dan standing her up?

"Would you be late for a date?" she blurted, without meaning to ask him.

"I don't date. But if I did, I'd be on time. I'd be early if the woman meant something to me, and I wanted her to know that."

Her stomach twisted. Wistfully.

That's what she wanted.

"Why don't you date?"

"No time for them. No desire, either."

Scarlett whittled her lip with her teeth, thinking about that.

"Yeah, same for me." She regretted accepting a date to prove she could get over Axel not wanting her. Dumb. Maybe Dan standing her up was a blessing in disguise.

"Why not? You're young and beautiful. You should have men kicking your door down to date you."

"That sounds very rapey, Axel," she smiled, and he half-smiled in return, softening his rugged features.

"You know what I mean."

"Let's just say I didn't have parents who allowed me to experience a teenager's usual journeys. You said Roux was wild, and you let her get away with a lot. My parents were the complete parallel to your parenting."

When she looked over at Axel, he was frowning almost angrily.

"Is that why you were homeless? You ran from a terrible home life?"

Scarlett swallowed, nervous under his watchfulness. "I don't want to talk about it."

Being on the streets for months had taught Scarlett many lessons she never wanted to go through again. She needed to forget that time had ever happened. And discussing it with a successful man like Axel, who'd probably never let himself get into that position. She felt shame sting her face.

The stirring air caught like a bushfire when his finger grasped her chin, forcing her to look at him. His voice was stern, yet reassuring at the same time. "Never feel bad about anything you've been through, Scarlett. Lessons, even hard ones, shape the person you are today. Whatever you've been through, you're kickass now; that's what matters."

He thought she was kickass?

Oh, pride swelled until her lips pulled tight in a beaming smile.

"I am, aren't I? I don't know if you knew this about me, but I once tried to steal from this big-shot MC president, and I lived to see the next day." She boasted, and Axel burst out laughing. He shook her chin a little.

"Smartass."

"Yep, I'm that, too. I've been taking lessons from Splice."

Suddenly the air was frozen around them as Axel's eyes flashed with unspoken words.

What happened? What had she said to make him look that way?

"Stay away from Splice, wildcat."

She thought Axel was joking until she studied his face and realized he wasn't smiling. He was deadly serious.

And the threat hurt like barbed wire in her skin.

Axel

"Why? Is your biker too good for me, boss?"

This is what he liked. Sick fuck he was, getting off on the burn of color on Scarlett's cheeks and her snarling teeth. She had a wicked, bratty mouth, and he enjoyed every word. Always had.

It was when Scarlet was spitting mad that he had her undivided attention.

And he fucking loved it. Loved it too much, but it didn't stop him from leaning in, inhaling the soft, intoxicating scent coating her neck.

"The opposite, wildcat. Splice is a dog."

She gasped, and some of the anger fell from her eyes. He knew what was coming next, and he internally smiled. Braced for it. Ever since she'd emerged from her shell and started back chatting everyone, she'd taken on the protector role over his men. If two were in an argument, she'd take up for the weaker one in the fight. She weighed less than a flower and barely reached his chest in height, but she'd puff up like one of those fighting peacocks in defense. If Axel gave a prospect a dressing down, he stuck around to watch Scarlett bolstering up his ego again like a mama bear.

It was fucking cute.

"Splice is your patched brother. You can't call him a dog!" she defended, all pouty lips and fiery eyes. *Fuck.* He wanted to stare into that fire while he plowed into her, ached to see her pouty lips when she was begging for another fuck, another orgasm, more of his attention.

Where had this side of him come from?

He'd never wanted to overpower a woman before. Never desired to take over her life, for that woman to depend on him for every little thing, even the air she breathed. But here he was, sitting in a crowded biker bar, holding onto the last vestiges of his control before he dragged Scarlett into his lap and made her plead for his hands.

She'd plead so sweetly; he knew that.

Without realizing it, she'd already reacted to his softer demands, and her compliance brought a visible reaction in Axel. He'd been constantly hard around her.

Could he give in?

Taste her?

Have her?

The need for Scarlett had gotten to a stage it was impossible to ignore, and he wanted her underneath him, gripping him with her thighs and crying out his name.

"He's still a dog, wildcat."

She sniffed. "I might like dogs. Did you think about that, boss?"

Boss. Oh, she was asking for it.

Her voice conveyed confidence, but maybe it was just because Axel looked closely at her; he always caught the slight tremble of her body. It was those signs he latched onto like a hungry predator. Salivating over her reactions, baiting her to give the sick side of him more of them to satisfy what he wouldn't allow himself to take.

But if she called him *sir* in her haughty, taunting tone, he'd drag her into the bathroom and fuck her in a stall, making her scream loud enough the bar would be issued with a noise violation from the city.

He smirked, bending in further, almost running his nose along her neck. Axel heard how her next inhale stuttered. Was the wildcat nervous? Turned on? He could work with that.

"I've seen you taking treats to Champ, so I know you like dogs."

"Just… just not Splice?"

"That's right, not Splice."

Good girl. Now she was getting it.

He didn't want no other dog sniffing around her.

Only him.

He still felt like a dirty old man, even entertaining carnal thoughts of her, but they were stronger than his will to stay away, and Axel would go fucking feral if he had to watch some joker romance her into falling in love.

No, she had to be his, and that's all there was to it.

"Come on, I'll take you home," he rasped, moving back before he took a nice bite from her throat and put his visible claim on her no one could deny. "Your date isn't coming."

She sighed. Even then, he didn't feel remorseful for spoiling her evening.

He was a bastard of the highest caliber.

That was okay. He'd let Scarlett take it out on his body one day. She could ride all her frustration out on him until she was a sweating wreck, sobbing pleasure all over him.

And now he was hard again. *Fuck*.

"I can't even do blind dates right. I might as well become a nun."

They made it outside, with Axel keeping a firm hold on her hip, navigating them through the crowd of people who knew him and wanted to talk. Giving only chin lifts, he got Scarlett to his parked bike.

"My mother would be so pleased to hear that." She said.

"She wanted you to be religious?"

It was probably the two drinks making her talk because it was the most personal info he'd gotten out of her in months. Scarlett was a butterfly with alcohol, even a whiff of 5%, and she was tipsy. Another thing he found cute about her.

"She wanted me compliant. Do as they say."

Taking her by the shoulders, he turned her to face him to help her into his leather jacket, her teeth were clacking from the biting cold. It swamped her, but it would keep her warm until he got her home. "Did they hurt you, Scarlett?"

He'd fucking kill them all. Every person who hurt her would regret the day they were born.

She shook her head. "Not physically. But there are many ways to cut a person with a knife, aren't there?"

Determined now, he needed to know all of her past.

What brought her to him? What actions had driven her to live rough?

Until now, he'd respected her privacy, but if he was right, and her family were cunts to her, he needed to know so he could make it right. Axel thought in black and white, right or wrong, wasn't a factor when he was exacting revenge.

And if there was revenge to put into action for Scarlett, he'd be the one wielding the knife.

If someone had hurt her, he'd punish them twice as hard.

His jaw hardened when he threw his leg over the seat, starting the engine. He craned his neck to find her watching, biting the corner of her lip.

"It's scary."

"I won't let you fall. Put your foot here, shuffle close, and hold tight to me."

She followed instructions deliciously, and Axel swallowed a groan, imagining how she'd follow his lead in bed. She would be the best sex of his life.

"Don't let me fall, Axel. These are brand new shoes."

The groan powered out of him as she banded both arms around his waist and tightened as though she thought he didn't deserve an ounce of air. He didn't mind. Her touch was fucking ecstasy.

"You don't care if we wreck my expensive bike?" he teased.

"Didn't you hear? These are new shoes. I haven't had anything new in forever; I want them to last."

The growl gurgled up Axel's throat, reminding him of how little she'd had so far and how happy she was with simple things. He was going to spoil her; he could already feel it happening. It was inevitable. He'd buy her all the shoes she could want. Perfumes, or whatever other feminine shit women adored. He still didn't know how he'd raised a girl, and Roux turned out okay. Though she was more tomboy than a fairy princess. Misogynists could learn this shit. Google search was invented for cavemen like him.

Stroking a hand on her knee, he licked his lips when she hissed, but he didn't stop as his hand traveled down her leg until he grasped her ankle and held it straight so he could see these shoes she needed protecting over their lives.

They were silver, thin heels, and sexy as fuck.

Then Axel remembered she wore them for another man, and his hand fastened tighter around her ankle.

"You won't wear these for another man again," he rumbled low, setting her foot down. He rested his cold hands against her clasped ones on his stomach.

The pinch on his stomach brought him out of his murderous thoughts.

"I'll wear them for anyone I want to, even dogs," she dared say. "Even Splice. I bet he'd like my new shoes."

"*Scarlett.*" One word. One warning and the brat pinched his stomach again.

"Oh, stop being cranky. It was *my* night in ruins. I got stood up! You should shower me with sympathy and chocolates."

He'd shower her alright. Bathe her in his come like the dirty fucker she was turning him into. He'd let it dry on her skin beneath her clothes, let everyone smell she was taken.

Swallowing his need, it was the hardest thing he'd had to do in recent times not to find a seedy motel room and unleash like he was the Kraken.

Patting her hands, he roared the engine pipes and felt her stiffen.

"It's okay, wildcat. I'll get you and your shoes home safely. Trust me."

"You're the only one I do trust."

Ah, fuck. A good feeling bloomed in his chest, and the ride back to the clubhouse went quicker than he would have liked because having Scarlett on the back of his bike was a pleasure he didn't know he'd needed, and now he wanted to do it again, but she'd already scrambled off the seat once he cut the engine.

"How was that?"

"Scary. Terrifying. Daunting. Cold. And fun. A lot of fun." She grinned at him. "Thanks for the ride, boss."

Nearing the entry door, he grabbed her arm, and she turned her large doe eyes on him. "Forget that guy. He's nothing. Not worth you kicking yourself and thinking anything is your fault. It's not."

"What if he was there, didn't like what he saw, and sneaked out?" Her lower lip wobbled, and *fuck him*, he liked her leaning in, seeking comfort from him. Sliding his hand behind her neck, his grip was firm to gain her attention. When Scarlett's eyes fluttered closed, he knew she loved the hold. "No man would look at you, wildcat, and take off. He'd run toward you and hide you in a dark closet so he could defile you."

Those doe eyes crippled him as they filled with tears, looking to him for reassurance. Not knowing she was feeling rejected because of him and his jealousy.

"Really?"

He waited a beat for the guilt to settle in.

None came.

It was better to ask for forgiveness than it was for permission.

If the day came, he'd bury his face between her legs and find forgiveness.

Until then. "Yes. Now get inside. You're shivering." He reluctantly set her free and held the door open for her to hurry through. She didn't look back as she headed to the kitchen area, wearing his club leather jacket with the logo on the back, ass swishing from side to side.

It was like seeing something for the first time.

Something he wanted.

Something he'd have.

Fuck his goddamn morals, however threadbare they were.

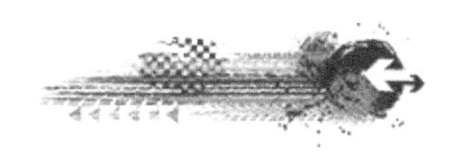

It wasn't long—maybe forty minutes before he got his jacket back. And it came hurtling at his face when the tornado that was Scarlett hauled ass through his office door. He caught it mid-air and arched a brow.

"You rotten snake. You downright rat. You absolute piece of dog poop!"

No longer intoxicated, she was alight with rage in the doorway. Beneath his desk, Axel had to adjust his straining cock.

"If you're gonna hurl insults, wildcat, you need to learn better ones."

"Don't get clever with me, Axel Tucker. I ought to scratch your eyeballs out."

Axel smiled now. He could guess why she was spitting mad, looking like a huffing dragon who'd lost its flames. Rising from the chair, he walked around the desk, approaching her.

She watched and tried to back up, coming up against the wall.

Now her breath was huffing in and out at speed, her cheeks mottled, and when Axel caught Scarlett around the neck, tipping her head back to look at him, he let his head fall a few inches, putting their eyes level.

"Slow your breath, and then you can tell me why you're angry."

"You... you..."

"I know," he smirked. "I'm a rat, a snake, and what was it? Dog shit?"

"Yes," she shoved at his chest. He held fast, crowding his weightier body into hers.

"Slower breaths. That's it, good girl."

Once calm but still throwing visual bullets at him, he squeezed her neck. "What's up?"

"What's up? I'm here to kill you."

"Are you?"

His dirty thoughts hoped she would kill him wearing less clothing.

With another shove at his chest, Axel let her go, strolling back to his desk to perch on the edge, arms folded.

"What did I do to deserve death by hostage this time?"

"I'm not your damn hostage. You did it, didn't you? Admit it."

"I admit it." He half-smiled and derailed her next tangent when her pink lips opened and then shut without words flying out.

"You downright dirty…"

"Rat?"

"Dan texted to warn me some thug threatened him if he didn't break our date. I thought he was full of tall tales until I asked for a description. Lo and behold, it was you."

"What a pussy," Axel curled a lip. He should have put his fist in the number cruncher's face.

"He was warning me I was in danger from a psycho."

"You're welcome."

She blinked, confused. "For what?"

"He wasn't right for you. No man that's into you would let someone else run him off. He put skid marks on the floor; he left that fast, didn't even give a token fight for you."

She stomped her foot and pointed her finger. "How could he be into me if we'd never met? You destroyed my night for no reason, and it was cruel, Axel."

He thought she'd run out of steam and stomp out, but she closed the door and threw herself down on the two-seater couch, deflated.

"I didn't even want to go on the stupid date. Monroe felt sorry for me, so I agreed. But it was upsetting when he never showed up."

Ah, shit. Inhaling, he held it for a second, accepting she'd get over it in a day. That accountant wouldn't factor in Scarlett's life.

"Don't do shit you don't wanna do again, Scarlett. Life is too short."

Look at him giving life lessons. Who the fuck was he again?

She looked over, and her face still displayed anger, but she was no less delicious. Axel took pleasure in looking at her far too much because she usually wore every feeling on her face. It was like flipping through the pages of a book, knowing what was coming next. He relied on seeing Scarlett every day, knowing she was in his space, became oxygen to Axel, someone vital.

His actions spoke volumes, but Scarlett's face had him on mute. The need to know what she was thinking was fucking him up.

Walking to the coffee machine, he went about boiling water and plopped in a tea bag, the kind she liked to drink. He'd started stocking it next to his coffee beans. She took the cup without a word, so he returned to his desk.

It wasn't the first time Scarlett sat in his office while he worked.

He didn't know if she needed company those first few weeks here, but she'd sometimes slip through the doorway and sit quietly, not saying much.

He remembered the day he cuffed her to the radiator when she'd thrown a snit. He'd done it as a joke, and she'd sat there, fuming, staring daggers at him.

He'd liked it. *Too much.*

The club still joked about the day he'd cuffed his hostage, and of course, it threw Scarlett into fresh fits of temper.

Wildcat was a tame name for her. She was more like a confined typhoon.

She sipped the tea and watched him, but didn't say much for over an hour. He was sending a text to Jamie Steele, the prez of the Apollo Kingsmen, when she spoke.

"Do you know I've never had weed? Or any drugs."

"Don't do drugs, wildcat. They're not good for you. There's a lot of other shit you can be corrupted by without turning into a junkie."

"I can't turn into anything if I never try it. I'm boring."

"Drugs don't make you cool. Being yourself does."

"You think I'm cool?"

"You stand your own in this place where most can't handle it."

"I didn't have much choice, remember? You said I owed you."

"You still do," Axel smirked and watched her face flush with color. Goddamn, she was pretty. Her innocence spoke to him like a siren. He wanted to slurp her up and taste every inch of her skin, learn the patterns of her hitched breathing, find out what got her off, and test out her scandalized boundaries.

He started with a small one by reaching into a desk drawer, bringing out an already rolled joint. Axel spotted her curious eyes when he lit up the smoke.

"Come over here, wildcat."

"I thought you didn't want me doing drugs?"

"I don't. This is second-hand and only with me. Don't do this with anyone else, got it?"

"Especially not Splice?" she guessed, sassing him.

If Splice put second-hand smoke into Scarlett's mouth, he'd hang that brother on the tree outside and let Champ piss on him.

Her steps were slow; she'd changed out of the sexy shoes, which was a pity; now her feet were socked. Axel didn't often smoke, one of those responsible things he'd changed when he hit forty. He could make an exception this once. When she was near, he pushed back the chair, indicating the space she could step into. Her brow furrowed, so he helped her along; grabbing her hips, he put her butt on the edge of his desk, directly between his spread thighs.

"What... what do I do?" she asked, nerves making her voice huskier.

"All you gotta do is open your mouth, and I'll do the rest."

"That sounds dirty. Don't shove anything in it."

"Wildcat, you'd know if I shove something in your mouth."

The way color raced from her neck to her forehead pleased Axel in a way he couldn't understand because he'd never been in a position to tease a woman into blushing over a sexual innuendo. Women he'd been with in the past were as forward as him, leaving no room for gentle teasing.

He smiled and put a hand on her hip just to touch her.

"Ready?"

She nodded, letting her lips open. Inviting him in.

Axel took a long tug on the joint and blew the stream of smoke directly into her mouth, moving closer until their lips almost touched.

"Oh," she said once the smoke dissipated. "It doesn't taste all that nice."

"You expected cherry flavor like a vape?"

"Do it again." Her lips opened again, and Axel's gaze dropped.

He needed to defile that mouth. Make it swollen and pink from overuse. He got lost in those deviant thoughts as he blew more smoke into her waiting lips.

"Enough," he said after the fifth time, stubbing out what was left; he'd had enough, too. A few tokes of the good shit wasn't nearly enough to affect his mood, but Scarlett was brand new, and it seemed it had gone directly to her head when she slowly blinked, her eyes opaque.

With some people, getting high mellowed them out. Or made them maudlin. He knew in three seconds how it affected Scarlett when she pushed two hands on his chest.

Unfortunately, it wasn't sexual.

It fired her temper even more.

"I could've had a nice thing tonight, but you wrecked it. Why won't people just let me have something nice for myself? What have I done so wrong to deserve that?"

She didn't give him a chance to question what she meant.

What people?

Who the fuck had hurt her?

And it wasn't him. She was pissed at him, sure. But missing the date hadn't broken her heart.

She slinked off toward the door. "I'm going to bed. Could you not talk to me tomorrow, boss? Or the day after, I will be mad at you for a while."

He bet she would, and he'd look forward to it.

But hours later, he couldn't get it out of his head.

Why won't people just let me have something nice for myself?

Scarlett

The Diablo clubhouse came alive at weekends.

Out-of-towners and other clubs who were neutral or on friendly terms with the Diablos. Women in their droves, hoping to bounce on a biker or two. Scarlett didn't judge, not when orgasms were needed. Toys were great and never acted cocky—pun intended—but they couldn't substitute for a warm body on top of you.

She said that like she had bodies on top of her every night. *Ha.* Chance would be a fine thing. For months, she'd been in a perpetual state of needing an orgasm, but not from any toy. Her fingers worked fine, but her body hungered for something she couldn't have. And that sucked. But she wished the new women who would turn up at the club tonight all the luck getting their big O's.

It was the main reason Scarlett organized a girls' night out for that weekend. Not only because it coincided with everyone's busy schedules, but she would have found any excuse to leave the clubhouse, so she didn't have to watch the influx of women trying to be the ones to capture Axel's attention.

"You look hot," Monroe smiled, nudging Scarlett with her elbow.

"It's your dress." She plucked at the borrowed thigh-length hem.

With her pixie hair styled close to her head, minimal makeup, and sexy shoes, she felt like a million bucks.

Monroe went to hang with Chains while they waited for the others to arrive. It was mostly a get-to-know-you for Reno's new girlfriend, Kylie. But again, Scarlett would have gone to the movies alone to stay out of the clubhouse tonight. She hitched her butt onto a bar stool and pointed the finger at the prospect Dillion behind her bar.

"Don't be messing up my system, you hear? I know every bottle, so you better remember where they go."

"Yes, ma'am." He smirked, giving her a little wink.

He was going to mess up her bar. She cast her gaze around, people were still arriving. It was only early yet. The hardcore partying wouldn't start until at least nine.

"So, uhm, where's Axel tonight?"

"Why?" leered Dillion, leaning both arms on the bar in front of her while he eyed her cleavage. He was close enough to catch whiffs of his cologne and count the number of whiskers on his chin. "You wanna show off your pretty dress to him?"

Yes, she did.

"No, I don't. Just wondering."

Dillion smiled like he didn't believe her.

But then the devil stepped into the room at that moment, affecting every molecule in her body.

It was as if all the air had sucked out of the common area. Scarlett felt shivers travel down her legs when Axel's gaze drifted over her dress and finally found her eyes. What he was thinking didn't translate on his face, and she mentally kicked herself for hoping he thought she looked nice. No, not nice; she wanted him to think she looked hot as fuck.

Every voice was overshadowed when he towered over her and asked, "Where are you going?"

Oh no. He did not get to play the overbearing card with her. Not when she was sort of, kind of still mad at him for spoiling her date. She hadn't spoken to him since.

"Are you my dad?" lord bless her rogue tongue. Not knowing when to shut the hell up.

He'd ended her non-date but didn't give a reasonable explanation.

She'd foolishly thought maybe he'd wanted her for himself. If Scarlett kept swallowing her delusional fantasies, she'd be full until Christmas.

He was probably looking out for her in the way an owner would a pet.

And that only pissed her off and made her sad he couldn't see what she felt. And worse, he couldn't feel the same.

Well aware they'd gained a crowd of eavesdroppers, Scarlett wasn't prepared for what he said next.

"You heard the saying; if you're not feeding, fucking, or financing me, what I do is none of your business?" Axel rasped in a growly tone hot enough to stain Scarlett's cheeks. He dropped his head and volume, his voice now scraping over her sensitive ears. Causing shivers to erupt all over. "I do two out of three for you, little girl. So I asked, where the fuck are you going?"

Did the ground shift underneath her feet?

Air locked in her throat as she stumbled over her words, stunned at the fierceness in Axel's eyes, daring to defy him. She didn't want to. But, *God*, she would obey his every growled word, within reason, if he let her. "We—we thought to go to Mike's."

One second and then two. She drowned in his intense stare. And then he broke it by looking over her head and giving off a shrill whistle, talking to a prospect. "Take two of the cages and drive the girls into town. You stick with them all night. You got it?"

"Sure thing, Prez."

"Hey, we don't need babysitters!" Scarlett protested, but it fell on deaf ears.

"You do not let them out of your sight."

With one hot, domineering streak of his eyes down her body, he turned and strolled off like they hadn't just shared that thing. What was it? Sexual passive aggression? Or something else? Making sure she was safe because she was his?

Ugh. "Asshole," she muttered beneath her breath, even as slithers of desire overrode her sanity.

"When are you two going to bang this friction? I caught hits of all the chemistry between you, and now I need to kiss my man." Proclaimed Monroe.

Of course, the girls teased her that night, trying to determine if her animosity toward Axel was lustful.

Axel was never far from her mind, and she witlessly checked her phone a few times during the night to see if he'd text her. He was most likely getting lap dances from the biker harem. Despite her sour thoughts, Scarlett enjoyed the night with friends.

As their lord and ruler ordered, the prospects stayed close enough and chased off packs of men who thought it was their lucky night. The girls didn't even have to pay for the drinks. According to Mouse, Axel called ahead to put anything they wanted on a club tab.

When she wanted to stay mad at him, he did something nice.

The fun of girls' night suddenly seemed to pale because she had thoughts of what Axel was up to and with who. The last thing Scarlett wanted to do was go home.

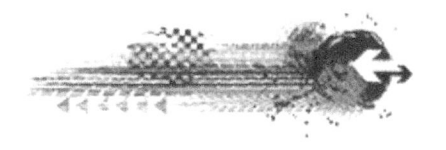

Axel

Watching Scarlett climb into the rig, the red dress rising further on the back of her thighs, he almost thumped on the window for her to come inside so he could eat her alive and taste the fire between her legs.

Only knowing he had shit to look into, he let her leave. The prospects had their duties to watch her and report anything back to him.

Back in his office, he ignored when Chains strolled in. Closing the door behind him, he placed two glasses of bourbon on the table while Axel waited for a call to connect.

He'd stewed for hours.

Now he knew what needed to be done.

"Steele, it's Axel. You got a minute?"

Chains, sitting on the couch, raised his eyebrows, curious.

It wasn't often Axel reached out to another MC. They weren't enemies of the Apollo Kingsmen; he and Jamie Steele had previously done a few mutually beneficial deals on stolen cars. But this was going to be the biggest favor he'd ask for.

And asking for favors was not something Axel did lightly.

On speakerphone, Steele answered, "How's it going over there, Axel?"

"I got no complaints. I'm calling because I need a favor."

"Am I hearing right?" the other prez laughed. "What do you need? I got an import of new sports cars if you need any. Real sweet rides, I'm tempted to keep one myself."

Chains motioned for him to get details, but he wasn't calling to discuss new arrangements tonight. "We might take you up on that another time. Listen, does your VP still keep his hand in the hacking game? I have a time-sensitive job for him."

"He does; he isn't cheap, though."

"That isn't an issue."

"Don't you have an IT guy?"

"We do, but currently, Primo is still serving time. He can only do so much with a smuggled cell phone."

Jamie Steele chuckled. "True enough. What do you need hacking? And if you say a bank, we'll decline. I got no time to spend in the clink right now."

Axel half grinned. "Nah, nothing so serious. I need some background info. Anything he can get. I don't have much to work from, though."

"My guy can dig up corpses with only a Myspace password. I grabbed a pen, go ahead, gimme what you have. He'll call you when he returns from a Denver run."

"Scarlett Bass, twenty-five. I think she's originally from Idaho, but that's uncertain." It was only what he'd gleaned from eavesdropping conversations. She could be lying. "I don't have much else."

"That should be enough. And you want a full background check?"

"Yeah. Parents, family, friends, boyfriends, where she worked, who she worked for, any records. Whatever Amos can get, I want it."

He wanted to know what circumstances drove her to homelessness.

Axel thanked him, knowing he'd pay Amos' cover of ten grand for a basic background hack five times over if needed. He'd been too patient waiting for Scarlett to confess her past. He was done waiting and didn't give a fuck what means he used to get that information.

Lounging in the big leather chair, he took hold of the glass and cast his gaze toward Chains. Waiting for the inevitable.

"Took you long enough. To be honest," he raised his amusement, "thought you'd cave months ago."

"I've given her chances to tell me."

"You think someone is chasing her." He didn't pose it as a question.

That was his concern. And he wanted to know who and why.

She'd never given off abused wife vibes if it was a bastard of an ex. Even so, Axel wanted to know so he could deal with it. No one was getting their hands on Scarlett.

They'd have to get through him first.

While finishing the bourbon, his cell chimed, and the tick worked heavily in his jaw when he got the first report from Mouse. He'd sent a picture he must have taken slyly of the girls sitting around a table, having a good time. His stare zeroed in on the redheaded siren. She had her head thrown back with laughter captured in time.

Utterly fucking beautiful.

In the background, a group of men were watching.

Axel: Anyone bothering her?
Mouse: Few chumps have been trying to buy them drinks, we got rid of them.

As much as he longed to do it, he couldn't shut down her fun night.

"You're giving in then?" asked Chains.

Was he? He didn't fucking know. All Axel knew was he couldn't stay away from Scarlett. All the same reasons he had months ago were valid. She was still too young for him. It hadn't stopped him this far from inserting himself into her life, and there was zero chance of him stopping now.

Without giving the answer Chains wanted, he said instead. "Do you know she watches cheesy 90s movies like it's the first time she's seen them? Because it is. She does the same with TV shows and junk food. Where Scarlett came from, what brought her here as it did, someone had kept her isolated from the world."

"A shut-in?"

"Not sure. My guess is someone had a tight rein on her."

"Damn." Replied Chains, having been through something similar with his wife and her cunt of a father who controlled Monroe's life. "You realize, Axe, if you uncover all her secrets, it could make her run."

Not. A. Fucking. Chance.

He wouldn't allow it.

"Or worse, cause a war with some unknown wacko."

"*This* is her home now." He said, determination coating every word. "No one takes Scarlett from her home."

"Oh, yeah," chuckled Chains, "you're so giving in. 'Bout time, brother. Roux will lose her fucking mind."

Axel groaned. He couldn't think of his rebellious daughter right now.

Not when he had brooding to do, wondering what douchebag with horny thoughts was creeping around Scarlett, trying to charm a smile out of her.

Those smiles were his.

Or they would be.

Axel lasted four hours before he strolled into the main party area, ignoring the curious eyes of the women. The updates from Mouse hadn't appeased him at all. He felt unanchored in his skin without Scarlett near to monitor her.

"Hey, sexy, you wanna dance?" some random chick asked. The sexual interest was evident in her heavily shadowed eyes and red lips. "No, you go ahead."

She pouted, sticking her chest out a little more, "aww, c'mon. I haven't seen you all night. I'm Billie."

"Not interested, Billie. Enjoy my club or go home."

"Your... club. Oh." Her eyes darted down to his club cut displaying the PREZ patch.

Finding Chains, Tomb, and Denver, he made his way through the crowd of party partygoers.

"I'm heading to Mike's. Who's coming?"

There was a chorus of agreeing voices.

"Fuck yeah." Boomed Devil, "Kelly is gonna be so sauced." He grinned like he knew he was going to be getting drunk sex.

All those with old ladies followed Axel out to the row of bikes. They got on the road within minutes and made good time by arriving at the biker bar not long later.

As though she was drawn to him, he knew down to the second when Scarlett spotted him. It made every part of Axel ache.

To claim.

To take her *now*.

Never dragging his eyes off her, Axel didn't notice his brothers dispersing to grab their old ladies. His stare zeroed in on one little redheaded pixie, forcing direct eye contact.

She had to have sensed his desperation to get closer; it was palpable in the air.

Every breath was dripping with desire.

And then, the sexy rebel jumped to her feet and disappeared through the crowd.

Axel smirked, following at a slower pace.

She wanted a cat-and-mouse chase, did she?

The little hostage didn't know what bell she'd just rung.

But she was about to.

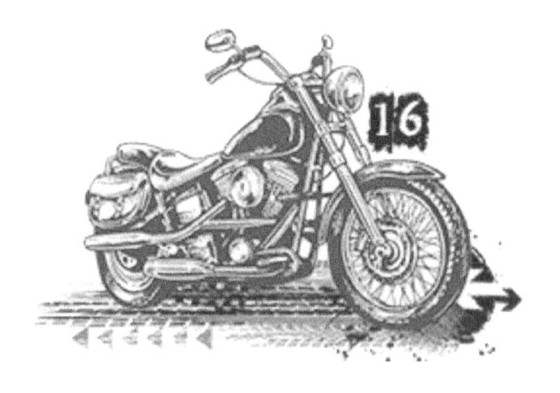

Axel

A rock of impatience rested firmly on Axel's shoulders while waiting outside the restroom like a peeping pervert.

Women came out, giving him speculative glances, but none of those women were Scarlett.

Tired of waiting, he pushed open the door with two fingers. "Get your ass out here, Scarlett, or I'll come in and get you."

She appeared seconds later, a scowl in place, and the burn of lust ignited in his gut.

Two women who were about to enter looked him up and down and said to Scarlett, "you okay, hon?"

Scarlett smiled when she realized the chicks were checking she was not in danger from him. "Yeah, this one is so impatient, aren't you, Sir?"

Another pulse of heat directly to his dick.

Reassured, the women disappeared, and Axel latched onto Scarlett's wrist.

"Hey!"

Pulling her down the dimmed hallway into a secluded nook, barely out of sight of anyone using the restrooms. He crowed her against the wall, and Axel only experienced calm drenched over him now that he had her close again. And when he looked into her eyes, her name flowed through his bloodstream.

"Why are you chasing me down like a bloodhound?"

"Have you behaved?" he ignored her question, asking one of his own. Knowing the answer already because of Mouse's updates. It was the only thing keeping him sane.

"Behaved?" her voice rose incredulously, her chin pointed up, ignoring their bodies pressed together. "Of all the nerve. No, I haven't *behaved*. I've been dancing on tables, kissing all the boys, even some girls."

"Little liar," he smirked, taking her chin between his finger and thumb and holding her in place.

"What about you? Did you have *fun* with all the new women, Sir?" she dared say with a bite to her tone. If she called him *sir* again, he'd fuck her right here.

But oh, he loved the snap of jealousy she was displaying. She could never hide her feelings, not even if her life depended on it. In that respect, Scarlett had always been a brand new penny in his world. And that's what he liked about her. She never tried to change herself to fit in. She was only herself. Wild at heart, uncoordinated, and a free, bratty spirit.

She'd love to know he hadn't looked at another woman since he saw her. Since she dug her claws underneath his skin.

Listening to his body, he pushed his pelvis into her stomach, letting her understand without words what she did to him, and he saw the moment her eyes rounded with insight and her breath left her slack lips.

"Axel…"

He couldn't wait any longer. The need scratched over his skin like a sickness, needing to possess her. To take her lips and taste and *taste*.

"Shut up, wildcat. Let me taste those sweet lies you just told me, huh?"

The adorable little thing might have been shocked at his words, but she soon tipped her head back against the wall. Expecting his kiss.

Axel couldn't kiss her here; he'd be more beast than a man if he got his tongue in her mouth. The one kiss they'd shared, she enjoyed sucking hard on his tongue, and for days afterward, just the thought of it sent Axel into a raging hard-on he had to take care of in the shower.

No, he had other ways and means and was ready to use them on her.

The hand on her chin dropped a few inches and curled his fingers around her throat, holding her in place. His other hand skimmed over the dress until he snatched the delicate hem.

"Axel… what?" she panted into his face, blowing sweet alcohol fumes. Even that wasn't enough to douse him in water. She wasn't drunk, and neither was he. But he was feral enough to steal a taste of her.

"Shhhh, little wildcat. Or do you want people to hear you? I'm fine with that; I'll carry you out now and lay you on the pool table."

She gasped, and it was filthy music to his ears.

Axel's intentions were terrible, and his denial exploded. He needed this. Needed her so fucking badly.

He didn't need to raise her skirt much more than a couple of inches. It was short already, and when his fingertips brushed her inner thigh, he swore he felt her whole body trembling.

"You wanna be bratty and call me sir now, hm? Go on, see what it gets you." he rasped, their mouths almost but not touching. He shared her breath and gave her his in return. Never once did she try to gain freedom from his throat grasp. If anything, Scarlett pushed into it, seeking more.

"You wouldn't dare," she tried, but her panting breaths told Axel what she needed.

Heading up, he touched the softness of her inner thigh, finding a sensitive spot right at the apex. Only an inch to the right, and he'd be caressing her pussy. He tormented that spot until she whimpered, feeling her hands gripping his waist.

"I'm going to break your habit of lying to me. Before long, I'll taste every secret you haven't shared with me."

She was actively seeking his fingers, popping her hips forward, trying to encourage his hand. Then, with a booted foot, he knocked her right leg wider, and that's when Axel knuckled past the edge of her panties and found the fucking bliss he'd thirsted for.

Sparks between them could have set fire to the gaudy bar wallpaper.

She was hot and wet. There was no way Scarlett could claim she wasn't turned on, not when his middle knuckle slid around her engorged clit the way it did.

Touching her brought peace, something Axel hadn't expected.

She made him feel like an animal he'd needed to keep under lock and key around her. But that lock had sprung open, and now he touched her like the demented deviant he was.

And while he did, she whined his name. He kept her head pinned to the wall to see her eyes glazed with desire.

She was a goddamn powder keg of lust.

If Axel did nothing else with his life, he would tame all that lust with his bare hands and bring his little savage alive, crying his name. He'd feed it fire and see it burn out of control, *only for him*. The thought was enough to make him groan as he brought her closer to the edge with faster strokes.

Footsteps approached. Axel's protective instincts roared to the forefront, but he was stopping for nothing short of a twister sweeping through the bar. He kept Scarlett hidden with his body; fortunately, the footsteps didn't venture further than the restrooms.

He wanted her mindless.

Shaking with want.

Crying his name.

And coming all over his hand.

"Shh, shhh, shhh." He warned, stroking her hammering pulse with his thumb while the other thumb took over the job of plying pressure to her clit so Axel could slide two lucky fingers into her pussy.

Christ, the first touch of her hot wetness and Axel nearly lost his mind. He throbbed behind his zipper; his dick wanted out and into her. He would lose the last of his control if her moaning continued. It did a number on his body.

Axel liked sex as any man with a libido did, but it had never ruled him, never been a priority since he left his twenties. In that darkened alcove where anyone walking down the hallway could see them, the urge to unzip his jeans and push into Scarlett thundered through his ears.

Need and want warred and blended, forcing him on.

Every lust-dripped whine past Scarlett's lips as she licked them—bit on them, was another second he couldn't hold on, but the feel of her tightness locked around his fingers as she gave him more wetness was something he wouldn't miss experiencing.

She was incredible.

"Your tight little cunt is hungry, Scarlett."

Anyone seeing them would think he was attacking her, seeing a man holding a woman by the throat while his hand was beneath her skirt, ramming his fingers in and out of her pussy. But it was far from an attack, not when she let out breathy pleas.

"Please. Please. Axel. *Sir.* God. *Please.*"

Axel was impossibly hard, to the point of pain, but he forgot his wants when he made Scarlett come in his hand. With a flick of his blunt thumbnail on her clit and a curl of his buried fingers right over the sponginess of her G-spot, she detonated on a strangled cry. The bar music would swallow up the sounds of her pleasure to any other ears, but Axel soaked them in, transfixed with the yearning look staring back at him.

Bringing Scarlett down was a pleasure as he slowed his fingers, eventually stopping and removing them. *Reluctantly.* Never had he wanted to stay inside a woman until now. Then he let her throat go, dipping down. He kissed her throbbing pulse once, twice, and then a final third time.

Then Axel did what he'd been patiently waiting for. He brought those two wet fingers to his mouth, sucking them in, cleaning her off them as he groaned.

"Oh, my God." He caught Scarlett wheezing as she watched him with wide eyes. He licked his fingers until there was nothing left, then switched to the knuckle he'd clit rubbed her with, followed by the pad of his thumb.

Dropping his forehead, a very turned-on Axel rested it against hers. She'd yet to let go of his waist; he'd probably have gouge marks on his skin. "Your lies taste so fucking sweet."

And he wanted more.

There was no reasoning this away.

Or saying it was a one-off.

"I can't believe you did that," she said.

"Believe it," he smirked, pushing away from the wall. He hooked up her hand and began the walk back into the bar. "We're leaving," he told her.

The others were assembled at one table, waiting for them to emerge. They stood when they caught sight of Axel. Grinning like trained monkeys, probably guessing what he'd been up to.

He paid no one any attention other than getting Scarlett into his jacket again and then onto the back of his bike.

"Don't kill me," she warned, fixing herself against his back.

Axel glanced at her over his shoulder, resting both boots on the wet ground, the sounds of his brethren roaring off into the night carrying their old ladies behind them.

"Say that again," his tone warned her about being bratty.

Far from being intimidated, she gave him a saucy smile. "Don't kill me… Sir."

Goddamn. Her tipsy eyes sparkled with laughter, and he wanted to lean in and taste her amusement.

His erection had only just calmed down, and now his cock thundered to life again.

"Better hold on tight then." He rasped.

The world could implode at that moment, and Axel would still get them both home safely because he had plans to see through.

Plans he'd sat on for months, willing himself not to follow through with them, let her find a decent man.

He was all out of patience and self-discipline.

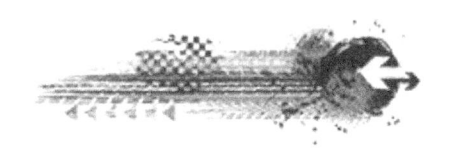

Scarlett

The moment she scrambled down from the back of Axel's motorcycle, while the engine was still growling, she escaped inside the clubhouse on fast feet.

Panting from exertion but mainly from the fact Axel had pinned her to a wall and made her come. The shock of that still had her trembling.

If this turned out to be a drunken-induced hallucination, she was kicking down walls tomorrow morning.

As Axel casually strolled through the entryway, letting the door close behind him, across the distance, their eyes locked, many unsaid things in that held gaze.

Why was she frightened now, suddenly?

She'd longed for something to happen between them, hadn't she? For weeks and months. But even after that one kiss, it seemed out of her realm.

Being finger fucked by Axel in a busy bar. Holy smokes, he'd been sexier than any man on earth. The rasp of his authoritative voice, the way he held her in place with a hand around her throat. She'd just about expired from sexual overload. But having his hand between her legs, Scarlett would never recover from that, not for as long as she lived.

He'd sent her into the next life with one touch and then dragged her back with a body-shaking orgasm.

It hadn't been a giant leap to know how carnal of a man Axel was. He was part animal, Scarlett was sure of it. Hey, she read books now; she'd heard of shifters, and he could easily be a wolf. An alpha wolf.

She shivered again as she watched his ultra-masculine walk.

Never did his eyes waver.

And then the beast man showed her he was sucking the pad of his thumb again, blasting heat into her sex like he was holding a smoking gun. Scarlett turned tail and took off.

She should head to bed, regroup and figure this out in the morning with a clear head. Maybe jump his bones. Could she do that now?

But her feet, unruly as she was, carried her into Axel's office.

She nervously shifted from foot to foot when he entered and closed the door behind him with a decided click.

She'd chosen, hadn't she? By coming in here, she'd put herself in his path for whatever he wanted to do.

And oh, Scarlett was *ready*.

So ready that he didn't even get a step nearer before she launched at him; she couldn't help herself. If she didn't kiss him right now, she'd die, and Scarlett refused to die before she got any piece of Axel Tucker in her mouth again. Luckily for her, he went back on his foot and caught her. His hands went to her butt while she shimmied up his body until Scarlett could wind her legs around his waist. *Oh, God*, it was a perfect puzzle piece fit, and she moaned when she clawed her hands into the back of his loose hair.

He was an animal.

A rogue pirate.

And the man of her dirty dreams was pawing her butt like he owned it.

Scarlett might have initiated the pouncing, but Axel crushed her mouth under his first. And one touch in became dangerously addictive, and he hadn't given her his tongue yet.

She moaned into Axel's mouth when she opened under his licking and coaxing tongue. He tasted of strong liquor and provocation. She followed his lead and let him kiss her with abandon. There was no structure to their kiss. He turned her head with his hand locked in her hair and moved her left and right, depending on how deeply he wanted to kiss her. Even in those few seconds when they parted to pull in much-needed air, she craved more of him. The passion for him was enormous, making her mindlessly weak under his hands.

It was heaven. It was hell. And Scarlett never wanted it to end.

Every kiss before him paled in insignificance. They were boys, and Axel was all man. A man in control of her mouth, sweeping his tongue through her seeking lips, letting her suck around it before he retreated, teasing her into chasing him.

Their kiss fast developed into a dance of war, and she was happily lost under his siege because nothing about Axel's mouth dominating hers said he was teasing her.

The moment was intense, like being dropped into a swimming pool and expected to breathe underwater. Scarlett moaned into his mouth, clinging with all her passion spilling over.

When she felt him shifting them across the room, the wall came at her back, and Axel held her there, pressing his massively dense body into her soft parts, squashing her boobs into his chest, making them ache.

"*Axel*," his moaned name was all she could manage; he'd fried her brain and left her a pile of horny mush.

"Tell me what you want," he demanded roughly, stroking his hand around the front of her throat.

"You." the answer was simple. She wanted him. Suddenly finding herself on her feet again, thank God Axel held her up, or her knees would have given out. He started pawing at the dress to get it off her, and the one logical brain cell she had left started flashing.

"Wait. Don't ruin this dress. It's not mine."

"Then take it off. Right fucking now, Scarlett." He growled.

Okay. Yeah. Whoa. Warm all over. She watched him pacing away as she carefully slipped out of Monroe's borrowed dress, folding it neatly and placing it on Axel's desk.

"The shoes stay on." His dark eyes gobbled her up, and she loved it.

The undercurrent in the room was uncertainty. He'd shaken the foundations beneath her with his flipped attitude, but was Scarlett about to derail because she didn't have answers? Heck no. Several steps returned her to Axel, and she was grabbed and taken to the couch, where he landed on top of her.

"Oomph, the shoes stay on, got it." she grinned, but he wasn't smiling; he stared down at Scarlett like he'd never seen her before.

Axel's past behavior meant he was a flight risk, likely to change his mind, putting her younger age yet again between them. She wouldn't let that happen, not now. Leaning her head up, she nipped his full lower lip, then ran her lips over his face scruff. Before he could pull away, she took two handfuls of the hair hanging down, drawing him in.

"What are you waiting for, Axel?"

Scarlett

Small kisses soon turned into kisses that snatched the soul out of her body.

Axel's mouth owned hers.

It wasn't as though she'd wanted to give her mouth to anyone else to keep.

As annoying as he was, as many times as she'd wanted to throw a desk chair at his head, Axel was it.

The whole shebang.

The man who made her body pop and fizzle.

Tonight had changed things; she wanted to know what he was up to, but after he fucked her brains out first.

And now his mouth was on a destructive mission to make her moan like a hippo in heat.

"*Concentrate.*" He growled, biting her lip a little, bringing Scarlett into the now. She groaned, fastening her legs around him.

"I am. I was thinking about hippos."

His groan of frustration vibrated against her lips, like he was so bothered by her wandering mind. But she couldn't help it, not when she had all that man meat on top of her. It sent her circuits haywire.

Scarlett grabbed Axel's hard chest and lifted her hips, feeling the evidence of his focus. So hard digging into her.

"I'm all yours now."

How true that was.

She wished it wasn't true.

Axel wasn't the guy to fall for.

He was a biker—nothing wrong with that. She had a lot of respect for the biker men she knew. But he also carried a lot of responsibilities and seemed to avoid romantic commitment. Being the president of the entire MC meant he messed with danger and she'd escaped to have an average life.

Oh, and the biggie was he had a massive hang-up about their age difference.

But, while their kiss turned hotter, she indulged in the sexiest man alive as he sucked around her tongue.

Because right then, she was the luckiest girl in the world. Axel wanted her, and she would not turn her nose up at a good thing. Even temporary.

She kissed him back and moaned when he slid his callused hand up her torso, pushing the cups of her bra up before discarding both pieces of underwear, doing some incredible groping until her nipples pebbled.

He tasted like pure masculinity, a taste she missed when he skimmed those wonderful lips down her neck. And then Axel's lips latched onto a nipple, sucking until she saw stars popping behind her eyelids. When he looked at her nakedness, she felt powerful as his eyes glinted with unmasked lust. Scarlett touched the ends of his long hair hanging down by his face. His features were masked by pleasure, and it swept the breath out of her.

He wanted her, maybe as badly as she wanted him.

For as much as Axel tried to avoid her, avoid the insane chemistry between them, it was unmistakable anyway.

A storm will always storm, no matter what.

And so would their lust.

Scarlett couldn't exactly recount how things happened in order after that.

Only that it was animalistic, frantic, and delicious.

Pain seized her. Oh, not because he was too rough, or he was hurting her.

She loved his roughness, how he didn't care if his hands left bruises on her skin. She was in pain because she couldn't wait any longer to be handled by him.

She gulped in his scent like an addict chasing a high, clinging to Axel, loving the solidness of his body.

"Now, Axel. *Now*." she moaned, enjoying how he sucked her entire areola into his mouth.

"That's not how you ask me for anything," he said, tracing his lips up to her neck, sucking hard enough that if he kept that up, she'd be marked by his teeth. And as a logical woman, she knew hickies after a certain age was not a good look, but Scarlett was drowning in leg-shaking desire, so she gripped him tighter with her thighs and moaned with her head back, offering her skin as his canvas.

His roughened words wrapped around her needy, lonely heart like barbed wire.

"Please. *Please*, Axel."

"That's better." He rasped. The noise of his lowered zipper sounded like gunshots ricocheting around his office, and she could have levitated from the couch if not for his weight.

His knee nudged her thighs wider, and then he fixed himself in place after dealing with a condom. She bent her head forward, unable to help herself from watching what he was doing. The rosy pink of his cock was a sight to see. Axel stroked himself up her soaked slit.

They both enjoyed that.

"Please, you said," he replied, resting a hand on the arm of the couch by her head. His cock nudged her entrance, and Scarlett thought she might die from wanting him. "Repeat it and mean it, wildcat."

She didn't hesitate. The richness of his dominating voice did syrupy things to her stubborn streak, melting it into a sloppy puddle. "Please fuck me, Axel."

He grunted and shunted his hips forward even before the last word left her lips. And then everything in her world was good again.

More than good.

It was *incredible*.

He stretched her exquisitely snug, so tight it pinched and burned only for a second, but the overwhelming pleasure soon overshadowed that feeling. It came at her from all sides, punching desire into her soul.

Oh, dear God, he fucked like a beast.

Hard. Merciless. Like he had a road map to all her hot spots.

"So goddamn soaked," he groaned. Axel's head dropped forward on his thick neck. Scarlett forced her heavy eyelids open to watch him. He was utterly gorgeous taking her, still dressed, with a silver chain glinting against his tanned throat.

Axel pushed back to the hilt, and that's when their mouths crashed together; there was no holding back the passion as she drove it into their messy, perfect kisses.

Their teeth clashed.

Axel moved and moved, slamming deeper with each thrust, and when he pulled back almost to his crown, her pussy spasmed to keep him inside her. He grunted and forced home again.

She wanted to tell him how good it felt, how perfectly their bodies aligned, but no words would come as she chased his taste with her tongue.

At some point, her arms raised, and he shackled her wrists in one hand. That's when her pleasure went nuclear, like Axel had known what she'd needed without asking for it, because she started to shudder.

And then a heavy knock rattled the door and startled her into squeaking. Her eyes pinged open wide.

Axel didn't stop moving, making Scarlett panic, because whoever was at the door could barge in any second and see the club bartender railed like a slut by the chief man.

"Axel, they might hear," she whispered desperately, wondering why he was still going. And oh, oh, *ohhh*, it felt unbelievable; her pussy fluttered around his drilling cock.

Their sloppy bodily noises became louder to her ears, sure everyone in the clubhouse could hear them, too.

She would die if anyone saw them.

Panic settled over her like rain, and that's when Axel forced eye contact, grounding Scarlett, as if reading her running thoughts.

"I would let no one see you like this, Scarlett," he pressed through his clenched teeth, pleasure clear on his rugged face. And while staring at her, still pushing, *pushing*, he yelled out. "You make a move for that door handle, I'll cut off your fucking fingers."

There was a chuckle. "Got it, prez. Amos from the Apollo Kingsmen is on the phone for you. He said you know what it's about."

"Tell him I'll call him back." He kept going, smirking down at her now, a man entirely in control, and because he was, Scarlett let out her held breath, melting beneath him. Axel approved and nuzzled his mouth to her lips. She opened and felt her orgasm blooming just out of reach. Right there, *right there*. Oh, yeah, it was there for the plucking, and his plunging cock seemed determined to find it.

She heard retreating boots and exhaled a sigh of relief.

But that relief was short-lived when Axel increased his thrusts, and a grunt of surprised bliss was forced out of her throat.

Her eyes widened, even as the motion was threatening to take her away.

It felt so good, and her body wanted to explode into a million firecrackers.

"Don't let people hear. Please, Axel." She would die a thousand embarrassed deaths if the people she saw every day heard her being railed by a sex God.

They'd never look at her in the same way again, and to a girl who pretended nothing ever got to her, the thought of it bothered her greatly.

Axel's eyes glinted. His fingers flexed around hers. "Then press your mouth to mine and don't let them hear your sexy whimpers." He commanded.

Like that was so easy!

She did it anyway, crashing her mouth into his, holding her lips open a little, and thought it was a terrible plan when his tongue dipped inside and made her moan even louder. This made him grin, and it only masked some of his savagery.

"Do you like it?" she felt stupid for asking and wanted to yank her tongue out of her head when she heard herself begging for reassurance.

His thrusts slowed and made her eyes open in protest, but all he did was change the tempo. Slow and steady. Hard and sure.

"You feel incredible, wildcat." His free hand skated up between her breasts and around her neck, stroking and holding, and it rocketed Scarlett to the moon. "Open your eyes. I wanna see it happen for you."

That one possessive touch and his raspy command brought her pleasure she'd never envisioned. Only remembering to smash into his mouth in the nick of time in hopes his perfect lips muffled her orgasmic war cries as shock waves barreled through her. But as he worked himself deep, there was little chance of holding the noises inside.

"*Incredible*," he rasped again, this time by her ear when he let her hands go free, and she clasped them around his neck, urging him with little bumps of her hips for him to bury deep, to bury hard and find pleasure in her body. She needed that more than anything.

Her world felt as though it hadn't stopped spinning for hours. She was surrounded by his scent, taste, and rough hands.

"Take it, wildcat. Give me another." Axel's persuasive skills were smooth, and everything within her longed to follow his instructions blindly, without question. Scarlett had thought her body was done, orgasmed out, but his mouth coasted against her lips, biting and licking. Holy shit, she loved the biting. And one shift of his hips as he lifted her leg higher on his waist, putting his cock at a different angle inside her, and she started panting. And then it was a full-blown cry as she arched, slam after hard slam.

"That's it. Good girl. Come all over my cock."

She did, with little persuading, but the *good girl* felt like a mouth-watering stroke on her brain, and she buckled with an orgasm. Less powerful than the first, but it still felt like she'd won the vagina lottery as her legs trembled. Her senses were buzzing, concentrating solely on Axel's finish. The thrusts came with a grunt each time he bottomed out, and the moment he buried his face in her chest, Scarlett murmured his name like a sacred chant as he came with one last shove, holding inside her, stretching her impossibly. Oh, it felt amazing, and she moaned again for the sheer pleasure of Axel's glorious cock being where she'd always wanted it. She squeezed around him, and he grunted again, lifting his face; his eyes were perfectly glassy.

For months they'd been boss and hostage, bickering frenemies who occasionally flirted, her more than Axel. But having sex and being under Axel's touch made them something new.

Or so she thought.

As Axel pulled free, holding the base of his shaft so as not to lose the condom, he went to his knees and climbed from the couch, dumping the protection in a trash can. His jeans were fixed next, and when he turned to look at Scarlett, she felt the blast of his blasé attitude as though the last hour hadn't happened. No snuggles, no after kisses.

Going back to the in-control prez, nothing rattling his cage. She held onto that one word he'd used.

Incredible.

He could withdraw all he wanted because she was sexed out. Her eyes closed and smiled; she luxuriated in the feel-good feelings swimming through her blood.

Fucked so good by Axel was a good tagline. And if she had a resume, she'd slap it on there.

"C'mere, wildcat, let's get you dressed so you can go to bed."

So you can go to bed. Not we. *Hmph.* Even that wasn't ruining her good mood. She cracked one eyelid open, Axel was staring hotly, raking his eyes all over her naked body on his couch like an all-you-could-eat buffet.

"I don't have a bedtime."

"Scarlett…"

"Come and give me a kiss, Sir." She held out her arms cheekily. Axel's brows instantly fell over his eyes, and she grinned wider. Oh, he was delicious. He reacted every time she used sir in the same way his praise made her wet.

Inhaling hard enough, she saw it stretch the black t-shirt. He strolled over, Scarlett's heart triple-timed, and she squirmed her legs, not at all shy to be naked in front of him.

Axel braced his hands on the couch, wrapping her into his intoxicating scent, and he tapped a slow kiss on her lips.

"Mmm, thank you. Such an accommodating boss I have. Guess I'll get dressed now you've had your evil way with me."

"Scarlett…" how he could make her name sound like a warning was a skill.

She was mistaken if she thought he'd toss her the panties and dress. Instead, Axel grabbed her panties from the floor and went down to his haunches. It was the sexiest thing in the world being dressed by him, and Scarlett was an obedient doll, gazing with hearts in her pupils as he pulled the dress over her head.

Questions swam like ravenous sharks around her mind, and maybe those orgasms had pumped some common sense into Scarlett because she didn't let one loose.

So, as an alternative, she leaned in and kissed Axel's cheek. "Don't forget to call the Amos guy back. I'm off to bed, you wore me out," she danced her eyebrows as he frowned. "Thanks for the good time, Axel. Goodnight."

Not prepared for the level of vulnerability, Scarlett let out a held breath once she was on the other side of the door, making her legs move, and they didn't stop until she was locked in her bedroom.

"I fucked Axel Tucker," she whispered to hear herself say the words.

Her smile grew until her cheeks hurt. The smile didn't fade while she went through her bedtime routine, showering and slipping into bed. Her inner thighs, particularly her vagina, felt sore and well-used. Though as the minutes ticked by, she hoped Axel had walked through her door. It didn't stop Scarlett from going into dreams, smiling, and thinking of him.

Axel

Two unfamiliar Harleys entered the gates, engines purring as they stopped before Axel, waiting at the clubhouse entry.

Fortunately, the snow had melted, but the chill nipped around his neck.

As the two men stepped off their bikes, he noticed they weren't wearing their club cuts under the leather jackets. It was a sign of respect. If Axel visited another MC, he would do the same. Stepping forward, he offered a hand to Jamie Steele and then his VP, Amos.

"Good to see you, man," Jamie said. "It's been a while."

"Yeah, at Tag's fight in Denver, yeah?" that was over a year ago.

"Fuck, yeah." Amos laughed, "I won big that night. I might not like those Renegade Souls much, but that monster can fight like his mama was insulted."

Steele added. "You don't like anyone, so that isn't saying much."

"True enough."

"Let's get you a drink. You could have emailed me the info." The two men followed Axel into the warm clubhouse.

"We were headed through this way, anyway."

"I don't trust email." Amos said, "unless your shit is encrypted, and I didn't think you'd appreciate me hacking to check," he smirked, pulling a white envelope from his inside pocket; he handed it over. Axel poured them a scotch, and the three men seated. "Is this everything?"

"Yep. I included it all, even the boring bits."

Unable to wait, he ripped open the envelope, scanning Amos' intel, and it wasn't far before he got to a specific part. His eyes lifted and met Amos'. "This shit is right?"

"Oh, yeah. I found that interesting, too. Who knew the cult life was thriving in Idaho, huh? It's Netflix, man. It gives folks bad ideas."

Fuck. Had his wildcat escaped from that?

"I dug deep, got my sticky fingers into that guy's business. He ain't declaring his taxes, by the way. Suppose that's something of interest to you. The sons are pieces of work; they got their fingers in a lot of illegal shit, mostly moving goods from A to B. That's where the Bass family gets their funds from. That and donations."

"Donations?" asked Axel, rubbing a thumb on his lip, scanning the paper full of Scarlett's history.

"On paper, they ain't a cult, get it? But they're sure as shit run like a cult. They don't like outsiders; newcomers are vetted extensively before they're installed in their little neighborhood. They pay a membership fee to daddy Bass, aka the cult leader. He has regular deposits in his offshore account, the same ten grand repeatedly."

"He rolling in it?"

Amos chuckled. "The guy is like a Washington political, his pockets are bulging. I couldn't even tell you what his job was. Far as I could tell, he lives solely on donations, but unless you want to invest in a P.I. to gather on-site intel, that's all I got."

"Nah, this is enough for now." Axel wasn't so interested in Scarlett's father unless he was why she'd been homeless. If it were true, Axel would ruin him.

"As a side note, how easy would it be to empty those offshore accounts of his, untraceable?"

Jamie looked at Axel and then Amos, who smirked. "If you know the right people, it's child's play. And you know the right people. Is that what you wanna do?"

"I'll keep it on the back burner. Just wanted to know."

"I smell revenge in the air."

Axel answered Jamie, "maybe."

He scanned the document again, and his heart thumped hard. Arranged marriage... the fuck. "Did you find a marriage certificate?"

"Nothing, and I looked hard. As cultish as those cunts are, they marry legally. It's not singing and flowers in the forest shit, so there would be a paper trail. The subject isn't married or engaged, but there was an email thread between the father and the fella groom to discuss terms." Amos whistled through his teeth as he reached for his glass and downed it in one. "He had a big hard-on for the daughter, offering all but the kitchen sink."

Motherfucker. Axel felt his blood boil, and his fingertips gripped the edge of his desk to stop himself from erupting and throwing the table across the fucking room.

Nothing on that sheet showed Scarlett had been loved or shown affection in her entire life. Likewise, nothing in the private emails Amos accessed displayed how her parents missed her or were even looking for her.

He read the money from her menial job went directly into the father's account, which told Axel she didn't see a penny. No car or an apartment. There was no dating history, lists of friends, or trips she'd taken. Her whole life had been in that small town in Idaho, without choices.

He was livid.

"I thought it was a regular background check for an employee shit," Amos started, "but the more I delved, the heavier it became. Axel, this chick you're looking into didn't have a fun life. There are a lot of women in that area, so if you wanna take down this guy, you can count me in; nothing I like better than destroying a shithead."

Axel chuckled, seeing the sadistic glee on the other man's face. Steele only rolled his eyes as if he knew his VP's nasty side. Axel would keep it in mind. As long as the Bass family stayed away from Scarlett, they could rot in their cult; he didn't care to play a crusader to save others.

He cared only about her.

"Were there signs they were still in touch with her?"

"Nada. I sneaked into mommy dearest's text messages, and she was telling some nosy bitch how her wayward daughter was a disappointment to the family."

Fucking bitch.

Scarlett thrived now. She was living her life her way.

Not long later, he took the men to the main area to get them fed; he sent a sweet bottom to the kitchen to make up plates.

"You got some pretty faces around here," Steele remarked, scanning the loitering sweet bottoms, but the bar caught his attention, and he strolled over, taking a middle seat. Every hackle Axel had rose like fog off his skin.

"Hello, beautiful darling," Steele said to Scarlett. Dressed in sinful tight jeans and a red band t-shirt, slouched off one shoulder, displaying creamy skin he could still taste in the back of his throat.

Before she could respond, Axel growled. "Off-fucking-limits, Steele."

Amused, Steele cocked an eyebrow. "Is that right?"

"Hey, rude!" of fucking course, she protested. He swore she'd argue with him about the color of the sky if he said it was blue. Little brat. "It's Scarlett, not off fucking limits, thank you very much. Hello, and what's your name?" she addressed Steele with a welcoming smile that lit up her eyes. "If you join the club, you should know Axel is grouchier than a skunk in a trap, but if you feed him, he's less of a monster."

Axel felt the increase of his heated growl crawling up his throat as she sent him a teasing glint. No one teased him, not as she did. It was a drug directly to his cock; he fucking loved it. Resting two hands on the bar countertop, he leaned toward her and watched her pupils dilate. *Good girl*. She hadn't forgotten a thing about last night, either.

"You wanna feed me now, wildcat?"

The meaning was transparent, and her face could not hide her shock or whatever dirty thoughts passed through her mind. Now he'd let the floodgates open between them; he was happy to delve into all her dirty thoughts and make them a reality.

At his side, Jamie Steele cleared his throat.

"This is Jamie Steele; he's prez of the Apollo Kingsmen. We don't accept his kind 'round here; his visit is temporary," he said with a half-smile, and Scarlett chuckled, offering her hand. Axel did not like the time Steele held it for.

"Good to meet you. Do I call you wildcat, too?"

"Do you wanna leave by the door or the window, my friend?" grated Axel. His show of possessiveness only made Steele snicker.

"My fucking bones are old, so I'd prefer to walk through the door."

"You can call me Scar. Can I get you a drink?"

At that, the sweet bottom came through with plates of food.

"Sassy, get behind the bar and get Jamie and Amos their drinks. Follow me, Scarlett. Help yourself to anything, Steele. Plenty of women around for company. I'll be back before you guys ride out."

"Not quite *anything*," he joked, his eyeline specifying Scarlett as she walked to the end of the bar. Yeah, that was *right*. No one could have her.

Instead of waiting for Axel, Scarlett scowled and then stormed in front of him toward his office. He was good with that because he could eye-fuck her tight little ass the whole way. His hands itched to get them on her again.

"If you're going to reprimand me for talking to the out-of-towners, then—"

Axel didn't allow her to get any further with her bratty mouth before he crushed it underneath his. Taking advantage of her astonished huff to slip inside and twine their tongues, tasting her like he hadn't had her in his mouth in months, pushing his tongue too deep, slaking his thirst.

He'd thought of nothing but fucking her since he'd sent her off to bed because she'd make him reel, like no one else ever had.

Sex so good, Axel had lost his ever-loving mind.

Scarlett was the dessert you ate even when you were so full because she was that delicious.

He tasted and ended their kiss by nipping his teeth on her lip; she groaned and listed into him. *Clinging*. Good girl.

"If I ever see you flirting with another man…"

"Was I flirting? Was *that* flirting?" she frowned, still clinging to him. Not that he intended to let her go, not now his hands found the suppleness of her ass.

"You *spoke* to another man. That was *enough*." He grated through his teeth without anger, going for her throat again; he enjoyed her fluttery eyes the moment his hand locked around it.

"No talking to men ever again. Got it. If I see a man, I'll run and hide or tape my mouth shut to show him I'm forbidden to share civil words."

"I approve of this method, good girl."

Bony fingers poked him in the sides, and Axel's reflex against tickling meant he let her go. "Oh my God, quit saying that unless you're prepared for a bear attack, I like it too much." He didn't let her go far. Axel folded Scarlett's hand into his and pulled her across to the leather chair, placing her on his lap.

"Ohh." She gasped. "This is new." And didn't she wiggle? Tormenting his already rousing dick. He'd been hard since he woke this morning and went to find her. But she'd gone to the wholesalers with a prospect. He didn't like the feeling of not having her within eyeshot, and he'd prowled around the club, watching the door like a hawk.

He thought she might be shy this morning, but when she leaned in and kissed his lips quickly, Axel knew there wasn't an inch of shyness in her.

"Are you feeling okay?"

"Can I say just one thing?"

Axel popped an eyebrow at her change of gears, but he was curious. Everything she said and did fascinated him.

"Can we skip the after-sex talk? I cringe when I read it in books, like it's unnecessary to have a play-by-play on everything, you know? I had a great time, and you came, so I think you did, too. We don't need more than that."

Axel's chest flamed with warmth as he gripped the back of her neck, bringing her close enough that their noses brushed. "I know you enjoyed it, wildcat. Your pussy exploded around my cock hard enough that I thought you'd killed me."

"Ohh.." she buried her face in his chest with an irresistible laugh. "Wow, so you said that. Okay then. Axel Tucker has no filter."

"None. And you don't need a filter around me, either."

She lifted her face, and her eyes twinkled. "But around other men?"

He growled. "Yes, around them."

"Got it, Sir." she beamed.

"I wasn't gonna do the after-sex talk, but I want to know if you're feeling okay."

"I'm great."

Moving his hand down between her breasts and further south, he didn't stop until he cupped the mound between her legs. Scarlett's breath whooshed over his cheek. "You sore here?"

Her wheeze was adorable. "Oh, jeez. No. I'm not sore there. Though, it feels like I've done some intense Pilates, stretching muscles I didn't know I had."

"Yeah?" he smirked, enjoying hearing that.

Her gorgeous face was so expressive and open, telling him everything he wanted to know. She'd loved last night and wanted more from him.

From the way she wiggled on his lap, she was about to get it again.

"You want more of that? What we did last night."

The moment she understood, there was a flash of passion in her eyes. Scarlett bobbed her head up and down. "Yes, please. If you do."

Though Axel still felt somewhat lecherous toward the much younger woman, he had taken the brakes off. No more holding himself back.

What the fuck for?

He skated by on so few morals.

Why change his attitude now? And not for someone he hungered for.

"Tip your head to the side, wildcat. Offer me your neck."

Instantly she complied, and he pressed his mouth to her pulse, feeling how steady and hard it was pumping life through her incredible body. The body which had kept her alive for months alone. He couldn't think of Scarlett living on the streets against the elements and not have the rage rise in him for what could have happened to her. He sucked hard and listened to her pixie-like moans. At the same time, his hand trailed down her body again, this time lifting the shirt's hem and sliding inside. Fuck him, she was braless. His palm curled greedily around her small breast, fitting perfectly.

"I'll give you what you need," he promised, nipping his teeth at her throat, a dark side of him wanting to leave marks behind. Axel had been a free spirit from a young age, partly beaten into him by the shitty hand he'd been dealt, somewhat because he couldn't envision himself with an old lady.

Scarlett fucked his head up, making him beast-like to put her in a cage and keep her for himself. Selfish thoughts stacked up as he ravaged her throat, and she trailed her fingers through his hair, murmuring his name and tormenting his dick with an ass wiggle.

"Not interrupting, am I?" an amused voice said from the doorway. Axel hadn't caught it opening. He was that deep in his lust for Scarlett.

As his mouth detached from Scarlett's skin, she squeaked in shock, tried to twist around, and fell off his lap, landing between his legs, her face level with his crotch.

"Shit," she cursed, looking up at him with wild eyes like they'd been caught screwing by a parent. Smiling at the panicked siren sitting between his legs, fingering the hole in the knee of his jeans, looking to him for reassurance. He gave it by cupping her face, feeling right to touch her.

"Do you think he saw?" she whispered.

Across the room, Chains chuckled. That asshole wouldn't move for all the beer in Germany.

"Yes, he saw, wildcat."

"Oh, shit."

"Up you get."

Once on her feet, Axel watched Scarlett push her shoulders back and scowl at Chains, who had a shit-eating grin on his face.

"This wasn't what it looked like. I was polishing the floor. Crumbs, you know? He's a messy eater."

Glaring at his VP, daring him to embarrass Scarlett, he thankfully got the message and winked at her. "Got it, babe."

She took her escape as though her fantastic ass was on fire.

"Polishing the floor?" Chuckled Chains once he closed the door and plonked on the hard chair in front of the desk. "Your hostage is the worst liar, brother."

Wasn't she just? He smiled to himself.

She couldn't lie for toffee, but she was the sweetest fucking morsel he'd ever tasted.

Axel

"Prospect." Whistled Axel to gain the kid's attention. "Go bang on doors and get everyone to church in ten minutes."

"Fuck's sake, I was already doing shit for Reno," Dillion indicated to the mop and bucket he was carrying. Reno was pissed off with the kid if he was on cleaning duty.

Axel narrowed his eyes and stopped in his tracks. "You'll watch what the fuck you say, prospect."

As if the younger guy realized who he'd been mouthing off to, he turned a mottled red and nodded. "Sure, Prez. On it now." He skulked off. As soon as he got his ass in his church chair, he waited for Reno. "You've got issues with Dillion."

"Don't I fucking know it? The bastard couldn't follow an order even if he were being loaded onto the Arc. I say we cut him loose."

"The prospects are under your ruling, so that decision is yours. How many hangarounds have we had coming by lately?"

"About forty. Few look like they could handle an arm wrestle with your hostage, let alone deserve the patch. However, a few have shown initiative."

Axel trusted Reno's instincts to know who to give the prospect vests to.

Waiting another minute for every member of his council to arrive, Axel stretched his neck; he scraped his long hair back and tied it in a loose knot. If he knew fucking a younger woman with the sexual appetite of a horny teen would make him feel old as dirt and ache all over, he would have swallowed vitamins months before Scarlett showed up to keep up with her.

Three nights in her twin bed, not much sleep, he was going for the sex title of the year.

Last night, after the fourth round, the first three being in the media room where she made him watch rom-com movies, he'd cuffed both of her arms to the headboard and told the siren to get some sleep and let his balls recharge. She only giggled and started pumping her hips in the air beneath the sheet as he shut his eyes. She drove him crazy. He'd lasted two minutes of her little moans before crawling between her thighs and eating her until she screamed.

She was killing him, and Axel happily signed his death certificate because he was hooked. When he wasn't fucking Scarlett, he was thinking about it, plotting how to get her alone and his hands making her moan.

The last of the boys shuffled in, taking their seats, and Axel's jaw cracked with a loud yawn.

"We keeping you up, Prez?" wisecracked Denver.

"Not us. But we know *who* is." added a smirking Splice.

"Take your clown act on the road, Splice." Deadpanned Axel, not giving his brother the satisfaction of biting or confirming that he'd been in Scarlett's bed the past few nights.

They all knew because Scarlett couldn't lie for shit. Her face wore every emotion she'd ever felt, and he loved that about her. But on this, for the first time, he wasn't giving his club brothers an inch of his personal life. He felt feral and protective over what he did to her body during the dark hours.

"Right, onto business. We've had nothing new drop on our doorstep in weeks from DeCastro. We can only hope he's gotten bored and moved on. The brothers," Axel pointed to Reno and Ruin, sitting stony-faced, "have been hunting him and coming up empty, too."

"You get anything from Fielding?" asked Denver. "The horny cop has to be better for something other than trying to get into your panties."

The table snickered. He wasn't wrong; her persistence grated on his last nerve. You'd think the woman would be happy enough with the dirty money she was earning against her measly cop paycheck and wouldn't beg for extra. Unfortunately, it wasn't extra cash the woman wanted. It was a piece of him. And that wasn't happening even if Hell split open and demons danced out.

"Since none of the dead bodies are connected to him, they're not looking for DeCastro, but she has her connections, legal and otherwise, and all of them are coming up empty."

"Is this guy Houdini or what?" hissed Tomb. "No offense to the grim twins, but this guy is a fucking moron and shouldn't be this hard to find. I want this shit finished before a body lands on Nina's salon doorstep."

Axel knew everyone could agree.

The club hadn't antagonized DeCastro.

He'd been in jail more years than some brothers had sat at this table. DeCastro was petty-minded. Instead of enjoying his second chance, having been released early for a technicality, he'd chosen revenge to punish Reno and Ruin.

As soon as church was called quits, Ruin took off first. Besides searching for DeCastro, he'd been holed up in his wood shop for days.

"You and Ruin good?" He asked Reno as the two men got to the door simultaneously.

"Yeah, Prez. This shit is what it is. Just wish it wasn't touching the club."

"We've been through stickier times, brother, and we will again in the future. You and Ruin hold tight, yeah? We all got your backs."

Until they found DeCastro, or he made a new move, there wasn't much the club could do except remain watchful. He got into the biker lifestyle because he wanted adventure. Primarily, he'd wanted money. But some days, he wished for a quieter life, if only for a goddamn weekend. But he'd signed on for this, and Axel was greedy. Now he'd tasted the money they could earn; there was no way he'd go back to an ordinary existence. Danger and trouble came with the territory, which was fine by him.

Especially when he rounded the corner and saw a piece of respite he could sink his teeth into and forget about hunting a murderer and cooking up dishonest deals.

He smirked, watching Scarlett's ass moving from side to side as she listened to whatever was pumping loudly through the earbuds. The moment she spun around with silent lyrics on her lips, she turned the reddest red and then smiled.

"Hey! You need anything?"

Yeah. You spread out on this bar with your legs thrown over my shoulders.

It felt too long since he'd put his touch all over her body, and something akin to craving tingled the back of Axel's throat. He advanced and saw the moment she knew what he would do, and she retreated until she hit a corner of the bar.

"You can't kiss me here," she whispered in a rush.

Axel narrowed his eyes. That wasn't the story she was singing early this morning when it took him over thirty minutes to get dressed because she kept attacking him for one more kiss.

"Is that so?"

Her eyes darted across the club as though she expected an audience. Was his wildcat still so innocent she had no clue that everyone knew about them already?

And then she flayed him alive.

"You can't kiss me in public, Axel."

"Why the fuck not?" he rested both hands on the bar separating them.

She wanted his kiss. She *always* wanted his fucking kiss, so this made no sense.

Her reason killed him further.

"I don't think people should know what we're doing because when you're finished with me, they'll feel sorry for me. Poor little Scarlett got dumped by sir prez."

Though she said it with a smile, Axel saw through it right down to her vulnerable heart, and he hated himself, knowing she believed every word.

Yet another reason he should never have given in to his baser self and taken her. One day he'd hurt her, which was the last thing he'd want to do.

He should give her up now.

Would he, though?

Not a fucking chance.

"Come out from behind there."

"Axel, I have things to finish."

"Right now, Scarlett."

"Jeez. Bossy much." She huffed, but walked the bar's length and came around to him. "Just don't drag me anywhere."

"Everyone is used to me dragging you off, so it's not a big fucking deal." He got hold of her hand and walked them to the entryway, hooking up her jacket on the way, making sure she was zipped in before braving the cold weather outside. The moment they were on the other side of the door, he flattened Scarlett to the wall and found her mouth so fucking sweet and willing that he grunted down her throat. The kiss lasted a minute at least.

"I'll kiss you when I want to kiss you, Scarlett. Have you been holding back from being kissed because of the shit you said?" taking her chin in his finger and thumb, he tipped Scarlett's head back and then ran that same thumb over her pouty lips. "These lips need kissing often. So when you want a kiss, you come to me, right?"

How she lit up with only a smile.

"Yes, Sir."

Axel growled.

If she weren't careful, he'd give the clubhouse more than just a kiss to spy on. He swatted her ass and made her move in front of him. "Get in the truck, bad girl."

"Oh? We're going somewhere?"

"Out for lunch."

"A date?" she all but screeched, scaring the local bird life. "An actual date with *the* Axel Tucker?" now she was grinning from ear to ear, and he arched a brow at her gorgeous silliness.

"You need feeding, and so do I."

"Yep. A date with Axel Tucker."

Days' worth of intense sex, and he hadn't even considered taking her on a date. He was adequately shit at romance, proven by how elated Scarlett looked at the prospect of eating food together in public.

He'd do better. Or try to.

Not having a permanent woman in his life, his default setting was always to put business matters first, but Axel admitted he could get addicted to putting a smile on Scarlett's face.

Once she'd scrambled up into his RAM, he waited for her to buckle in, but she surprised him when she attacked the second his ass was in the seat. Her mouth attached, and he got the kiss of a lifetime in a whirlwind of her taste and seeking tongue. Half prone across his lap, Axel fixed his hand on her ass.

"You said I should get my kisses." Licking her lower lip like a seductress, arrowing his gaze down to her mouth. It was like Scarlett had the magical button to switch his brain off and to focus entirely on her.

Regardless of his shy wildcat, Axel didn't give a damn about being caught when he lifted Scarlett into his lap, splitting her legs so she had a knee on either side of his thighs.

"You need anything else before we go?"

She got his meaning because her breathing changed. Desire pooled in the depths of her eyes. She was so easy to read. The thirst for her never quit. And in these quiet moments over the past few days, Axel realized how he relied on Scarlett to bring normalcy to his life, even with all her chaotic temper or when she was silently sitting in his office watching him.

Things with Scarlett were easy, and he never knew how addictive easy could be. Now he squeezed her ass cheeks, feeling how she wiggled against his crotch.

"What's on offer?" she dared ask, biting the corner of her lip like she didn't know it drove him feral.

"I'm not a decent man, wildcat, don't look at me like that, or I'll have my hand in your pants before you can blink."

Her hands fisted into the back of his hair the way he liked her tugging at it. It meant she was turned on and so ready. She came inches from his mouth, brushing sweet air over his lips, and then the little brat dared him. "Bet you can't."

Nah, there was no way he'd leave that bet hanging; he'd get his prez card revoked. Leave Scarlett wanting something from him? Not a fucking chance. Like the vulture he was around her, he palmed the back of her neck with one hand, giving her a nice long squeeze. And then, after opening the button, he delved his other hand down the front of her jeans, surprising a giggle out of her as she popped her hips forward the moment his fingers slid into her panties and met wet heat.

If Axel had a dream lover, Scarlett was it.

She was aggressive enough when she wanted to be, telling him what she needed, but when she was in his hands, she trusted him to deliver precisely on his promises, knowing her pleasure was *his* fucking pleasure.

She melted like ice, and he'd only stroked her clit a few testing times.

"Axel. Oh, God. That feels good." her head dropped forward onto his chest.

"It's about to get better. Lean your hands on the wheel." He wanted to see her eyes when it happened. It took next to no time; he loved how Scarlett reacted to being touched, how she flew apart on a wave of heavy breathing when he curled his fingers inside her and tormented her g-spot. Axel latched on to her sweet lips to taste her orgasm when she splintered apart. Feeling her shudder was his reward. As much as Axel wanted to strip her bare and fuck her raw—and one day soon, he'd do that in his truck—he wouldn't compromise her shyness by doing it in broad daylight, so he removed his fingers and did the next best thing.

Painting her lips in her juices, he sucked them clean until his dick hurt from the need to fuck her and *fuck her*.

"Oh, wow, I sometimes forget you're dirty," she laughed into his mouth.

"The kind of dirty you love."

"Mmhmm. I do."

One swat on her ass, and he moved her back to her seat. "Buckle in, wildcat, before I show you how dirty I can get."

"You say the nicest things, Sir."

His dick twitched, and he had to adjust the seam of his jeans or risk blood loss to her favorite appendage.

"Keep calling me sir, and we won't get out of here."

Scarlett laughed, laying her hand on his thigh. "Yes, Sir."

Little brat, but Axel was smiling while he backed the truck out.

And not long later, Scarlett sashayed her ass in the café diner when he opened the door for her, like she was on a runway and hadn't just been coming around his fingers only minutes before. His mouth salivated, watching her.

The hunger never quit.

It folded a tight fist around his heart, demanding more.

And the longing to be around her was growing like a virus.

She was still tight-lipped about her past life, but it didn't stop Scarlett from talking about everything else, and lunch went by fast.

For the first time in days, Axel was solely concentrated on the woman in front of him, eating her weight in tacos, instead of thinking about a deranged asshole out to get the club by littering dead bodies.

Once outside, Scarlett slipped her hand into his, and he latched on tight automatically. The last thing he expected to hear was.

"Hey Axel, I need to talk to you."

His head turned to Sofia Fielding, out of uniform, staring at Scarlett specifically. Because he'd been dealing with Sofia for a while, he caught her facial cues damn quickly, and he understood the flash of irritation when she looked at Scarlett.

Hell fucking no. The bitch was not throwing her venom at his wildcat.

Letting his eyes roam up and down the sidewalk, checking no one else was looking over and seeing him talking to a cop, he shifted his body, half hiding Scarlett, keeping her hand firmly in his.

And then he leaned in and lowered his voice. Deathly quiet.

"You got memory loss? If not, then you know what I said to you already. You never fucking approach me in public. I don't know you. You don't know me. And you don't try to ambush me when you see me with my woman. Hard rule, Fielding. I pay you to spill your guts." Her alarmed gaze flew to Scarlett. "She knows who you are; if your twisted mind was coming up with ideas to ambush her alone and bend your narrative to suit you best, I'd rethink it quickly. We have a good thing going, Fielding, don't let your jealous hormones spoil it. You know what would happen."

Angry color filled her face before it was gone in the next second. She was a damn good chameleon; he'd give her that. But he'd trust that woman about as far as he could throw Ruin across a room.

"But I have something you need to know."

"Not here. Not now."

"It's fucking important." She snapped.

"Then get in touch the usual way." He left the cop there on the street and didn't look back as he walked Scarlett back to his truck, helping her in, he was pissed off.

"She was…"

"She was something, alright." Axel finished for Scarlett. "if she ever approaches you when you're on your own, don't ever fucking talk to her, you got it?"

"But aren't you working with her?"

"I buy information. She isn't a friend, Scarlett. She's not a friend of the club. You listening? She would use you, put poison in your head; she's good for what she does, but don't ever trust her."

Unfazed by his warning, she put her hand on his thigh again, instantly bringing calm to his coiled body, and his fingers covered hers.

"It's not my first rodeo dealing with sly people, Axel. I got it, I understand. Besides, I don't want to be friends with anyone who wants to get in your pants."

He snorted and cast her a sideways glance to see her grimacing.

"Jealous, wildcat?"

"Only in the same way you'd be jealous if I spent time with Splice."

The growl came unbidden, and he brought her hand to his mouth, nipping his teeth on Scarlett's inner wrist.

"Exactly," she beamed. "Have you slept with her?"

"No."

"She wants to, though."

"So do you," he half-grinned, loving seeing how her face, "the difference is, you've fucked my brains out and will again soon as I get you home."

"Oh, yay." The brat chuckled and made him laugh. She did that a lot. "Take us back to the club, Sir. I have brains to attend to."

"We're not going to the clubhouse." He told her, and one more thing he liked about Scarlett Bass when she only sent him a sunshine-filled smile across the cab at him, trusting him to take her wherever he wanted to.

This woman was everything he had never expected.

Scarlett

"Hold up. Why didn't I know you had an actual house? I thought you lived in the clubhouse."

He'd stopped in front of a two-story house in a sedate neighborhood, parking the truck under a porch. It was red brick with a long pathway and looked adorable with its lush green lawn.

She stood gaping at the house even as Axel locked the truck and grabbed her hand. The hand-holding was new, and she was giddily happy about it.

"I keep a room at the clubhouse, but I've lived here since Roux was a kid. Come on; I'll show you around." He took her to the backyard and what looked like a massive extension.

"This whole back end was blown off a few years ago."

She gasped. "Like exploded?"

"Yeah, some trouble with the Mexicans. It's all fine now," he added when he expected her next question. "So while I was rebuilding, I added a few extra rooms. One upstairs and an extension for when Roux and her family come to stay. They have a ground-floor suite now."

"Aww, you're a wonderful daddy, Axel. And this house is beautiful."

The inside was the same. It was decorated in whites, blues, and grays. Large couches you'd expect in a man's house. Lazy boy chairs in front of a built-in TV wall. He had a lot of family photos on a unit that took up the entire back wall.

It was like looking into the secret cave of Axel Tucker.

Scarlett's heart beat faster. He'd brought her home. That meant something for a man so private.

Axel let go of her hand but stroked it down her back instead. She shuddered and listed into his body. "I know you're dying to poke your little nose everywhere. So go ahead," he half-smiled. "I'll make a pot of coffee."

"You don't mind?"

"Got nothing to hide, wildcat."

"I won't touch anything," she promised, excited to explore his house.

"Sure, you will."

She laughed. He knew her.

With a brief kiss pressed to Axel's lips, she took off, deciding to start on the top floor. She walked around his house like she was going to evaluate the property. Not a nook was left unexplored. There were three bedrooms, four if she counted the one he'd built for Roux downstairs. Two bathrooms and a nice office/library, but it was his bedroom she was most fascinated with. Of course. She was in his lair, and it smelled exactly like him. She tested his bed by putting her butt on the edge and bouncing slightly. So sturdy. It could withstand their sexcapades.

Had he brought her home to stay the night?

Oh, no, she didn't even have a toothbrush with her.

Shut up, Scar, that doesn't matter. She'd use her finger if it meant she could snuggle in Axel's colossal king-size bed.

She wound through the house and ended the tour in the kitchen. More family photos and drawn pictures, obviously from his grandbabies, decorated the front of the double-sized silver fridge. Seeing them made her heart swell. He was such a cute grandpa. She'd been around him only a few times with the kids and saw only pure love.

She got along with Roux. But that was before she started sleeping with her dad. What would she think of Scarlett now?

She brushed that scary thought aside because she didn't fancy getting on the wrong side of Roux Savage.

All worries fled when she made her way back to the living area.

"Oh, Axel, I love your house," she started, "it's so—"

Her tongue dried.

And her heart thumped out of her chest.

Axel was lounging in one of the black lazy-boy leather chairs. His legs spread wide, he'd kicked off his boots, and now his feet were beautifully bare. His hair flowed around his shoulders, and swear to God, his long brown hair was an aphrodisiac to her. It reminded

Scarlett of men from another era who went to war and came home and put babies in their wives' bellies. His masculinity was over the top and made her mouth water.

With his arms above his head, his eyes tracked her slower steps across the living room.

"You like my house?"

"Yeah," she croaked.

His gaze was eating her alive. So low-lidded and sexy, she hardly breathed as lust built like kindling in her body.

What urge made her drop to her knees in front of his spread legs? She couldn't say only that she *needed* to. Instantly, Scarlett put her hands on Axel's thick thighs, feeling how the muscles beneath her fingertips flexed.

Still, he watched her silently as if gauging what she would do.

There were only two reasons to be on her knees, and because Scarlett wasn't a religious zealot like her mom, it wasn't to confess her sins. No, she had more pleasurable ideas in mind.

Loving Axel's command over her body. When his hands were on her, she gave her soul to him. She loved him making the moves and initiating sex. Sure, she could tell him what she wanted and didn't feel shy about it. Axel handling her was so hot.

Now he seemed pretty relaxed, allowing her to explore him. And she was overjoyed at the prospect.

Up and down, she stroked his thighs until she went for the zipper on his jeans. Oh, sweet Jesus, his cock was already hard. The only reaction she got from Axel was an invigorating grunt when she rubbed the heel of her hand over the bulge. He helped a little by angling his pelvis back when she went too hard on the zipper and button and couldn't immediately open them. It was heaven when she finally had him in her hands.

Stroking Axel was paradise.

But making him make those little breath sounds was beyond heaven, and she rubbed him faster, harder, tighter, almost choking the life from his dick until dribbles of pre-come appeared at the plump crown. There was no doubt she would fall on his length like a ravenous beast. No doubt, at all.

"You keep licking your lips like that, Scarlett, and I'll blow all over your hands."

Those two hands of hers halted briefly before he shunted his hips forward and got them moving again. Trying to span his cock in a pull-stroke motion, using his leaked pleasure for a better handjob.

"Not yet," she husked, though watching him come all over her fingers was something she needed to see. He was so good at making her come, she wanted to do the same for Axel.

She licked her lips again, leaning forward. Axel groaned. His eyes were extra low-lidded now, sexily watching her with a tightness to his lips as if holding on. That thought only spurred her along and produced giddy excitement inside.

"I want to do this so badly, but I have to warn you, I might be bad at it because I have a weak gag reflex. Like I have to nibble a banana. It's that bad."

He half-grinned and then reached down to stroke two fingers gently on her cheek. The move was so sweet and romantic that she nearly swooned off her knees.

"There isn't anything you could do with that gorgeous mouth that I won't like, yeah? You wanna suck me deep and gag? It'll be sexy as fuck, Scarlett. You wanna lick and torment my tip? Send me to hell now because I know I'll love it."

Oh, wow. He blew her mind open.

"Don't say sweet things like that, Axel. I could so easily fall for you."

It was too late. She'd fallen.

She was felled.

Completely over her feet for him.

She dared not look at his face at her declaration for fear of what she'd see looking back. She'd over-spoken but didn't care, not right now. Not when she bent over Axel's lap and engulfed the broad tip of his cock into her mouth, not starting slowly. No, Scarlett sucked him hard, and the grunt he emitted reached down between her legs and stroked her into a sodden mess.

"Fuck. *Fuck, Scarlett.* Suck a good suck. Fuck, keep going."

His praise sent her spiraling to another dimension, where she was his sex slave, and he used her long and hard.

Fuck it, she thought. If Axel wanted her to gag on his cock, she'd give him anything he wanted, so she slid her lips down until she couldn't possibly fit more of his tree-trunk-sized length in her mouth. It was obscene to be this loved by God that Axel got his share and some other dude's share of the penis.

This was no porno, and of course, she gagged, but when Axel's hand cupped the side of her neck, stroking her cheek with that thumb, she hummed around him, retreating only a little before trying again. It was bliss. She never thought giving head to someone would feel as good as being finger-fucked in a truck, but it did.

She got off on making him feel good, so by the time he warned her he was coming and to take her mouth away if she didn't want to swallow, she was already rocking her hips. Axel helped by rubbing his foot against her sex.

She didn't remove her mouth, and the spurt of his orgasm, as he groaned her name and gripped the back of her neck, took her by surprise. But every drop was swallowed reflexively.

She would have kept on sucking. It was Axel who gently pulled her head back, detaching his spent length.

"Jesus, you little savage," he rasped, breathing hard. "You nearly killed me. I'm a goddamn old man, wildcat, and you sucked the life out of me."

That sent her into a round of giggles as Axel tucked himself away and lifted her across his lap. She laughed into his chest at the idea she could kill a gorgeous man by giving him head.

"I guess you liked it then, hm?"

"Fucking loved it," he spoke with his mouth pressed into her hair. Beneath her hand, his heart raced, bringing little tears to her eyes. Thankfully, they never fell, or she'd feel like a silly idiot crying because she'd pleasured him.

Because Axel didn't mind when she snuggled all over him after sex, she slipped her hands behind his back and buried her face in his neck. Content to sit in a lazy boy chair with the man she loved.

Inevitable. Or fate. It was all the same noise.

Scarlett was where she wanted to be for the rest of forever.

Scarlett

In the dim storage room, Scarlett was trying to find a water bottle only moments ago when a solidly built body pushed her against the shelving.

Fortunately, she recognized that body and didn't have to go into Kung Fu Panda mode, so she became only flesh and sensation as lust wired its way through her lower extremities. The all-consuming need took her out like she'd been hit with a bat. If only she could bottle the powerful, pussy-twinging feeling Axel gave her, she'd have women all over the world day drinking.

"This is sexual harassment, old man." She moaned as a hand, full of sin, skated lower and lower until Axel cupped her crudely between her legs. The thinness of the yoga leggings was hardly a deterrent.

"I'm the old man, but you're the one who falls asleep during sex."

Scarlett gasped. "It was one time, and it was between sex, Axel! I was taking a little power nap to recharge because the way you fuck me is so good I was worn out. Besides, it was the first night I stayed over at your house. I was overstimulated."

The way he chuckled curled her toes, even better when he ran a finger along her pussy lips, greedy for his attention. "Nice, save, sleeping beauty."

That first night together had been over seven days, and she'd had the best week since. Only once had she been in her bed at the clubhouse. The sleepovers were at Axel's house the rest of the time. The night they couldn't was because he was out on a run with his road captain and VP, and he'd wanted her safe within the MC.

"I gotta head out of town for a few hours." He told her, rubbing until she panted, his mouth following a similar path on the back of her neck.

"So, this is my goodbye? I approve, Sir."

Already knowing Axel was a fan of handcuffs, at least, using them with her, they'd played some sinful games this week in his enormously comfy bed. Calling him sir brought its own trouble, and no law in the land would stop Scarlett from making Axel unruly with domineering rage to overpower and fuck her silly when she used that title.

He grunted in her ear. "You'd be put on your knees for that if I had the time to shove my cock in your throat, bad girl."

"Promises, promises. Later?"

"Yeah," he rumbled, kissing her throat again, making her soft. "We'll play later and see how much of an old man I am. You gonna be able to stay awake?"

Scarlett spun around and pushed her hands on his chest. "You're never going to let me forget that, are you?"

Even in the dark, she could see him smirking.

"It didn't stop you from fucking me again."

"You were wet with my come, splayed out and moaning my name in your sleep. You practically led my cock home, Scarlett."

She flushed like he'd set a match to her clothing. She was such a horny tramp for Axel Tucker and couldn't even rouse a second's worth of shame over it.

Being fucked while she slept and waking with her body trembling with pleasure while Axel churned between her thighs was a newly discovered kink. Now she couldn't wait for the next time he brought her awake.

Learning all these new things about herself with a beautiful, long-haired biker was the funnest part of all.

"Be safe, okay?" there was no telling what he and the boys would do unless Axel talked to her about club things, she never pushed the boundaries. Though he always guaranteed she was safe, she wanted the same for him.

He dropped a slow kiss on her lips. "I will."

Not wanting to appear clingy, or act like a girlfriend, when she still didn't know what they were or if they were something other than sleeping together, she reined in her worries and kissed Axel one last time before sneaking out of the storage room. He came out a second later, holding a water bottle for her. Oh, yeah, she'd forgotten that. She grinned at him with thanks. Then watched his spectacular stride as he walked away from her.

Scarlett had it so bad for him and didn't want to ruin it by assuming they were important if he wasn't there yet. She could out-wait Axel Tucker. That was a solid fact. Wait for him to fall in love with her? Easy peasy.

She went about the next few hours with a spring in her step.

That was, until a prospect found her crouched behind the bar, reattaching one tap to a brand-new beer keg.

"Yo, hostage," *ugh*, she'd never get away from that title, would she? She appeared behind the bar and glowered at Samson, her least favorite prospect. He was always in a constant bad mood. "You got mail," he smirked, tossing a plain white envelope on the top of the bar, and then strode off, grabbing one of the sweet bottoms sitting nearby. Tucking the envelope in her back pocket, Scarlett fed Champ some treats. Only when the dog was happily eating did she reach for the envelope. She assumed it was a flyer from her phone company; it was the only mail she'd ever received.

Her stomach dropped, seeing the return name on the back.

Sheeran Bass.

Her eldest brother.

Oh, God. Oh, shit. Oh, fuck.

They'd found her.

But how?

When?

How long had they known where she was?

She'd been so careful. When she cut the Bass family out of her life, the cut had been complete. She'd figured she might reach out to her mom in a few years when she was settled.

Scarlett wasn't aware of shaking until Champ trotted over, whined a little, and rested his shaggy head on her lap. She absently stroked the furry crown as she stared at the letter.

Tossing it into the fire would be the right option, but she was too nervous not to know what Sheeran had to say, so she tore it open, feeling her heart pulse loudly in her ears.

What she read made her feel sick.

Dear sister.

I can't say you haven't led us, your family, a merry dance trying to locate you. You've caused our mother untold pain and worry. And we've wasted a lot of money to find you. I hope you got this pathetic rebellion out of your system because it ends now.

It's time you did right by your family.

I could have walked into that place and taken you many times, but I trust you will do the right thing. I don't need to remind you, do I, my sister, that father is friends with judges and police chiefs and can bring a lot of trouble to the Diablo Disciples' doorstep. I know you don't want that.

Do the right thing, Scarlett.

It's time you came home to where you belong with your people.

No more will be said about you running away.

All will be forgiven in time once you've paid for the consequences.

But please, don't make me do something I know you will regret. And trust me when I say I will happily bring the law down on the bikers you're living with until every one of them never sees daylight again.

Don't test me on this.

I'm staying in town at the Points motel.

Do not keep me waiting, Scarlett.

Sheeran didn't sign off the letter, but he didn't need to. He'd made his threatening point quite clear. Pushing Champ out of the way, Scarlett made it a few feet to the outside trash can and lost her stomach in seconds, vomiting her anger and fear. Those alone feelings from months back, the debilitating lack of freedom, came crashing down until it felt as though Sheeran had strangled the air from her lungs. Wiping her mouth on the back of her hand, she grimaced at the foul taste left in her mouth.

Champ was openly whining now, rubbing against her legs like he sensed how upset Scarlett was. "I'm okay, boy. You're such a good boy, aren't you?" she hugged his neck and refused to cry.

Fuck Sheeran.

He could go directly to Hell and not collect $200.

But his threat had landed in the right place because thoughts were flying around Scarlett's head as she sat on the ground with a whining dog comforting her.

Would he cause trouble for the club if she stayed?

Could he?

She'd known of her father's associates, but did he have enough pull to go up against the Diablos?

For the rest of the day, she was ineffective at anything other than worrying. Though she worked and served drinks, there was only one topic on her mind, and it was nothing good.

Luck always ran out, eventually. A heavy sigh weighed on her shoulders, and hers had run out before she was ready.

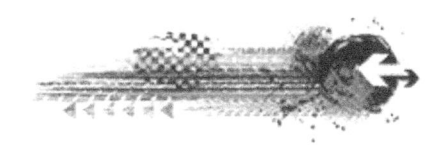

Axel

Axel didn't know what he'd done to deserve to find Scarlett asleep in his bed at the clubhouse. She never ventured into his room without him, so he smiled at her sleeping form after closing the door.

Quietly kicking off his boots and leaving his cut hanging over the chair, he unbuttoned the jeans and sat wearily on the bed. The run had taken longer than expected, but he'd needed to be there to meet with the Murphy's. All was good, and he'd ridden back to the club, almost double the speed, knowing who he was riding home to.

She had him hooked; that was a fact.

There was no point in lying to himself, not now. He was around her little finger and happily so.

Leaning down, he skimmed a kiss across Scarlett's soft, warm cheek as she slept almost childlike, with a hand tucked under her chin. She hadn't climbed under the covers, and that bothered him.

"Wake up, baby."

He steered his lips on hers this time, and she came awake, startled and panic in her eyes. "Hey, it's me. Settle down." A hand on her stomach was the only thing stopping Scarlett from bolting up. She was a deep sleeper, but he'd never seen her come awake like that.

"Bad dream?"

"Eh, no. Sorry. Hey." She rubbed at her eyes. "I didn't know you were home."

"Just got here," he said. Just like she couldn't mask her happiness or desire, Axel sensed her hiding shit from him when her gaze avoided him. "Something wrong?"

"No, nothing." She tried to sit up, but his hand on her stomach kept her down. "Well, I got my period today and am in agony. I shouldn't have fallen asleep, sorry."

Two fucking sorries from his wildcat in a minute. Now he knew something was wrong, and he'd find out what.

"I was only meant to change the sheets, but I think I sat down and fell asleep."

"Why wasn't the house mouse changing the bed?"

"Because she wanted to send up a sweet bottom, and I don't want them in your room, Axel," she scowled. She was so fucking petty; he grinned and kissed her lips.

"Possessive little thing."

She huffed and ignored his claim. He knew it anyway, and he dug she was possessive of him. With his hand on her stomach, he pressed in a little and rubbed left to right. Instantly, he felt the tension in her body sag.

"How long have you been in pain?"

"Most of the day, it'll pass."

He hated how easily she swept her discomfort aside, like it didn't matter. It mattered to him until he couldn't stand her hurting. He rose to his feet, her big doe eyes following him. "Get undressed and into bed."

"I don't have my sleep shorts up here. I should go to my room, Axel." she didn't want to be anywhere else but where he was, and it was the same for him. So he went to the drawers and pulled out one of his t-shirts and boxer briefs. "Put these on; I'll be right back. I'll spank you if you're not in bed when I come back."

When he returned, she was in bed so that he couldn't redden her ass. Ah, well, he'd find another reason soon enough. His mouthy wildcat always gave him a reason, but she needed tender care right now as he watched a grimace play across her pale face. She was curled up on her side with her legs raised to her stomach.

"Did you eat dinner?"

"Yeah, Tomb made burgers."

Leaving only the lamplight on, Axel sat on the side of the bed and pulled the covers down; she looked edible in his clothes. Though he had no hangups about fucking her while she was bleeding, he had to remind the fiend-like side of himself that Scarlett was hurting and didn't need him mauling her. He rubbed her belly again and ate up her little moans of comfort. Then he placed the hot water bottle he'd filled on her lower abdomen.

"Oh, god yeah, that's nice." She sighed. "Thanks, Axel. You must think I'm a big baby."

"You're a goddess, a fucking tough one at that. Open up." She opened her mouth without question so he could drop two pain pills on her tongue; he helped her with a sip of water, holding the glass to her mouth.

For over three hours, Axel held Scarlett through the worst of her cramps, changing the hot water bottle each time the heat diminished or rubbing her stomach when she asked for his hands instead.

He kissed her head when he thought she'd drifted off to sleep. The need to take care of her hadn't sneaked up on him. It had been a roar through his ears from day one, but only now had it become more critical.

"Axel," Scarlett's honey-coated voice cut through the silence. Just his name and his brow furrowed because she sounded so tiny and delicate.

"Yeah, baby?"

"I need help. I must tell you something because I've brought trouble to the club."

He'd sensed something had been off about her demeanor, and he had nothing to do with her period pain. His arms tightened around his woman, and he showed he was fully present, thoroughly focused on slaying any demons she had by saying two words.

"Tell me."

Scarlett

When trouble came knocking, it sure as shit came knocking loudly.

However, the noise in Axel's navy-colored clubhouse bedroom was deafening.

She'd told him everything.

Every detail of her pitiful life, Axel now had all the receipts.

How she'd lived, the stifling and controlling. Her escape and resulting homelessness.

Everything up to receiving the letter, which he now held in his hand, while she waited, holding her breath, for him to say something.

He hadn't spoken while she poured out her life in a spluttered, emotional rush. She tripped over words, not wanting him to hate her, when she reached the climax.

"I'm sorry," she said from the side of the bed. "If I'd known being here would cause you problems, I would never have stayed. I swear it, Axel. I don't want my shitty family to make waves for you."

"This arrived at the clubhouse?" he spoke finally, still gripping the letter between two fingers, his head hanging low over his knees. She wanted to crawl into his lap, repeatedly tell him sorry, and beg for forgiveness.

"Yeah, in the mail. Samson gave it to me. I don't know how Sheeran found me. I've been careful, Axel."

"It sounds like they hired a P.I."

"I'm sorry. I'll go, of course. But I didn't want to take off without telling you the truth. I just wanted to be free, that's all. I would never have gotten you guys in trouble; you're like my family, the true family I chose for myself." Now she cried and hated the weakness. She hadn't cried all this time, even when she was alone. She hastily dragged the back of her hand over her eyes, and that's when she was lifted from the bed and put on Axel's lap.

"You listen to me, Scarlett. What I'm gonna say will sound like I'm angry, and I am, but not at you, okay?"

She watered more from her eyes and nodded.

"You got this mess today and came to me about it. That was the right fucking thing to do, baby. You came to me so I can sort it out."

Her eyes went impossibly large. What did he mean? No, she couldn't get him mixed up in her mess. There was no way she'd hurt Axel; she'd hurt herself first. She'd marry that fucking horrible man; or live under her father's ruling before she hurt Axel or his MC.

"No, but…"

"This motherfucker, even sharing the same blood as you, has tried to take what belongs to me. *Belongs to fucking me*, Scarlett." He growled loud enough to rattle her rib bones, and Scarlett shivered at the severity of his meaning. "You understand what I'm saying? He's threatened you. Trying to force you back into a life you don't want, you actively ran away from. And he dares to fucking send a letter to my club, issuing you to crawl to him like you're a goddamn dog? That shit doesn't fly with me. He was trying to frighten you, and it worked. So now I sort it out."

"But what does that mean? You saw what he said."

"You think I fear who your father knows, baby? I could give a fuck who he golfs with. I'm the bigger dog in this fight, and I fight dirty. When it concerns someone who is mine, I fight fucking messy. And you're mine, Scarlett."

"Of course, I'm yours," she cried, putting her head into his neck. "That's the only thing I'm sure of."

"Then who do you trust to make this right?"

"But…"

"Scarlett," he growled, gripping the back of her neck, but she didn't feel anything but cared for. "Who?"

"You, Axel. Of course, you. But think about it for a second. It's not worth it. What if he knows some powerful cops who can mess with the MC? I'm not worth that."

Another growl, and she trembled.

"That's for me to decide. Are you mine?"

"Yes."

"You're my woman?"

"Yes, Axel." Her voice was firm now because she only had the truth to give him.

His eyes were so piercing, so filled with rage, it shouldn't cause her to become wet or to want him to throw her down and fuck her into a coma, but those feelings were there anyway, swirling hotly through her body.

"You had no one, Scarlett. That asshole has screwed up big time because now you have me. Now you have the weight of the MC behind you. You're not alone anymore."

The tears came again, and Axel gathered her into his brawny arms while Scarlett cried. She cried while he put a call through to his VP despite it being after two a.m. in the dark hours. She cried because not being alone sounded the best thing she could have ever wished for.

Axel Tucker was the wish she didn't know she'd wished for.

And she trusted him to untangle her from a mess she was happy to leave behind for good.

Blood didn't make a family.

Good people who would stand up for you in hard times and good times made a family.

"What are you going to do?" she asked once he was done with the call, bringing Chains to the clubhouse.

"Do you want me to kill him?"

"No." was her immediate answer; she could never live with that on her conscience.

Axel nodded. "Then I won't kill him, but he won't be in my town come morning. Climb back into bed, baby."

"But…"

"Trust me."

She exhaled and trusted him, lifting her face for him to kiss. He gave her a perfect kiss.

There was no sleeping after that. Instead, she took a shower, climbed into some clothes, and waited in the dimly lit common room, watching the doorway.

Sheeran was not a fighter; she'd never once seen her brother raise his fists to anyone, but he had a vicious tongue and a cunning streak that made him very manipulative.

But he was nothing compared to Axel Tucker.

And if she cared about her brother in the slightest, she'd feel sorry for what was about to happen.

But she didn't.

So, she waited quietly for her man to come home.

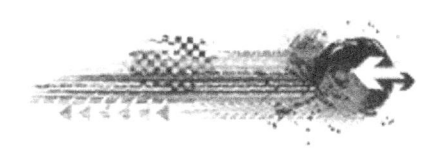

Axel

"Man, it's been a while since we did an old-fashioned beat down. I'm excited." Chains bleated with a grin as they strode with long steps towards the motel room. It took only one glare at the motel manager to find out what room Scarlett's fuckwit of a brother was staying in. "We got a plan?"

"Yeah. I make him bleed, and he fucks off. You're only here to make sure I don't go too far and kill him."

Chains snickered again, "sounds good to me. Little bastard threatening Scar, what the fuck does he think we are, a hobby club? Like we wouldn't take a threat to one of ours personally."

Axel was glad Chains agreed. He was barely holding onto his last drop of control. He wanted to end her brother and not leave a crumb of his existence behind. Only for Scarlett would he leave the dick-for-brains still breathing. But he was about to get his message across as he thumped hard on the door and didn't stop thumping his fist until it swung open.

"It's the middle of the night. You've got the wrong fucking room." the blond guy snarled, dressed only in shorts.

"Right room," Axel snarled, "right fucking person." His fist appeared like a tank, and he used all his force to punch the asshole in the face, knocking him to the ground like he was made purely of jello. He couldn't even stagger to his feet and attempt to fight back.

"See to this trash, brother. I got eyes outside." Chains said, and as Axel stepped into the darkened motel room, Chains closed the door behind him to stand guard.

Violence sluiced through Axel's blood, burning him with the appeal to finish the guy groaning on the thick carpet. His promise to Scarlett forced him to rein that in as he dragged Sheeran Bass from the floor.

"Do you know who I am?" He asked with a calm tone.

Bass was from bleeding from the nose.

"I don't fucking care who you are," he groaned, wiping a hand under his nose, smearing the blood, "you're about to be arrested."

Axel grabbed him by the hair to stop the guy from reaching for his cell phone on the bedside table. Almost bored because Bass was so pathetic, he saw it now up close. Whatever threats he had thrown out to his sister, he had shit to back it up with. "I'm Scarlett's man, and she sent me with a message. Can you guess what that message is? No? I'll tell you."

The guy didn't see the knee coming to the ribs. Blow after blow, he said, "she wants you to know she won't be coming home. And if you try to contact her again, and I strongly advise you not to, she'll send me again. And I'll keep coming, and my messages will be more brutal than the last."

With one last hit to the temple, the guy was done for. Laid on the floor like a pitiful blob of bloody nothing. Axel stepped over him.

"Scarlett is mine, and she wants you to fuck off and forget you ever knew her."

Axel opened the door, and that's when Chains came in. With less than a minute, he had Sheeran Bass packed and his shit tossed into the rental car outside, and the bloodied man poured into the seat behind the wheel.

"Now you're gonna go home to your little weird as fuck cult and pass my message on. My brother here will follow you to the outskirts of town to make sure you leave. And you tell your daddy I have enough shit on him to sink him for good. Keep that in mind when you get a wild hair to come here again."

Axel ignored the bubble of blood-soaked words the guy tried to say. Blah, blah, it was white noise. He had nothing he or Scarlett needed to hear.

Once the car started and it pulled away, Chains offered him a fist bump, and Axel pulled out a bandana from his back pocket to clean the blood from his hands.

The brainless douchebag better heed his words because Axel had no limits or threshold he wouldn't cross to stop him and the Bass clan from hurting Scarlett more than they already had.

Mess with his woman, make her unhappy or scared, and they'd meet the dark side of Axel.

And he'd end them happily.

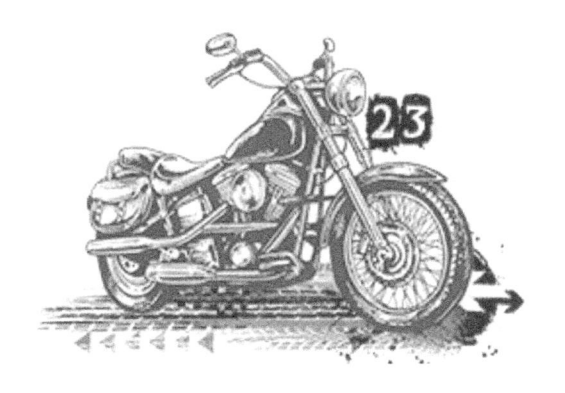

Scarlett

Worrying made Scarlett pace around the clubhouse until she knew the exact number of steps to reach the kitchen.

The sun came up and Axel wasn't home.

When the men started arriving for work, she rushed around as usual to deliver takeout cups of coffee and whatever snacks they wanted, but her mind was wholly on Axel, waiting for the familiar sound of his motorcycle.

To stop from going insane, she decided to boil in a shower hot enough she might forget her worry for a while. It didn't help, but she only had a few minutes alone underneath the spray when roughened hands claimed her waist and scared a scream out of her.

"Settle down; it's me." Axel rasped by her ear. His chest plastered to her back, and she exhaled in a rush, realizing he was naked in the shower with her. She spun around to survey the damage.

Not a scratch on him.

There was nothing like relief to dissolve all her bones, and she flung herself into Axel's naked arms. What did it say about her as a sister that she didn't care what state Sheeran was in, as long as Axel looked unharmed?

His wet hands cupped each side of her face, tipping her head back, and they just looked at each other for a long minute.

She'd never felt such love for another person before. It poured through her eyes and skin to coat all over Axel.

"Look at you, so worried for me, baby. You're so fucking beautiful."

"What happened? Are you okay? Where is Sheeran? What did he say?" all the questions she'd held at bay for hours came bubbling out in a rush. Axel placed a thumb over her lips.

He looked the same yet different, and then it all became clear. There was nothing but feral longing on Axel's face.

Wild longing for her.

He wanted her.

As water poured over his dark head, his bared teeth let her know he would take her. *Now.*

Suddenly, Scarlett's knees became weak, and she clung to his forearms.

"I'll tell you everything later. Right now, I need to take my woman."

His woman, in that husky tone, almost put Scarlett into orbit, and she all but levitated onto her tiptoes, though she still only reached his chest. God, he looked incredible, all bronzed and wet with the smattering of chest hair arrowing down to his groin. Tattoos graced Axel's arms and chest and some on his back. It was always like looking at a piece of sinful art when she was this close to his naked form.

Right when his mouth was inches from hers, and his hand was doing something fantastic to a boob, she remembered with a gasp. "Wait, Axel. I, erm, I have my period, remember?"

She didn't know if he was funny about sex while menstruating. She couldn't say she'd had an opinion on it either way, having never had sex at her time of the month, but with Axel, she would sex him up whenever she could have him.

"You care about that shit?"

She blinked at his roughness, butterflies in her stomach, unable to look away from what looked back at her. His lust-soaked eyes. Words were lost, but she shook her head as his hand caressed down to her belly, where he rubbed slowly.

"Are you still hurting here?"

"I don't feel anything but you." the truth.

He smirked then, like the dirty man she knew him to be.

The man in control.

This man took her to heights she could never reach alone.

She didn't think she could elevate higher in her lust, but Axel's mouth waged war on hers, and she folded on a moan. Then, in her heady state, she grabbed onto his erection, already standing out of his pelvis, thickened and long, and when she gave him a hard stroke, passing him through her palm, he grunted.

But then the show was all Axel's after that. His thumb found her clit, and he teased the first climax out of her while they kissed like their mouths couldn't bear to be apart.

"Turn around, hands on the wall," he issued with a growl hot enough to turn her hair to pure fire. "Now, wildcat."

Lost in his eyes, she nearly lost her footing in the wet room until he caught her around the waist, moving hair from her face.

He caged her in with his size and two arms up on the wall, making the air evaporate from her lungs. For the longest minute, he didn't speak, his eyes speaking loudly, though; for once, she wasn't a mouthy brat at him.

Not with Axel this close.

Turning her head, she couldn't stop her greedy eyes from wandering over his bulk, finding his gaze low and hooded when she reached his stubbled face.

"Do you know what it does to me when you eye-fuck me like that?"

Heat went manic underneath her skin until she didn't know if she had bones left.

She was melted.

Eviscerated.

Surrounded by his masculine fragrance, she almost turned her nose into his arm to get a better sniff.

One kiss.

It took only one kiss, and Scarlett felt the gates of freedom burst open.

She tasted everything in his mouth.

Rich smoke and masculinity.

Danger and fire.

An all-consuming impulse to cry nearly overtook her senses.

Then she was bodily spun around, and Axel moved her hands until they were braced on the shower wall, water still cascading over their bodies. It was seconds later, she felt him knocking her legs wider. "Keep them open for me. Tip your ass back. Fuck, such a good, teasing girl."

She was encased in him. His tongue at her neck and ear, the warmth of his back and arms, and especially his scent. Scarlett was eagerly panting his name, asking silently for everything he had to give. Forgetting any embarrassment as he notched his thick crown to her opening, stroking only an inch inside before he pulled back, repeating endlessly to drive her insane. If he didn't care if she leaked, then why should she? Not when they were in this powerful moment together.

"So tight," he grated in her ear, holding her by the stomach, and before Scarlett could say anything, he thrust so hard her hands slipped on the tiled wall.

Their height difference meant that with each slam of his dick, Axel almost took Scarlett off her feet, but by God, he made it work, pushing her on and off his magnificent cock.

The feelings were indescribable.

She moaned like a whore.

Probably begged him like one, too.

She knew he'd ruined her for other men if this didn't last.

There would be no one after Axel.

"Stop thinking, wildcat, when I'm fucking what's mine."

She puffed a breath and arched her back. Axel groaned and fucked her harder.

"I'm here," she reminded him and herself. She was here with Axel, he was safe.

It took next to no time for them to come. It was at the last moment that Axel pulled free of her greedy pussy and spilled over her ass, holding her close with his mouth locked on her neck, murmuring the dirtiest things.

Thank God for the steamy room, because she was already red all over.

"So good," she whispered as she descended from the massive high.

"Love fucking you, wildcat." He told Scarlett, and she burned all over, and while the hot water still flowed over them, he took the separate showerhead and washed his pleasure off her, and then the sweetest man on earth turned her around and soaped her up, taking his time to clean everywhere.

She watched and fell more in love.

He aimed the shower spray between her legs, and though she was sensitive, she bucked her hips forward, and he grinned wickedly. "Feels good?"

"Yeah."

That was all Axel needed to know to make her come from the tingling water spray, and she did it crying his name with her head thrown back.

Then he cleaned her up again, helping her out of the shower to dry her while he stood deliciously naked, a feast for her greedy eyes.

Once dry, Scarlett took care of her other needs. The moment was intimate and not shameful as Axel watched her slip her tampon in place and then pull on a pair of panties and a t-shirt.

By that point, he was dry and wearing boxer briefs; he kissed the top of her head and roamed a hand down to her stomach. "Hurting here?"

"Nope." She grinned. "I think orgasms are the answer to cramps."

He chuckled. "Happy to help, baby."

"You're dirty, Axel Tucker."

His superior dark eyebrow popped up. Holding her eyes with his intense stare.

"Are you complaining?"

"Not even a little bit."

And wasn't that the truth? Axel could get dirtier, and she'd beg to be on the other end of all that delicious dirt.

Orgasms aside, she had a burning question.

"So, what happened with my brother?"

"He's gone, Scarlett. And he won't be back to bother you."

Once she knew the gory details, she touched his wrist. "Thank you, Axel. You didn't have to do anything, but you did, and I can't thank you enough. I feel like I can breathe now."

"You tell me everything. You got it? I can't do shit about anything if you keep secrets from me." He was so serious, she flashed a smile.

She loved this man more than it was possible to love anyone.

"Yes, Sir."

He growled and snatched her around the waist. Lusty fire in his smiling eyes.

"I knew I should have put you on your knees. Get to it, brat. Show me how sorry you are for mouthing off to me."

Oh, God. She trembled so hard as she got to her knees, so eager and started peeling his shorts down past his growing arousal.

There was no one on earth less sorry than Scarlett. Axel knew it, but boy, she tried to convince him otherwise with her mouth and enthusiasm.

Orgasms shook her bedroom walls for the next few hours. It felt as though Axel needed to convince himself who she belonged to, and no one was walking into the clubhouse to take her away.

Love.

Love.

She loved him so much and gave him everything his domineering hands demanded of her. His growled erotic words, his tender hands, and his forceful mouth. She packed it all up in her memories.

It wasn't orgasms that rocked the club foundations just days later, though.

And no one could have expected it.

Axel

After untangling business with the Mexicans a few years ago, Axel had been careful about who he got into bed with. He might run the MC in unlawful ways, but it didn't mean he'd deal with any maniac with an ego complex and deep pockets.

That's why they'd been living well lately without looking over their shoulders, and then Jensen Fucking DeCastro got out of prison and started a campaign of vengeance against Reno and Ruin, which meant against the club, too.

It hadn't bothered Axel too much.

But he'd underestimated the deranged guy when he seemed to have disappeared weeks back. The call no MC president wanted to get came while he parked in a service station filling the tank twenty miles from the club.

Mouse sounded like he'd been running. "Prez, it's bad. Fuck, it's bad. I saw it too late on the cams."

"Calm down, prospect, and tell me what's going on?"

It was long after one a.m. Didn't anyone sleep anymore? He'd been planning to get home and slide into bed with Scarlett; now, his brain was alert.

"Someone called the hotline asking if Reno was around. I thought I saw him earlier, so I said yeah and asked if I could take a message, but you know I get the twin brothers mixed up sometimes, especially looking at them from the back." He stumbled over his words.

"Prospect, get to the point."

"There was a fucking explosion, Prez. It's gone, it's all gone, it's like wrecked the fuck up."

What the fuck had gone?

Axel unhooked the nozzle, swiped his card to pay, and threw his leg over the seat, ready to take off.

"I didn't see him in time on the cams, Prez. Someone was sneaking around the back of the buildings, behind the fence. And then, before I could check it out, I thought it was teenagers. You know how they sometimes like to wander around there. I didn't even get outside, and the fucking wood shop just blew up like something from a movie. It knocked my ass out."

FUCKING HELL.

He was too far away from home to do anything.

Mouse rushed on to tell Axel he didn't know if there were casualties, but some hangarounds were hurt by flying debris, and the emergency services and Chains were on the way.

"Do you have eyes on Ruin?"

"I don't—*fuck*, Prez. I think Ruin was inside the shop. The light was on like he was there working. The place is rubble. I don't... I don't know how he survived if he's in there."

"Listen to me. Get your head together, Mouse, and then you get every pair of hands to dig through to find him. I'm riding now."

"What about Reno? Do I call him in?"

"No, I'll handle it." In the background, Axel heard emergency service sirens arriving at his club. The instant he hung up, he called Scarlett's number, confirming she was okay. His worry tripled when it rang without an answer.

There was no way he could envision what carnage he'd return to, but he needed to get to his club. For privacy, he rode his bike down the street and pulled over to make the harrowing call to Reno. He sounded sleepy when he answered, and Axel hated what he had to tell him next because he didn't know much.

"Jack..." he started. And then dropped the bad news on his SAA.

It was probably the worst one-minute conversation he'd ever had.

Whatever Axel expected to see when he arrived back at the Diablos compound in record time, it wasn't the disaster zone that took his breath. An upstart cop tried to stop him from going through the gates. "It's my fucking property, asshole."

He instantly saw Chains and Tomb standing shoulder to shoulder; he parked where he could and surveyed the damage that had once been Ruin's personal space. Now a gaping hole, piled high with bricks and debris.

"What do we know?" he asked of his men.

The sound of rumbling bikes arriving became louder as everyone was held back while the fire services worked diligently to secure the area and pick through the wreckage.

It looked fucking bad.

His gut was nothing but dread-filled, picturing Ruin trapped underneath it.

Chains filled him in, but there wasn't much info. "Do we know for sure Ruin was in the shop?"

No one had an answer. The guy was such an introverted loner, even being their enforcer, he preferred his own company, and instead of pushing him to fit in, they'd left him alone. *Fuck's sake.* Axel should have done more for Ruin.

He scraped a hand through his hair, casting his eyes over the other buildings. Small offices and storage sheds, with small amounts of damage, but nothing like Ruin's wood shop. Fortunately, the garage was untouched on the other side of the courtyard.

"It looks like a deliberate hit on the shop, Prez." Offered Denver, coming up to his other shoulder. "What a goddamn mess."

It had Jensen DeCastro all over it. Why only hit one small shed, not the main clubhouse, which would have caused the most damage to everyone?

Nah, this was personal. DeCastro was trying to hurt his brothers.

"Does anyone have eyes on Scarlett?" all answers were no.

The cops were all over his place, and Axel made his way through them, casting his gaze everywhere, looking for a pintsize redhead.

Once he reached the club entryway, he searched like a madman on a mission. Her bedroom was empty, bringing a fresh wave of panic for Axel.

Why in the hell wasn't she in bed?

The longer he searched for his woman, the more dread he felt as each room came up empty.

It was pandemonium outside, but thank fuck they'd found Ruin. Though unconscious, he was alive. Axel waited until the ambulance rig carted him away. Reno followed with a few brothers. Axel and Chains dealt with the cops, but he knew they'd be at his place like uninvited guests for the next few days. It wasn't new, but he couldn't think of that intrusive shit while still searching for Scarlett.

The relief he felt in his rapid heart when he went down to the second kitchen and saw her tending to cuts and scrapes on the prospects. He didn't care that she was in the middle of checking minor wounds. Forger's forearm would have to wait because Axel grabbed her and pinned her to his chest, reassuring himself she was okay and not crumpled beneath a fallen building.

"Where the fuck have you been, and why the fuck weren't you in bed?"

"Whoa, that's a lot of fucks, boss." She muffled against his chest. He might have laughed if he wasn't so wired, but the fear of losing her was still real. When she freed from his hold, her eyes were red-rimmed like she'd been crying, but her hands were steady when she stroked them up his chest.

"The enormous boom woke me up, and I didn't know what was happening."

"So, you walked toward it?" he growled. Her little ass would be sore if he spanked her right now.

"No, smartass. I dressed and came downstairs. I thought maybe we were being raided, and you wouldn't want strangers to see me in my underwear." This last part, she whispered, but the prospects still heard and chuckled.

That was a good girl. Good thinking.

"Then, when I saw what had happened, Forger made me come inside where it was safe; he even dragged me when I wanted to help."

He was going to give that kid a bonus.

"So, I helped where possible and started grabbing the medicine box to fix scrapes. I also started the call tree to the old ladies, keeping them informed of what was happening."

Jesus. She'd dove right in without caring for her safety. If Axel had ever thought she wasn't a right fit for the club or him as a queen, he was sorely mistaken and would beg on his knees for forgiveness one of these days.

She was perfect.

Only now, as she was in his arms, she started shaking, as if the adrenaline began seeping out of her.

"It's okay now." He stroked her back gently.

"Did they find him? Ruin? Is he okay?"

"They got him out, but I don't know what kind of state he's in yet. I gotta head to the hospital."

"Right, okay, I'm coming with you."

"Scarlett, you're staying here where I know you're safe."

"I'm coming with you," she said forcefully, staring at him. The truth was, he wanted Scarlett with him, with eyes on her at all times, within a distance of being able to touch her. He would never recover from those minutes of being unable to locate her.

"Grab a jacket. Prospect, you and the others secure the building. Bash is coming in; he'll take point once he's here."

"On it, Prez."

The Ruin news wasn't great when they arrived at the hospital.

After hours of waiting with Reno and Kylie, the doctors gave Ruin's brother the grim information that he was in a coma and didn't know how long it would last. He was stable, which they considered good. But there was nothing good about being in a coma. The news was fucking bleak, and he heard Scarlett hiccup at his side. She wiped a tear off her cheek when he looked over and his heart stopped. He hooked up her hand, fuck her reluctance for people to know about them. They already knew. And he held on tight. She held on tighter.

"He's gonna be fine, baby," he told her quietly, and she nodded. She repeated those words when she let go of his hand and went to Reno, trying to reassure him with a hug.

Reno looked like he was half dead.

However much of a loner Ruin was, he was part of their family. They weren't only patched brothers anymore, and Axel felt responsible for them both. He'd been the deciding factor in allowing the twins to prospect and patch. Ruin's unhinged nature had given the other brothers caution, and some hadn't wanted him. Sure enough, though, he'd proven his worth these years later, but that same responsibility hadn't left Axel.

So, he waited for everyone to gather around Reno, showing support. Then, finally, Axel sent most of the men home or back to the clubhouse. He called in a prospect to collect Scarlett in a rig; much to her protest, she was dead on her feet and needed sleep.

The nurses wouldn't allow Reno to stay with Ruin for more than a few minutes while they continued to monitor him, so Chains went to get coffee, and Axel sat his ass on the hard plastic seat next to Reno.

"I know it's a shit question, but how you doing, brother?"

Reno scraped a hand over his tired face, his arms on his knees, eyes on the floor. "I don't know, Axe. I've killed no one, but I wanna rip that motherfucker apart with my bare hands. I want to watch him bleed out on the floor. But it won't help my twin, will it?"

"Not in this second, it won't, but long run, we'll make this right, yeah? He's not gonna get another chance like this to fuck with either of you again." Axel put a hand on Reno's shoulder and squeezed gently. "We got you, Jackson, yeah? You and that sleeping maniac in there. I know your instinct is to close off and turn to only each other. It's what you were used to, but you got all of us, whatever you need. Family sticks. Jensen is not and has never been your family. We'll show him what family does when you fuck with one of ours."

Reno made an agreeing noise and clashed eyes with Axel for a second, understanding looking back.

"Ah, fuck, did I miss one of your rousing speeches again?" Chains announced his presence to break the tension, making Reno chuckle as he accepted the hot cup of takeout coffee.

"You're an asshole, you know that?" Axel told him with a half-smile. His VP plonked his ass down next to him.

"Born and raised, Axe. So, who is volunteering to kiss sleeping beauty in there? Dibs, not it, I heard he's a biter. But I think one of Monroe's sisters wouldn't mind the job."

Whatever troubles came to their door only made their forged-in-titanium brotherhood all the stronger.

He'd need to deal with the cop's questions later and see to rebuilding his compound. But for hours, while the sun crested, Axel sat with his brother and waited.

Because that's all they had in their arsenal.

To wait and hope that Ruin used all his psychotic strength to pull through this.

Scarlett

Why was the longest week in history also the busiest?

Scarlett felt like her feet hadn't touched the ground in days.

The MC was still under lockdown. No newcomers or strangers were allowed inside. All old ladies, girlfriends, and kids were not permitted outside their secure homes or, like some brothers, brought their families to the clubhouse until the all-clear was given.

It was pandemonium most days. Loud and messy, but Scarlett got stuck in, helping where it was needed and loving every minute of that noisy family.

She watched cartoons with the group of kids and helped to cook massive amounts of food with the old ladies and house mouse.

She poured enough drinks to sink several ships.

But what didn't happen was seeing much of Axel.

Sure, they saw each other in passing. A stolen kiss here, a tight hug there. But Axel was busy overseeing the reconstruction of Ruin's shed, plus making the other buildings surrounding it structurally safe again. Though the blast didn't altogether take them out, it had left lasting damage. There were police interviews, so many.

Scarlett gleaned during an overheard phone conversation that day on the street when the lady cop ambushed Axel; it wasn't to flirt. Or it wasn't *only* to flirt and utilize her female dominance over Scarlett, but also to tell him DeCastro had been spotted blocks away from the MC.

The news sent Axel into a spiraling temper she'd never witnessed before, as he blamed himself for the bombing.

Even now, days later, after finding that out, Axel was still in a piss-poor mood, and she approached him on quiet feet as he stood watching the construction crew clear out the carnage before they could start to measure and rebuild.

"Hey, boss. I brought you a coffee."

He grunted, wrapping his ringed fingers around the white mug.

Scarlett touched his side, waiting for those devastatingly gorgeous eyes to turn her way, but he remained staring forward. "Are you okay? You haven't slept much."

"Shit to do, can't sleep yet."

They hadn't shared a bed since before the attack. Scarlett tried not to take it personally. Axel had a lot to deal with. Not like romance could be at the forefront of his mind. But her insecure side felt as though he was pulling away again.

"I know you're busy, Axel, but will you come inside at lunchtime for something to eat? I made quiches with Nina, and you need to eat more than you have been."

Each day, someone took fresh food to Reno and Kylie, who were camped at the hospital. But no one else was making sure the stressed president was eating. She frowned when he started thumbing out a message on the phone, answering absently. "I'll grab something later."

"Yeah, okay." She replied.

He was busy.

Worried.

Had a lot on his plate.

Whatever Axel said, she'd find him later, bring him food, and make the freaking stubborn biker eat, even if she had to sit on him and force the food down his throat.

Swallowing her feelings, she turned to head back inside.

"Baby?" he called out. Scarlett spun around with her begging heart all open and raw for his hands.

"Yeah?"

"You look fucking beautiful today."

Her heart flew. And she flashed him a smile.

It wasn't a declaration of love, but it felt like enough, for now.

Besides the obvious, there was a glaring reason she felt the distance between them. And that was because his daughter and family had arrived days ago and were staying at Axel's house. And when Roux wasn't at the hospital, she was around the clubhouse; she fit back into her MC princess role like she'd never been away.

Scarlett had met Roux in the early days and liked the woman, but she was also intimidated by her. She was a force to be reckoned with, that was for sure, and she whipped the bikers into shape with only a few cursed words. It was clear they adored her and her kids. Not so much her handsome biker hubby from another MC, but Scarlett thought Butcher was great. Though loyal to the Diablos, she'd never met a friendlier biker than Butcher. So, when she saw him sitting at her bar, she smiled and offered him a drink.

"I'm on kid duty, but I'll take a soda," he answered. He was a dad to three-year-old twins, and they were freaking adorable. Crew was the quiet twin, and Coco was the mischievous one. Scarlett almost died of an ovary explosion the first time she saw Axel squat down so the two babies could run to him.

Death by GILF. Granddad I'd like to fuck.

Had fucked.

But no one knew that.

It was her diehard secret.

"It must be strange being around a different MC," she said, sliding an icy glass of Coke his way. He grasped it with his tattooed hands. She noticed he had ROUX across one set of knuckles. And a cookie inked into his thumb. Cute.

Butcher chuckled and sipped. "You could say that. I never know who's gonna try to strangle me for marrying Roux every time I step foot in this place."

Oh yeah, she giggled. She could see the boys would hold it against him, but you'd have to be blind not to see how much Butcher and Roux were devoted to each other. Scarlett felt a pang in her chest when she thought about it. Longing for that kind of love and connection. She wanted it sometimes more than her next breath.

Would she ever have it with Axel, or was she hoping for unicorns sitting on rainbow clouds?

"You're good for him." Butcher cut into her stray thoughts, and Scarlett looked over, trying to figure out what part of the conversation she'd dipped out on.

"Excuse me?"

He grinned that handsome biker smile she bet Roux loved seeing. "My father-in-law, Axel. Your man, if I'm not wrong? You're good for him."

Well, cut her up and feed her toes to the fishes. Scarlett was stunned silent.

Open and shut, her mouth moved, and her tongue refused to work.

How the heck did Butcher know anything if Scarlett had been super-secret? Like real damn secret about her relationship. She was so secret; she reckoned she was a spy in a past life.

"How... what... how?"

His laughter cut across the bar. "Don't worry. My Roux hasn't figured it out because she doesn't see her dad as someone who would date."

"We're not dating. We're only..." she exclaimed and slapped a hand to her mouth. *Jeez, admit it all, Scar.* "Forget I said anything, okay?."

"As I said, you're good for him. Whatever makes that miserable bastard happy, so he doesn't wanna kill me every second." His eyes twinkled, and Scarlett, despite her panic, laughed.

"He is a grumpy guts sometimes." She loved that about Axel because it never stopped him from caring for her in his way.

"What you guys talking about?" butted in Tomb, sliding his ass on a stool, and asked for a beer. She turned her back one second to grab it, and in that time, the freaking bikers were gossiping like hens. "Oh, Axel and his hostage fucking? Yeah, we knew that. They're always at it."

The gasp Scarlett let go of was straight from the nineteenth century as she held imaginary pearls at her neck. "I will pull your head off and spit in your neck, you giant gossip."

"What?" he laughed. "You thought that shit was on the hush-hush, girlie?"

Yes, she fucking did.

"Chicks," Tomb rolled his eyes; a playful glint said he was teasing her.

These bikers were something else. Cut from a different cloth to other men.

Good thing she was trying to be a biker chick.

Well, a biker chick to one biker.

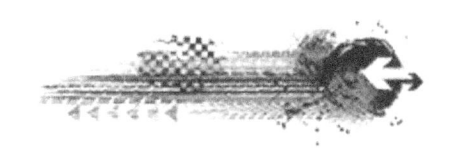

Axel

Fifteen days.

He was done having his kid cockblocking him.

Axel loved having Roux at home. Especially his grandbabies. They put life into the old house again. They were noisy little demons, full of naughty mischief, and he loved each passing moment watching them grow. If he had his way, they'd move from Colorado, and he'd build a house nearby so he could see them every day.

Having said that, he goddamn missed his woman.

Holding her against his body while she shivered from the cold or orgasms. He missed her crazy laugh while she discovered new movies. He missed creepily watching her sleep and being there while she looked for him in her tiredness.

Axel was done tiptoeing around like Scarlett thought they were a secret.

Only she thought that.

So, while Roux was out of the house with her brood, he sneaked Scarlett in like he was a fucking teen boy. She was soon out of her clothes and clinging to him, and he could breathe again.

"Harder," she moaned. "Go harder, Axel." She went for his mouth like he held her life in there and wanted it back. Swirling tongues and grabbing hands, he fucking feasted with no end in sight.

And then he made her scream while he worked her on his cock, holding Scarlett up with his hands and her back at the bedroom door.

She moaned.

She cried.

She bit gouged marks into his shoulder and cried again on her third orgasm. That was when Axel lost his soul, ramming his pleasure into her with the hardest grunt. She latched tight around his cock, all her limbs fixed around him, and he came hard, like never before.

His wildcat succeeded in killing him finally. After that, he couldn't do anything but bury his face in her sweet-smelling neck, waiting for the world to steady beneath his feet.

Laying Scarlett on the bed, he couldn't get enough of looking at her. Flushed all over with sweat, a radiant smile on her sex-satisfied face.

She'd stepped up since the explosion. Helping where she could, assisting the old ladies, and always visiting Ruin. She fed the construction crew and Champ and was always there shoving food and coffee at him when he was out dealing with business and keeping his people safe.

This woman was so deep in his skin that he couldn't think of the time he'd held back from her. Leaning down, Axel brushed kisses on her cheeks and lips. "You want water, baby?"

"God, yes, please. I'm parched."

He knew why. They'd gone at each other like untamed animals; he had the claw marks on his chest to prove it. Slipping into a pair of jeans, he left them open and told her to stay there.

Axel didn't expect to be greeted downstairs by a scowl that was a mirror image of his own. Roux was standing with her arms folded.

"I can't believe you brought a club skank back here to our family home, Dad!"

"Watch your mouth, kiddo. This is my house; I bring anyone I want here."

"So it's not my house, too?"

"You know it is," she followed him into the kitchen, where he got two bottles of water from the fridge, "but you don't live here anymore."

Again, she followed him to the stairs. "You're too old to be fucking around with random skanks," she raised her voice, no doubt for his company to hear. He could picture Scarlett with her red face, probably hiding in the closet like a beautiful, shy little thing.

"Roux, I love you, kiddo, but I'm three seconds from kicking you out if you don't watch how you talk to me."

He recognized that look on her face. She got her foul temper from him, after all.

But then the sweetest voice interrupted what would be a Tucker showdown.

"Oh, my God, stop yelling at each other. Roux, it's me, Scarlett. I swear I'm not a skank." Standing at the top of the stairs was his bold and brave wildcat, wrapped only in his bedsheet, her red hair a mussed mess. So fucking sexy.

It was probably the first time in her life Roux was stunned silent. She blinked up at Scarlett and then at Axel, who smirked.

"Now I know how you felt when you caught me with Tad," she announced. And Axel laughed. The irony of it hadn't swept by him. "You're with Scarlett? All you guys do is argue."

"And all you and Butcher do is chase each other. It's foreplay, kiddo."

"Ugh. For God's sake, Dad. I could have gone my whole life and never heard those words from you. I'm out. I need an exorcist to take this from my brain."

To mess with his kid, he smirked. "I'll hang a tie on the door next time."

"You suck," she declared, moving like the wind, slamming the door behind her.

At the top of the stairs, Scarlett was giggling, and he sent his gaze upward.

Beauty and perfection. He started up slowly.

"Shouldn't you be laid on the bed waiting for me?" he growled low.

She snapped to attention and then smiled to put heat in his belly.

"Yes, Sir."

Axel had time to make up. He was far from done with his bratty wildcat.

Scarlett

Four weeks into the Diablos compound's reconstruction, things looked like they once had. If not shinier with new buildings.

Reno was working hard to replace all of Ruin's tools and pieces of wood so his shed would be useable if—when he woke up and came home.

There was still no positive news on the Ruin front, but there was also no bad news.

Last night, they'd had an impromptu cookout at Axel's house to regroup for his men. It had been a good respite for the boys, who were worried for Ruin and still working diligently to find the evil brother, plus keep everyone safe. It was easy to see how worn out they all were.

Axel had put her on his lap, warning her to dare try to move. Sheesh, her biker boss was so bossy, but she kept her ass in his lap. Later that night, she'd been half asleep, and she barely heard him tell the others he was going to carry her to bed.

This morning Axel cooked her breakfast and then took her into the club before he went to the hospital. Few people were around. Prospects, as always, doing their tasks. The other bikers were out at other businesses or working over in the garage. So, when she heard the rumbling of many bikes turning into the compound, she rushed to the window, hoping it was her man, but these were bikers she didn't immediately recognize. Thankfully, the entryway was locked, so she called Forger, who was guarding the gates.

"Hey, it's Scar. There are a lot of new bikes parking outside."

"Yeah, babe, they're Kingsmen. You can let them in; they're here to see Axel."

Knowing that, she went to the door and recognized Jamie Steele from the last visit, once he'd hung the helmet on the bike handlebars. The man was a walking dream for women, all ink black hair, stubble, and a physique you'd only see in the Olympics. His pearly white smile would devastate, but didn't do anything to Scarlett's belly butterflies. She keyed open the door and let his crew pour in. Men and women.

"Axel isn't here yet, but you can wait in the main area." She told him.

"Thanks, sweetheart. How you doing?"

Scarlett tried not to judge anyone, mainly because of where she'd come from, but some ladies accompanying the Kingsmen crew looked like they'd been picked up on street corners. Skirts up to their breakfast and tops low as their kneecaps. In this cold front Utah was experiencing, they should wear UGGs and thick sweaters like she was. Well, not the UGGs; she wore a pair of buckle leather boots that made her feel badass and part way to being a biker bitch.

She served drinks and fetched food for everyone.

Most were pleasant enough, except for the ladies, which was par for the course, as she'd learned quickly from the Diablo sweet bottoms, who, for whatever reason, saw Scarlett as competition for the biker's affection.

"I'll be with you in a minute," she smiled as an older blonde lady chose a middle bar stool to sit on. Before serving her, she went to the other end when she noticed Reno had come inside from the shed.

Seeing how troubled he was about Ruin was upsetting. Ever since she'd known Reno, he wore a grin. He hadn't smiled in weeks.

"Can I get you anything, Reno?"

"Nah, I'm fine, babe."

"Would it be okay if I visited the big guy later?"

He was still crunched down over his clasped knuckles. "Yeah."

"I gotta update him on the latest episode of the Housewives, I'm on season four."

Now Reno cranked his head up, and she smiled. "Didn't he ever tell you we're best buds?"

"Yeah? Funny that Monroe says the same. Funnier how my brother has chicks making him their best friend, the most unsocial man in Utah."

"What can I say? He's a good listener."

She'd do anything to make the MC whole again, to have Ruin, as scowly and frightening as he was, home again, so everyone was happy. But she was powerless. Everyone was. It was down to the excellent care of the doctors and Ruin's fighting spirit. Scarlett reached across the bar and squeezed Reno's hand, lowering her voice.

"He's going to get better, Reno. And be badder than ever, scowling at everyone."

He half smiled like he was trying to believe it, too.

She went to serve the blonde when he took off to keep Jamie Steele and the rest company.

"Sorry to keep you waiting. Do you want a drink?"

"That one your man?" she asked. Up close, she appeared to be in her forties, but the good kind that made her look thirties at most with her light tan, curled hair, and makeup.

Being a nosy question and without even a hello, Scarlett ignored her and waited for the woman to say she wanted a neat vodka.

"This place doesn't change much," she remarked, tapping long red and white striped nails on the top of the bar as she looked around. "The bedrooms still upstairs?"

"Eh, yeah, some. You've been here before?" not in the last year, or Scarlett would have recognized her.

"Long time ago, but everyone knows me, honey." She smiled with ruby-red lips, taking a small sip of her drink. "Are you with one of the bikers?"

"Yeah, I am. I also run this bar."

"Wow, they allow their women to do more than lie on their backs now?" she laughed scornfully, and the nastiness took Scarlett by surprise.

"Lady, who even are you? You can't say shit like that about people you don't know."

"Oh, they know me, honey. They know me well."

Ugh. It probably meant the blondie had been on *her* back at some point. That explained the outright pettiness. Plus, she'd arrived with another set of bikers and wore no PROPERTY OF vest nor a wedding ring, so Scarlett could only surmise the older lady was a sweet bottom in Jamie Steele's MC.

"Maybe you should sit with your MC circle."

"I'm good here, honey, just resting. It's hard sitting on the back of a bike for hours. Are you in this lifestyle for the long haul or just a passing fancy? It's a hard life, honey, so get used to your ass hurting in more ways than one." She winked, sipping again. "Have they shared you yet? That'll come, so be prepared for it. All bikers are the same. Some are sweeter than others and treat you nicely for a while, but they all get tired and want fresher and younger. Like a younger bitch can do the things I can. But they're stupid, you know? Men think with only one thing, and it's not their brains. So if you stick around, learn some tricks now, make sure you're the one they always turn to when they tire of the young ones with the hard tits and plastic lips."

Unfortunately, her lecture was far from over. "And I'll tell you this for free because the biker sisterhood needs to stick together and look out for one another. Learn to be wise and get as much money from them as possible while they're feeling generous because that giving well soon dries up. And you can only rely on yourself."

Flabbergasted, Scarlett didn't know what to say or how to react. The woman sounded like she had an axe to grind and a vindictive list a mile long.

Why was she hanging around with bikers if she didn't like bikers?

"Why are you here if you hate this lifestyle.?"

"Who said I hate it?" she chuckled, bangles jingling on her wrist when she brought the glass to her lips. "You can love something and still be realistic about it. Being a biker whore isn't rainbows and soccer mom rallies. It is what it is. Fun and sex, but you know your place, and even if you get an old man and his property patch, he isn't going to be faithful. None of them ever are. That's being realistic and accepting this is what you signed on for. These men don't live by the rules out there, honey. Inside here is their world, and they can do whatever the fuck they want, and they'll always have each other's back. You think they're your friends? Think again. You say you got a man, yeah? That man could fuck around on you, and none of the others would tell you. They'd lie to your face to cover for his brother. That's their world."

Whoa.

That was a lot of info dumping all at once, and from a total stranger who may or may not hate bikers, she couldn't tell. But it was bizarre and made Scarlett feel uneasy, listening to her tirade.

"Sounds to me like you need a change of scenery or a fresh set of people to hang around with. Even if you had been here years ago, the Diablos aren't anything like you described bikers to be. They're loyal men to their partners."

The blonde lady shrugged. "You'll understand, eventually. We all learn at different paces. But you can still have fun. You'll see a lot of the country and sit on many biker's laps."

Ew, no, she would not. She had one biker lap to sit in, and that was it.

Oh, thank God, Scarlett breathed a sigh of relief at seeing an actual friendly face coming through the door. She loved Nina, Tomb's wife, and waved her over, hoping the other woman would rescue her from this God-awful conversation.

But it wasn't Scarlett Nina was looking at. Glaring at.

Her steps increased, as did the anger breaking out on her face.

She got closer, and her voice shouted across the space as she pointed a long finger at the bar lady.

"What the hell are you doing here, Selena?"

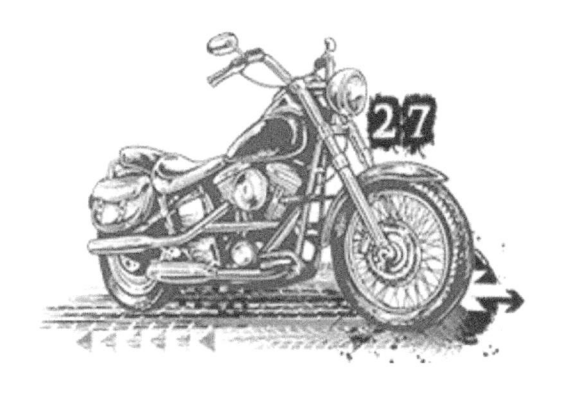

Scarlett

"Nina, sweetheart," the other woman greeted. "It's been how long? Six? Seven years?"

"Not long enough, bitch. What the fuck are you doing here?"

Whoa. The animosity from Nina was like a tidal wave and surprised Scarlett. Not that she hadn't seen the woman blow up many times in the last year, she had. But it was usually a sexy fight with her big hubby man. Now Nina looked ready to pull out her earrings and throw down with the bar blonde. Selena.

"Just passing through, as always, thought I'd check in with a few old friends."

"Nasty whores like you don't just pass through. You land like an atom bomb to cause as much destruction. No one wants you here.

And from how you're sitting like you think you're welcome, I'm guessing Axel doesn't know you're in his club."

Axel? What did he have to do with knowing Selena?

Deep within her roiling belly, she found the answer and what she suspected because it would be the first time she'd come up against any of Axel's exes. When the sweet bottom women talked about their biker exploits, Scarlett mostly tuned them out. If Axel had slept with any of them, she didn't want to know, so she'd kept her head firmly in the sand, and thankfully, Axel never offered information about his past. What had come before her didn't matter, but Scarlett didn't want to face someone with ties to Axel.

The hatred became thicker and more boisterous as she stood by and watched Chains and a few other boys come through the door; they clocked who was sitting at her bar, and they all made a beeline. Anger palpable.

Oh boy.

"What are you doing here, Selena? Don't give a rat's ass what wind brought you this time. Get your ass up right now." Chains snapped, none of his jovial tone present. Instead, he sent his eyes to her for a second, and Scarlett could only shrug. She knew nothing about what was going on.

"Isn't there a house in Oz you're supposed to be buried under?" Bash asked, sitting his ass at the bar. Okay, another biker who wasn't a fan of this woman. What on earth had she done?

"Nice to see you guys, too. Nah, don't show me any hospitality. Why change the attitude of a lifetime where you mistreat women?"

"Fuck you." Spat Tomb, standing behind Nina with his hands on her shoulders, "We treat shit the way shit is meant to be treated. Do yourself a favor and get out before one of us has to do it for you." He then directed Nina away from the bar before she could have another say.

Selena didn't look bothered about the less-than-welcoming treatment; she grinned and wiggled her fingers at Tomb. "He's still hung up on me."

"I don't call trying to fuck up his relationship with Nina hung up on you, woman." Said Bash.

She shrugged. Unbothered. "If she didn't have her Diablo blinkers on, she would have seen I was trying to show her you can't trust anyone around here."

"You got that right." Glared Chains. "Get the fuck up, or I'll toss you out."

"I don't think so. I haven't seen my family yet."

"You have no family here, bitch."

And then all Hell broke loose.

The statement came from a fresh voice.

Scarlett didn't notice Axel, Roux, Butcher, and their two kids coming into the club entryway until Roux descended on the woman like a thunderstorm.

Scarlett's eyes found Axel instantly. He held a lively Crew in his arms, but Axel looked at Selena. His face was dark and hate-filled. That coiling in Scarlett's belly got tighter as the atmosphere became unbearably tense.

"Did you hear me? You have no family here." Hissed Roux, Butcher holding her back, his arm around her waist from behind, all the while he had his sleeping daughter on his shoulder.

"Roux, darling. Don't be like this. I've come all this way to see you." A calmer Selena said, but Scarlett recognized the insincere saccharine tone. Her mom would use the same with people she wanted to impress.

"Is she for real? You came all this way to see me? Listen here, cuntasaurus, you're delusional. Get the fuck on your broomstick and get out of my club; you're never welcome here."

Over the past year, Scarlett had seen Roux handle the bikers, usually with loud yelling, but she obviously loved the guys. Now her shaking rage was pure hatred for the blonde woman. Axel stepped in, but her reflexes were tested when he handed Crew across the bar to her, wordlessly telling her to hold his grandson. But he was staring his fire at the woman.

"You've got some balls coming to my club."

"This is how she talks to me, Axel? You've done a fine job of turning our daughter against me."

Our daughter.

Oh shit. It was worse than Scarlett suspected. An ex-lover, maybe. Or a sweet bottom who had done the club dirty. Selena was Roux's mother. Axel's ex-girlfriend, since she at least knew he'd never been married.

"She's not *our* anything, Selena. She's mine. Always has been; you've had nothing to do with her since you ran out, couldn't be a whore and a mom at the same time."

She'd seen Axel handle shit. Calm and assertive were two words she'd use to describe him. But she'd never heard that voice before. Rasping with gritted anger leaching from every pore. He looked ready to murder. Chains got in the frame with him, and Selena laughed. "Always up his ass, aren't you, Chains? Things never change much. Is it a wonder I never came back for her when she had you two filling her head with poison?"

"You did that all on your own," answered Axel.

Between Roux and Axel, the noise levels rose. Scarlett shushed the toddler in her arms. He was a hefty boy, and she shuffled him up her hip as he lay his sweet head on her shoulder, a thumb in his mouth. She absently kissed his forehead while watching Axel with his hands on his hips. Even now, he was beautiful, and her heart crawled toward him to calm him down. But Scarlett felt powerless to help.

She was a spectator to his past. *The fuckening.* Fireworks were going to fly.

"Why are you here?"

"I had to hear from someone else that our daughter has kids now."

"And what?" Axel laughed scornfully. "You thought you'd waltz in and play the doting grandma?"

Selena grimaced. "They can call me Selena."

"Over my dead fucking body." Snapped Roux, and then she broke free of Butcher's one-armed hold and got in Selena's face. "Get a clue, lady. You're nothing to me and less than nothing to my children. You didn't want me twenty-five years ago, and I don't want you now. You're too fucking late. So pack up your fake act, get out of town before I show you I'm Axel Tucker's daughter, and knock your head through the wall."

Scarlett heard chuckles and approving whistles. No matter who she was married to, Roux was a Diablos through and through, and those men would always have her back.

The arguing went on, back and forth.

Crew fussed in Scarlett's arms as the noise level escalated.

"Axel," she tried to gain his attention, but he was too busy staring at Selena. "Axel." She said louder, and he turned his head. "Not now."

Not now? What did that mean? If not now, then when? "Axel, maybe everyone should take a break. The babies are here."

"Not *now*, Scar." He grated with thunder to his voice, and she was taken aback by his delivery of anger toward her. Scar. He'd never, not once, called her Scar as everyone else did. Whatever crossed her face, Selena read it correctly, and she laughed.

"Oh, honey, this is the biker you're with? Do you remember everything I said? It goes double for him. You see how he's treating me now when I'm only trying to see my family?"

"You have no family here," he growled, "and don't fucking talk to her. You don't look at her." Then, because their argument had gained an audience, he stared at Jamie Steele. "Did you bring this trash in with you?"

Steele shrugged, "not sure." Then turned to his men. "Who did this chick ride in with?"

"Me, Prez." One of his men answered, "met her in that last dive bar we were at; she said she had family here. Didn't think anything about giving her a ride."

"Family? The fucking audacity. You're not welcome. How many ways do we have to tell you? Crawl back into your selfish hole, and don't come back." Roux's temper climbed until her husband stepped in, pulling her back. "That's enough, sweetheart, getting you out of here." He switched his daughter to Roux's arms and came to Scarlett for Crew. Before any more yelling could transpire, Butcher, probably the only calm man there, ushered his family into the back rooms.

Selena was far from done and didn't look like she had a mothering bone in her body when she didn't even try to plead with Roux. Was it clear to anyone else she'd only come to cause trouble? Because if it had been Scarlett in that same situation, she'd be doing much more begging than combative snapping.

"This is the way you've raised her, Axel. She has no respect for me at all."

"Respect is earned, and you haven't done a thing to do that."

"I want to move back to town and get to know my grandbabies."

Axel laughed then, but if Selena were smart, she would have known her statement didn't amuse him.

"I'll rain hellfire on you before I let you anywhere near my family."

"You can't stop me. Not anymore."

"Can't I?" he asked calmly, staring at her.

Oh, God. Scarlett's belly clutched. That was his *dare me* tone.

"Axel, this isn't helping anything. Jamie will take her out. Maybe check on Roux." Or catch a breath before he exploded and committed murder in front of everyone. She only tried to defuse his anger, but he turned it on her without warning. Pointing a finger. "I told you not now.

Stay the fuck out of this; it's none of your business, Scar. Go and be somewhere else. *Now*."

The stab of his words went through Scarlett like physical pain, and she stepped back, her spine hitting the wall of spirit bottles behind her.

It was probably the first time since knowing him she didn't have a ready, locked, loaded retort on the end of her tongue. Because, like all other times, Axel had never spoken to her in anger. Their bickering was just that, done in fun and foreplay.

His attention turned back to Selena.

"Listen to me, Selena, and listen well. This is the last time you turn up here to drop your landmines and fuck with what's mine. You're less than fucking nothing to anyone here. Roux is *my* kid. She was my kid when I begged you not to abort her. When I had to plead with you to pump milk for my starving daughter, she was my kid because you were too busy partying and getting high. And she was my kid when you packed your shit and took off and didn't see her again until she was seven years old. In fact, that was the best damn decision you've ever made, so keep making it and stay gone. It's too late to make amends with her, and I'll do anything in my power to make sure you don't upset her again."

Her face fell. "You know I wasn't ever gonna be a good mom, Axel. I told you that. It's not my fault."

"It never is. You made your bed, Selena, lie in it."

She stepped off her stool and approached him. "We could talk and make things right." Scarlett saw red the second Selena put her hand on Axel's arm. She felt physically sick, and that's when she finally got her feet to move, striding down the other end of the bar to get out from behind it.

The last thing she heard was Axel laughing. "Not in your wildest dreams. Now grab your shit and get the fuck out."

Scarlett was done listening to what Axel had told her. Nothing to do with her.

She went to check on Roux, who was sitting on Butcher's lap in the kitchen, the pair quietly talking, so she didn't disturb them. And she kept walking until she was outside. Champ came out of his kennel, padding over to sit with her. Scarlett put her arm around the dog, stroking his flank, taking comfort from his nearness.

Sadness stung her throat, but she refused to cry and feel weaker than she already was.

No matter how angry Axel had been at Selena for showing up unexpectedly and upsetting Roux, Scarlett shouldn't have been a target for that anger. Not when she'd never treat him that way.

She sat there long until Champ grew bored and ran into the wooded area to chase rabbits.

Sitting with her knees to her chin, loving and hating that angry man. Then she realized that the home she'd loved for the last year wasn't her home.

Stay the fuck out of this, it's none of your business, Scar. Go and be somewhere else.

Axel

With twenty-twenty clarity came calmness.

As soon as Axel had all but shoved a pissed-off Selena into a cab, giving her one last warning to never step foot on Diablos property again, he strode back into the clubhouse and cleared his lungs of the last remnants of his anger.

That woman riled him in the worst way because of how it affected Roux.

There were no lasting feelings. He'd barely had feelings for Selena in the first place other than a seventeen-year-old kid getting pussy from an older woman. Older by five years, and by then, she was a well-seasoned party girl who'd taken a shine to a then-prospecting Axel. If not for a broken condom resulting in an accidental pregnancy, he wouldn't have thought of her once he'd bedded her a few times. But now he'd been trying to shake her off for the past quarter century.

She got a flea up her butt every few years, trying to return to their lives. When Roux was still a kid, Selena had tried to get back with him, and he'd put done to that most bluntly. No way did he want that woman in his bed again. She was a parasite. A veteran sweet bottom who only tried to latch onto the biker with the most power.

He pitied Steele if she'd chosen the Kingsmen as her latest sport, but better his club than Axel's.

"You good now?" Asked Chains, resting both elbows on the bar while Axel poured himself a scotch and downed it in one. He poured a second.

"She upset my kid again, Chains. How else am I supposed to feel?"

"Roux handles her own. You taught her how; she put Selena in her place, and I don't think she'll try coming back around anymore. Roux is more than done with her."

He agreed with a grunt.

"So, you're good. Roux's good 'cause she's got us at her back and her Renegade Souls man. What you gotta ask now is Scar good?"

Axel frowned. The glass paused to his mouth as he stared at Chains. "What's it got to do with Scarlett? Selena's bullshit won't touch her."

"I don't think it will either. Though, if you took any notice before you charged in like a bull and started roaring the place down, Selena was sitting at the bar, chatting with Scar. You don't know what shit she said to her before you went Mad Max."

Fuck. He hadn't even thought of the before shit, only that he hadn't wanted Scarlett to witness Selena's brand of passive-aggressive poison. She was too naïve and sensitive for a woman who made it her career to get what she wanted by any means necessary.

While he was ruminating on that, Tomb and Nina approached, Tomb's arm slung across his wife's shoulder. They knew better than most how Selena worked because she'd tried to convince Nina she'd slept with Tomb multiple times a few years back. And this was when she'd tried to persuade Axel to let her work things out with Roux. Of course, that had been a lie; she rolled into town like a foul smell, causing as much trouble as she could before sweeping out again with whatever man she could attach to. It was her M.O.

He found out seconds later Nina was pissed off at him.

"We're taking off, Prez." Tomb spoke.

"You've got a nerve talking to Scar the way you did," Nina said, her voice as cold as ice. "A sweet girl like that, who's always stood by you, didn't deserve it."

Axel frowned. "How I spoke to her?"

"You basically told her to fuck off and that nothing in this club is anything to do with her. She looked like you'd stabbed her in the heart."

Axel locked gazes with Tomb's unreadable face. He gave a slight tip of his shoulder. "You were pissed, Prez. She'll get over it."

Nina elbowed him. "Don't excuse bad fucking behavior, or you'll sleep at your mom's tonight."

"The fuck did I do? I'm only saying. Selena is a bitch, you know she's a bitch, and she stirs the pot. Axel was dealing with her shit."

"So that excuses him for treating Scarlett like a doormat, huh?" she huffed and knocked Tomb's arm off her shoulder. "fucking men," she added and strode off, her heels clicking with every furious step.

"*Jesus Christ*. You get pissy at your woman, and I get the consequences from mine," half-laughed Tomb, who jogged after his woman.

He couldn't figure out what shit Nina had spat at him until it felt like he'd been hit on the head with a hammer.

Stay the fuck out of this. It's none of your business, Scar. Go and be somewhere else.

Ah. Fuck.

Shit.

Fuck.

He'd said those exact words to his woman without thinking of their meaning. Because he didn't mean it in the way it came out, his only instinct was getting her out of reach of Selena's vapid lies. And now Chains had reminded him Selena had already been in the clubhouse, for however long, talking to Scarlett, filling her head with more lies and her version of being the cast aside mother of the year, no doubt.

The rage came rushing back through his lungs, and he punched the bar. "Fuck!"

Goddamn his fucking short temper to hell.

He could picture Scarlett's hurt face. And he'd been the one to hurt her.

"Which way did she go?"

"She'll be fine, Axe. She's stronger than she looks. Just let her kick you in the balls," smirked Chains.

"Which fucking way?"

"How do I know? I was too busy waiting to stop you from putting a bullet in Selena's ass."

"I should have done." He growled, stepping out from behind the bar.

He already could see his redheaded siren was not in eyeshot because if she were, his body would know it. It came alive for her. His heart did, too.

Now he needed to say sorry and kiss the breath out of her.

"Roux and Butcher headed down to the kitchen. Maybe your hostage is with them. Now that the drama is over, I'll see to Jamie Steele. Guess we left them hanging there for a while. They already got a good show out of us."

Axel couldn't give ten fucks what Steele and his club members saw. They'd brought that vacuous bitch here, and he wasn't in the mood to play nice with them now. He was already starting on the stride down the long hallway of doors leading off to different parts of his clubhouse. He stopped first in the kitchen.

The kids saw him and yelled, "Grampy!" Coco jumped down from the table and hugged him around the legs. "Hey, how's my sunflower?"

"Eating gwapes. Want one?"

"Nah, baby, you have 'em all."

"Nommy." She toothily grinned at him and shoved two grapes in her mouth. Axel grinned and then caught Roux's eye. "You good, kiddo?"

"Yeah, why wouldn't I be? Did you kick her out?"

"Yeah, she won't be back."

"Ha. Bad stinks always come back."

That was true, a lesson he'd taught his girl years back, always to be prepared for the worst-case scenario. He hadn't helped to protect her heart from a neglectful mother, though, no matter how much he'd surrounded her in love. If he'd thought Selena was halfway decent or meant any of the shit she'd said over the years, he would have let her in Roux's life. But she'd repeatedly proven that she didn't care for her daughter.

He pulled Roux into a half hug and felt her arm go around his waist when he landed a kiss on her temple. "Love you, kiddo, you know that?"

"Yeah, Dad. Love you, too."

"Butcher, why don't you take your family back to the house and start the grilling."

"Never a dull moment when we come visiting," smirked Butcher as he rose, Crew in his arms.

"You knew she came from a wild family. So deal with it," advised Axel, turning on his heel in time to hear Butcher bark a laugh, and Roux yelled she wasn't fucking wild.

He left his feral kid behind and went to find his soft-hearted woman.

It didn't take long, and when he saw her hugging her knees, sitting outside where it was too damn cold, his gut locked up tight.

He'd done that. He'd made her look so small and alone.

She noticed his approach as his boots crunched on the gravel, and her shoulders stiffened, but she didn't look around.

Scarlett ignored him like he didn't exist, which twisted inside him. She was always happy to see him, giving him smiles and beautiful eyes. Going down into a squat, he rubbed her knee.

"Baby, come inside. It's cold enough to freeze. You're gonna get sick out here. Fuck. I'm sorry for what I said; I didn't mean—"

"You can shove that apology right up your ass, Axel Tucker. I no longer care."

Scarlett

Hearing Axel's voice caused a painful yet lovely sweep of emotions deep within her chest, where she housed all her love for him.

It was a lot of freaking love.

Too much.

No man deserved all that love.

Except Axel Tucker did. Until he hurt her.

And logically, she could reason he had been in a foul mood brought on by seeing someone he hated for hurting his daughter over and over. She got it, okay? She understood.

But a sore heart didn't come with logical understanding.

All she felt as she walked through the clubhouse to get on with the job he paid her for was a deep sense of no longer belonging. That she'd been put in her place, and that place wasn't here.

Looking at Axel in those few seconds outside while he got down on his haunches to apologize made her ache. She was hungry for his love but was angry at him, so she quickly shut down that emotion. And then she'd climbed to her feet and walked away from him with her chin held high.

Before Scarlett, the woman she was before she came here, would have accepted that apology, probably told him it was no big deal, and then taken responsibility for his actions and cruel words. But that wasn't the Scarlett she was today. Ironically, Axel's care and attention made her a stronger woman who could stand up for herself and protect her heart.

"You gotta talk to me, baby, and let me apologize," Axel stated from behind her as she grabbed her cleaning supplies and started polishing the bar until she could see her miserable face on the surface. "I'm so fucking sorry. I'm the biggest prick walking for snapping at you. You gotta know I didn't mean it." he tried to put his hands on her waist, and she jolted with loving shivers, pushing his stupid hands aside.

Spinning around, she looked up into those beautiful eyes and saw he was sorry. Axel never said things he didn't mean; he'd told her that, hadn't he? So she had to believe, even mad, he meant it when he told her it wasn't her business, that seeing people she cared about being upset and wanting to help wasn't anything to do with her.

Okay, fine. She accepted it.

"I don't want your apology. You said what you said, and at the time, you meant it. So, unless you're firing me, please leave me alone so I can do the job you pay me for. I don't want to talk or to listen to you."

"Jesus, fucking Christ." He muttered, "you're gorgeous when you're angry." His eyes flashed, and her heart jumped. He went to grab her again, and this time, Scarlett backed up. Holding out her *stay away* hand.

"I'm going to say this one thing, and then I'm sending you where the English people send people they don't want to talk to ever again, you're going to Liverpool,"

Axel's lips twitched, and she saw he was fighting a laugh. The absolute audacity of the man, thinking this was a laughing matter.

"I think you mean Coventry, baby. It's something to do with ostracizing."

Scarlett seethed and pointed a finger. "Don't you biker mansplain to me, Axel Tucker. Liverpool, Coventry, or the depths of hell, it's all the same. I'm sending you there because you hurt me. And you were the only person I trusted not to hurt me, and you did it anyway without thought. You can't take it back, and I can't forget it, so be ostracized and leave me alone."

Even now, she wanted to lurch toward him and bury her face in Axel's chest, knowing how good he held her.

The air deflated out of Scarlett when she thought he'd listened, but only moments later, she felt him press his chest to her back, holding her steady with an arm around her waist until he turned Scarlett to face him.

His expression darkened enough she felt a rise of love for him.

Next, his head lowered, pressing their foreheads together.

"I would never hurt you intentionally, Scarlett. *Fucking never.* If you believe anything, believe that. I wanted you away from Selena because I know how dirty she can play, and I will always protect you from anyone who might damage your tender heart."

Ah, God in heaven, that felt nice to hear, and Scarlett's jealous heart wanted to fall all over Axel like the slut it was. But she was stronger than her heart; she had to be.

Old Scarlett was a pushover for anyone walking over her feelings.

New Scarlett would hold grudges forever and be damn good at it.

Not that Axel was getting her memo for icing him out. He cupped the back of her neck, using a weakness against her like a weapon because he knew how much she loved that hold.

"You can be mad at me."

"Thanks for the permission," she snapped, and he grinned a white-toothed grin.

"You can be mad at me, wildcat, and I'll earn your forgiveness. You tell me when, okay?"

Ha. He could wait one hundred-fifty-six days, and she'd still hold strong and stubborn. She could tell him his sweet talking wasn't working. Much. But she'd shoved him in no man's land now, where conversations would not be had, so instead, she made a huffing sound and looked away.

Axel only laughed, capturing her face in his hands and kissing her lightly. Oh. What a kiss. She tried hard not to pucker her lips.

"You're everything to me, Scarlett. Gonna start telling you that more. Should have been saying it from the start."

Her soul straight up leaped out of her body at his declaration.

"Don't care if you're mad at me, wildcat, 'cause, at the end of every day, we're gonna be together, you and me. I fucked up and hurt my girl. But my girl has the biggest heart and will let me win it back."

Another kiss skirted across her lips, and she was powerless to stop him because all those words, those beautiful words she'd longed to hear, he was finally saying them.

"Gonna give you a little time to mope and plan my murder, baby. But I'm not gonna be far away. You're mine, Scarlett." If she'd had any wind left in her sails after that, it would have been gone when he said, "I'm yours."

She was slack-jawed when he walked away, but scowled when he turned around and winked at her. That devil was coming at her with an attack he knew she couldn't resist.

And he came at her from all sides for the rest of the day.

An hour later, he brought her lunch. Though she refused to talk to him, he still kissed her neck and told her to eat everything. Hmph. He'd gone to her favorite Tex-Mex restaurant and brought her a rice-loaded Chimichanga with guac dip. Of course, she'd eat everything. She practically licked the container clean of crumbs.

Just because she had Axel in the doghouse didn't mean being the president of a growing empire stopped in its tracks. For the rest of that day, she saw him in a meeting with Jamie Steele before the other biker prez took off for pastures new, or back home, wherever he hailed from. Then he strode across to the garage to help with a backlog of cars to fix. But he never once forgot about her. He traipsed back through the entry doors every hour and headed right for her.

It was like being attacked with affection.

"Everything good, baby?" he asked, cupping her face even though she showed no interest in being touched. Lie, she always wanted to be handled by Axel. It was a need, but she wasn't letting her tongue free to tell him. Being in the doghouse meant just that. "Don't be doing any heavy lifting. That's what we have the prospects for." Another few face kisses, and he trekked off to work again.

This happened several times before dinner time.

Against every intention, her eyes followed him out until she sighed.

"I'd slash his tires if I were you, girlie." Bash approached the bar and straddled a stool; he was already holding a coffee mug. She liked Bash a lot. He was one of the quiet, introspective bikers who didn't say much until there was something to say. "If you wanna do it, I'll alibi you. You were with me the whole time," he flashed a grin, making Scarlett laugh.

"Aren't you meant to be bro-loyal?"

A smile touched his lips. "I can be both. Especially when it's funny to see Axel bust his hump to fix his shit."

"You're mean," she answered with a smile. "I like you."

That wasn't the end of the bikers giving her sage advice over the following days. In between Axel plying her with food and whatever else he thought she might need to get through the day, and while she pointedly ignored him and all his affectionate touches, the bikers came up to her one by one or sometimes in a group.

"You're not being mean enough, Scar."

"Make the prez work for it. You could burn down his house."

Absolutely not. She was no firestarter.

"Or make him buy you a villa in Spain."

Oh, she liked that one.

"You could make him rage with jealousy and go on a date with me," offered a smirking Splice, and Bash thumped him on the back of the head before Scarlett could answer him. "If you want your dick cut off, keep saying shit like that to prez's woman. Axel would rip you limb from limb."

"Only trying to help the cause."

"You're a bad boy, Splice, and one day when you catch feelings for someone, we'll all stand back and watch you lose your mind," Scarlett said. Splice visibly grimaced.

"No, thanks. I like my adventurous ways better. Why have one bed to sleep in when you can have many?" He winked.

"You could seduce him," Forger spoke. "Be all sexy like, and then when he thinks he's about to get some, you say only joking, motherfucker."

This earned the prospect a thump on the back of the head from Splice. "Prospects don't get a say in this."

"Ow, fuck! I was helping Scar get back at the prez."

Mouse joined the rabble gathered at her bar. "Put snakes in his boots."

Holy shit, where would she even get snakes from? She screamed at tiny bath spiders; there was no way she could hold a snake to stuff it into his boots.

More ideas bounced around, and she thought they were crazy, but it didn't stop her from laughing.

"What's all this?" a rough voice asked, and Scarlett's body jolted.

He was back.

She'd only seen him at breakfast when he accosted her in the kitchen for a full kiss she had hardly participated in before she escaped.

"Nothing, Prez. Just talking to your hostage, guaranteeing she doesn't pack her bags and take off for the hills." Said Splice, sending a wink her way. That dirty suck-up, playing both sides, he was a crazy loon.

"Scatter, let me have a minute with my hostage."

En masse, the ramble of bikers, who'd been plotting with her only minutes ago, fled the scene, leaving her alone with Axel.

Of course, she ignored him. She even walked to the other end of the bar to rearrange some bottles, but that didn't deter him.

"It's been a busy morning, baby. Come kiss your man."

She scowled over her shoulder. Her lips tingled. Her brain got sluggish when he was around, and she found it hard to remember being hurt and angry.

"Fine, I'll come to you," he announced and did that sexy thing of vaulting himself bodily over the bar by spring boarding using his hand. Whoa. He was beside her in seconds, crowding her against all the bottles. Axel's body heat was blistering her resolve.

A hand curled around her nape but twisted to the front; her throat swallowed as he held her. Her kryptonite was working against her because she didn't shove Axel away. "I'm gonna make it work between us, Scarlett."

"Nope," she said and nearly snapped her tongue off for talking to him. Axel grinned, brushed a wisp of hair away from her eyes, and trailed that finger down her cheek.

The way he looked at her was one of sweet awe, but there was nothing sweet about Axel, and his possessive glint told her he was being friendly right now, but soon he'd take her over. The all-over body shiver made him smirk. "Yeah, gonna bust my ass off because I've never had something so good before, someone I wanna keep and make mine."

Damn him for saying what she wanted to hear.

She relented a little.

Let him pet her only a bit because his touch was paradise.

He left her with a kiss and a promise to see her soon.

Soon wasn't enough, and Scarlett was pitiful because days into icing him, she was ready to crawl into his jeans and beg for his love.

But she was more intrigued about what he'd do next to woo her into forgiving him.

So she waited.

Axel

"How's my sweet and sharp little wildcat?"

Scarlett stiffened because Axel flattened himself to her back. She was so damn small; he was almost hunched over so he could touch her with two hands on her stomach.

With each shudder, he felt it.

"Don't you talk to me, Axel Tucker. I'm icing you out. You're in the freezer! You're ice cubes to me."

"He's ice cubes," someone over his shoulder repeated, followed by rumbling laughter, but he ignored anyone around them. He'd been winning her around for six long days in front of the club members, not caring if they thought it made the president weak. Axel had received the worst lesson of all, and that wasn't how fucking macho he might look to others, but how not to hurt his woman's feelings.

He growled right by her ear. "You wanna call me Axel Tucker while I push deep into you? Nah, you enjoy calling me sir, don't you, bad girl? It gets your thighs all slicked up, doesn't it?"

He couldn't help talking filthy to her. It seemed to be the only thing she reacted to all week, and like a starving man, missing his woman in his bed curled all small and sweet against him, he gorged on those reactions.

Even as her eyes fired and lips pursed, he'd see how the pulse hammered in her throat. Other times, he'd catch how she followed him with her eyes.

Yeah, baby, I'm hungry for you, too.

With a kiss on her neck, he smacked her butt and grabbed her hand before she could escape. "Come on. We're going out to lunch."

"No, I'm not."

"You are." He kept his long stride, making her jog at his side even as she tried to pull her hand back. No chance Axel was letting her go.

"This is kidnapping," she huffed when he lifted her into the truck. Unfortunately, it was too frosty to take her out on the bike.

"Can't kidnap my hostage," he winked, and she went wide-eyed.

"You finally admit it."

"I never denied it." Axel smiled, starting the engine, bringing her hand over to lie on his thigh. "You're mine, Scarlett."

She let that go. At least she wasn't denying it now.

Just when he thought she'd returned to giving him the cold shoulder, he drove the truck through the first gates, and she turned her head toward him. "Axel, I'd prefer to stay at the compound. I feel safer here."

Safer? His throat got thick, seeing the look of uncertainty in her eyes. He idled the truck and grabbed her hand, tucking it inside his.

"Safe from what, baby? You know I won't allow another explosion. I've put guards in place, and there's been no sighting of DeCastro in weeks."

"I'm not scared of that. But what if my brother or some of my family are in town?"

Those fucking scum still had a stranglehold on her.

He kissed her palm and then took it to his neck, letting her feel his steady pulse and that he wasn't stressed about her shit family.

"I got you, Scarlett. No one is getting near you who you don't want close to you. If we see any of them in town, you look through them. They don't exist to you unless you want them to."

Her light fingertips stroked his neck. "Just like that?"

"Yeah. Fuck 'em. I'll deliver them all back to cult town individually and not be so nice about it."

She chuckled and took her hand back. Pity it was getting him revved up.

"Axel Tucker being nice, I'd pay to see that."

"I'm nice to you," he smirked before she replaced her smile with a scowl. His fiery girl forgot she was supposed to be mad at him.

"You said something about food."

"Yep. Fish tacos." Her favorite. "Then we're going to the store to stock you up on new DVDs."

He saw the joy in her eyes. "You can't buy my affection back, Axel Tucker. It won't get you into my panties."

A heated growl crawled up his throat as he put the truck in motion again. Then, grabbing her hand, he put it back on his thigh. "If all I wanted was to fuck you, wildcat, I'd pull onto the side of the road and be buried in seconds, and you wouldn't stop me. We're more than sex, more than those shaking orgasms you're addicted to."

She huffed, cheeks pink, her eyes suddenly so sex filled. "Like you aren't."

"I am if they're with you. I can wait, Scarlett, because I want my woman back. I want her sweet with me again."

She stared at the side of his face while he drove, but said nothing. He didn't need her to. Axel was playing the long game, whatever it took.

However slick and cunning he had to get to win her back. He'd do it.

There was no trace of her family in town because he was having them watched, and her slink of a brother hadn't moved since he'd arrived home. When shit settled down, he knew he would employ Amos to empty Bass' offshore accounts and give every penny to Scarlett. Axel had revenge in his heart.

Sofia Fielding saw them as they came out of the store, Scarlett gleeful with all the shit he'd bought her, Axel holding her hand. The cop was coming out of the coffee shop with her partner; she stared across the street at them but wisely didn't acknowledge them.

Stopping work in the middle of the day to go to lunch and a shopping trip wasn't the shit Axel was used to. Thinking of someone else's needs hadn't always been at the forefront of his mind. Showing

Scarlett how important she was to him—vital had become his key priority.

The realization he'd hurt her and could lose her turned him cold.

And it wasn't something he wanted to face.

His beloved hostage belonged to him. Let her try to leave him.

He'd get her heart back, her love, and her fucking soul because Scarlett Bass was going nowhere without him.

Scarlett

Scarlett needed sex in the worst way.

If she didn't get laid in the next few minutes, her vagina would turn to dust. Or something equally dramatic.

She wanted to get nasty, and Axel was the only man she wanted nastying her up.

So what choice did she have but to take matters into her own hands and make it happen?

It didn't mean he was forgiven. No siree. Okay, fine, he was forgiven days ago.

But he'd probably go berserk if she even considered getting her needs met elsewhere. And ew, the thought of another man's hands on her hips, holding her down and sliding his big cock inside her, made her skin chill.

There was only one man for Scarlett, so he'd have to take it while she got hers.

Her mind was as filthy as Axel's, and she'd never been shy about wanting him sexually, so when she burst through his office door like she had hounds on her heels, she was a little out of breath because that first look at Axel and her body flamed.

She had the hots for him in the biggest way.

Her man.

The love of her perfectly ordinary life.

Axel's eyes rose when she'd whirlwind through the door, and now he sat back in that big leather chair he spread his bulk in and watched as she locked the door and started pulling off her boots. Looking like a king on his majestic throne. The boots were tossed aside before she attacked her plaid shirt, pulling it out of her jeans, almost bursting the buttons open to get it off.

He understood what this was about.

"I'm in charge. I'd prefer you didn't talk and ruin this for me. I have the portal between my legs that makes you wild, so you have no power here."

The sexual grin he flashed nearly knocked her dizzy.

She got out of her tight jeans so fast he would have to be a dummy not to catch on to what would happen next. But there was only lust in his low-lidded eyelids as he watched. And then he pushed the chair back, silently inviting her over.

Why, thank you, sir. I will graciously accept such an offer.

She counted the steps to reach him because she was nervously excited, unable to keep her breaths steady.

Her heart raced.

And she had greedy fingers, aching to touch him.

Axel got to touch first when he grabbed her around the waist as soon as she was close enough and brought her onto his lap.

"Sweetheart, I might be a dumb idiot, but having you nearly naked on my lap, you wanna tell me something?" he smirked, looking good enough to serve between two pieces of thickly buttered bread.

"This doesn't mean anything," she replied quickly, going for his belt with grabby hands.

"It means everything. It means my woman is horny, and she came to find me. You trust me to give you what you need. Anytime. You hearing me, Scarlett? You come to me, and I will give you what you need from me."

All the air in her lungs evaporated, and she jolted as though he'd zapped her with electricity. The look in his intense eyes set the fine hairs on her body alight, and that's when she attacked Axel's mouth.

The kiss exploded in soft sparks, leaving shards of lust all over the room.

Every callus on his roughened hands was known, so when he rubbed them over her hips, grabbing on hard, Scarlett shivered with delight. She loved how he handled her; there was nothing soft now as she wrestled his dick from the confines of his jeans. She only hesitated a second when she had Axel's length in her hands, breath shoving in and out of her dry lips.

He was busy, too. Flicking open the tiny clasp of her bra. It disappeared, and then he shuffled off her panties, tossing them on the floor. He was so good at that.

"This what you came for, baby? So take it." His eyes showed a flash of aggression, but it was not to dissuade her. Axel knew how to motivate Scarlett; she maneuvered herself to her knees, bracketing either side of Axel's thighs, and her hands instantly returned to his length. He didn't help, just watched her with a hooded look.

He'd been patient, more patient than she'd expected from him.

So when she stood his cock up and impaled herself in a slow push, they breathed into each other's mouths.

The bliss was acute.

She liked how Axel took her body; he knew how to work her over to the highest highs, but riding on his lap was an extra pleasure she reveled in.

His hands clasped her moving hips.

His mouth tattooed patterns on her neck.

Helplessly, she reacted to his devastatingly soft kiss because Axel had always been everything she'd ever wanted. And his taste was the highest high.

And missing him all week, although he'd hardly left her alone, had gouged a hole in her chest. Scarlett clung to his broad shoulders, and she rode him. She rode him with every piece of love she felt for the crazy, gorgeous man beneath her.

"Jesus, baby. Look how beautiful this pussy is. I wanna die up inside of it."

Her hips rolled. The pleasure gaining speed. "Axel, that isn't the romantic gesture you think it is," she half-laughed, moaning in the next breath when he swept a rough finger over her clit, pulsing her orgasm right down to her curling toes.

After a long minute of holding her to his chest, he pulled back and dipped in to kiss her. "I don't have a romantic bone in my body."

"You do in your Axel way. But try not to die inside my pussy, old man. I'd have a hard time explaining that to a coroner."

Her pulse floated when Axel lifted her free, his still-hard cock a beacon for her eyes as he laid her ass on the desk in front of them. Lord, she hoped her bare skin wasn't squashing a gas bill.

But thoughts fled when he rose to his feet, pushing his jeans down only so far to fully free his cock. The incredible sight made the air vanish in the room, and she inhaled hard as Axel fixed his body over hers. Balancing his hands by her hips.

His hanging hair around her face and his intoxicating stare felt like a cat attack surrounding her. She all but purred, reaching for him, his hands clasping around her wrists, pinning them to the desk.

Her thirst shot up to cloud level. Only Axel could seduce her pussy into running a river.

And then it got even better when Axel rubbed his nose against hers in a lovely gesture.

"We're gonna fuck again, baby. Then we talk." It wasn't a question. Emotion locked in her throat, so much love for him, she nodded in return.

He was as good as his word because there was no hesitation as he widened her thighs and pushed into her. Oh, God, he slid in and in and didn't stop until he hit bottom. It was exquisite. Heaven on earth.

Axel groaned, rolling a hand around her neck like he knew firsthand how it affected her. Then, buried inside her, Axel brought their mouths together, whispering her name into her lips like a divine mantra.

Just that sound and she fell deeper in love.

"Fuck me, please." She begged back in the same hushed tones.

And so he did. *Ruthlessly*. Rearing his hips back, Scarlett's breath shunted out of her body when he brought his next thrust, and it didn't return until the last shudder left her.

Axel fucked them to peak orgasms; he hit every pleasure spot and dragged her over the edge of bliss until she sobbed into his mouth. She should have been prepared for how *insatiable* he was after a week's dry spell.

Leaving her sprawled on his desk, Axel did the clean-up and tossed the wet tissues into the trash can, then he helped her back into her underwear before putting her on his lap, holding her securely.

Because she was blissed out, she cuddled in. She'd missed him so much. Not just the sex, although that was mind-blowing. But this part, when she felt it, was their hearts connecting their skin and souls.

"Missed you, wildcat."

Oh, how her heart rolled over.

And he didn't stop with that sentiment. Obviously, an alien had captured her gorgeously bossy but most often tight-lipped biker, because the next thing he told her almost poured Scarlett onto the floor.

"I love you so fucking much. I want you to stop being mad at me."

Wait. Her ears buzzed. Did he just say…? Scarlett pulled back to look at his face, and he appeared so earnest, so freaking adorable, as his brow folded in and stroked the side of her face.

"You love me? But I'm a nuisance."

A grin cracked his lips, and Axel leaned in to kiss her. She latched on and devoured his mouth.

"You're a goddamn pain in my ass, Scarlett. But I've loved no one the way I love you. It's consumed me from the inside."

"Like a parasite," a giggle erupted, and lips pressed to her neck, bringing a halt to the laughter because anytime Axel's mouth was near, it derailed her.

"You forgive me yet?"

The time of reckoning was here.

She missed Axel, being around him, and showering him with her affection. Even yelling at him across the room. But she didn't want to be the girlfriend who hid her feelings. So she didn't.

"You hurt me; it took me by surprise more than anything. And I'm afraid it will happen again when you get pissed off at someone else and take it out on me. I don't want to hide my opinion when you need to rein it in, Axel."

"I don't want that either, baby."

"I get Selena makes you feel a type of way because of how she affects Roux. You go into daddy-protect mode. My mom defers to my dad about everything, like she doesn't have her voice. He's the decision maker, and she has to accept it."

"Sweetheart," he said, cupping her face. "I was an impulsive prick, and I'll probably be that again at some point. You know I'm not perfect." Scarlett snorted, and Axel smiled in return. "But you gotta call me on it, punch me in the balls, but I'd rather you didn't. What I mean is, we're gonna clash, but you always got a voice, I promise. We won't always agree."

"I don't think we've agreed on anything so far."

Axel tapped her lips with a kiss, stroking her hair back.

"You are fucking precious to me. I would never intentionally hurt you. If you think I'm being a dick, you let me know. If we're arguing and I say shit you don't like, say shit back. I'm nothing like your dad, Scarlett. I want an honest relationship with you. Good, bad, and ugly. Different opinions splattered all over the floor. I'm not pig enough that I can't admit when I'm wrong, and being apart from you this week has been torture. I don't enjoy sleeping away from you."

"I don't like that either. Okay, so we can agree. If you lose your temper again, I can punch you in the balls."

His smile grew, and she saw love in his eyes. "I'd prefer you didn't."

"Nope, you said it now."

"You're such a brat," he tugged a wisp of hair, and she nuzzled his nose.

"Your brat who you love, though."

"Yeah, baby. I love you."

It was like she was tasting colors and feeling the air move through her lungs for the first time. Happiness lassoed around Scarlett, binding her to the big man holding her on his lap.

"I love you, too. You dragged me into your world because I did something wrong and was made to pay for it. I stayed because I wanted to be in your world, to be around you. I went to your bed because it's what I wanted to be more than anything. You treat me right, spoil me, and show me how I can have everything. You gave me freedom and trust. And when I say you're the only person I trust in this world, it's not light words. So don't ever dare treat me less than your equal. I'm not a sweet bottom looking for scraps from you, and I'm not a whore, unless we're roleplaying." She burst with the words, peppering him all over with kisses. "I love you the most and the best."

"Fucking finally." He breathed and pressed his face into her neck. "Your life belongs to me. Not because you owe me shit. You never did. I brought you home because I wanted to keep you even before I knew what a sassy-mouthed brat you were. Long before I realized you brought my soul alive, I had to own you."

She was being given a miracle by seeing Axel emotional, and it was a gift she would never squander. As tight as he held her, she held him tighter, stroking a hand over his hair, letting him know how loved he was.

"We better get you dressed." He said after a long minute, depositing Scarlett on his desk so he could fetch her jeans and top, which he helped her into.

"So, no prancing out there in my undies, then?"

He growled, and she grinned bigger. "Don't start. I can still spank you even now that you love me."

"Ha. I always loved you from the start, which never stopped you from whacking my butt."

The controlled Axel was back in the room. Looking larger than ever, smirking, and about as beautiful as a man could get. He stroked a finger down her cheek and reached behind him to bring his chained wallet from his back pocket.

"If you're paying me for services given, I will start punching balls, Axel Tucker."

"Put a lid on it, wildcat," he chuckled and came out with five bucks.

"This is the same one you tried to steal from me." Axel rubbed the money between his finger and thumb. "I carry it with me, baby. I will never spend it because it reminds me of what it brought into my life."

Her heart went into free fall, and she was going to cry. "What did it bring?"

"It brought me you. It brought me my love."

The waterworks started, and she buried her face in his chest while he scratched the back of her head with comfort.

Who said you couldn't teach an old biker new tricks? Especially if those tricks were all about loving, wanting, and belonging to each other.

She might have attacked him with kisses if not for the commotion outside the door. Axel frowned, and Scarlett followed him into the hallway with her hand locked inside his.

"What's all the fucking noise?" he asked, seeing people whooping and hollering, clearly celebrating. Did someone win the Powerball this week?

And then they saw Reno fly out of the back rooms at a full sprint.

"What the fuck?" Axel remarked.

Reno didn't stop running, but he shouted over his shoulder. "Ruin's awake."

Oh, my giddy God. Scarlett clutched Axel's hand, feeling the same joy everyone else was experiencing.

It was three months to the day that he'd fallen into a coma, and now Ruin was finally awake.

Axel

When the club traveled in a group, with Tomb as their road captain leading the convoy, it was always a sight for the locals to see. That sight didn't end on the streets. It piled into the local hospital and reached the twelfth floor, where Ruin's private room was.

Axel's men prowled into the waiting area, still shocked that their enforcer was conscious after months of being in a coma the doctors couldn't explain. And from the sounds of it making a holy disturbance. At least his lungs still worked.

"*Aurora!*" they all heard coming from down the hallway. "*Get me Aurora. Get me Aurora.*"

"Who the fuck is Aurora?" inquired Bash. A half-smoked cigarette was hanging from the corner of his lip. A nurse dressed in green scrubs left her station and gave him the stink eye. "Sir, you can't smoke in here. Take it outside, please."

"Little darling, I'll do anything you tell me to do." He flirted back with a smile. The nurse rolled her eyes, unaffected as if she'd heard all the same guff before, and Bash stubbed the cigarette out in a trash can. He followed her to the desk, but Axel pulled his gaze away. He didn't care who Bash had his eye on now.

"Do you think he's okay?" Scarlett asked, worrying a lip with her teeth.

"He's awake."

"And fucking loud," chuckled Chains, sprawled beside Axel. Ruin's same litany continued.

"He's gonna be fine, baby."

"Yay. The gang's all back together."

He kissed the side of her temple. She was straight-up sunshine to his otherwise black heart, and he felt settled again now he had her back in his arms. It didn't suck that she was all over him with touching. Since leaving the club, she hadn't taken her hands off him. He laced their fingers on his thigh and waited for an update.

The update came a while later. Reno looked reborn with relief. They were all relieved that tests so far showed no lasting damage to Ruin's brain. Axel knew that big, menacing bastard wouldn't let a little thing like a coma diminish his demonic personality.

When Axel pulled her into his lap, she snuggled deeper into his chest.

His girl broke the tension. "Listen, guys. I need to tell you something. And I don't want to shock you or anything. So you maybe want to take a seat." She said earnestly as his men grinned.

"I wanted to be the one to tell you that me and Axel are a couple. Now I know you'll be surprised by this news, so don't faint, okay?"

Collectively, the laugh started around the waiting room.

"Scar, whatever you do, girlie, don't ever join the FBI because you're shit at keeping secrets," Bash teased.

Axel palmed the back of her head and kissed her temple.

"Don't listen to 'em, baby. You're fucking good at secrets." He supported as a good man would.

"I know, right?"

Axel took Scarlett home not long later. Now that Roux had returned to Colorado, his house was empty. He planned to fill it soon, but first, he rode through the club gates, closely followed by the rest of the boys who'd left Reno at the hospital. Once Ruin was home and back in the clubhouse, he could scrub one worry off his list. Unfortunately, the thing kept on growing. DeCastro on the top of that list. When he'd thought the maniac was only out to cause minor inconveniences, Axel hadn't put his total weight and brainpower behind ending him. But he'd crossed a line and hurt one of Axel's men. He'd been on their land and planted an explosive device. Since that night, Axel had put all his effort into ending him. If it meant death or jail, he was fine with either.

He had some theories which pulsed an angry tick in his temple if it came to pass. When he kissed Scarlett, watching her little ass get behind the bar, he winked over when she shyly sent him a grin.

That woman was his making and his unraveling.

Some men thought love weakened them. They were wrong. Loving his kid had driven Axel to the success he was today. Nothing short of love would have motivated him to get off his ass and make something of his worthless life.

He appreciated money and growing an empire. The danger came with the territory. It wasn't as though he deliberately set out looking for enemies, but they kept coming like a bad date who couldn't take a hint.

Loving Scarlett was a new motivation.

To keep her safe and sound.

To make his world bulletproof.

The explosion had taught him a lesson he didn't want to repeat. And that was his world had been penetrated. Someone had gotten in through a crack in his armor. And while he strode to his office, he engaged a call on his cell phone.

"Fielding, any of those leads pay off?"

"You're gonna love me."

Axel rolled his eyes and closed the office door behind him. If she was going to start with her flirting bullshit again, he was about to bribe a new cop. One with a dick who didn't try to climb into his pants.

"Oh, relax." She snapped at his silence. He could almost see her arrogant eye roll. "I'm dating a lawyer now. You're no longer on my radar."

"I'm thrilled." He deadpanned. "Now tell me."

It took only a minute, and Axel's jaw clenched when he hung up. The most crucial part of Sofia Fielding's new intel concerning

DeCastro and his whereabouts repeatedly clanged through his gray matter.

"Your club has a rat, Axel."

The name of that rat—someone with access to his club for months had been put in place as a traitor, forced a snarl on Axel's face. He needed to call a church meeting and discuss it with his council of trusted brothers.

Axel's knee-jerk approach was to kill the guy on the spot. But he wanted him to hang himself out to dry, to tie himself in so many lies and disloyalty before his punishment came.

If he and his brothers played it right, they'd get their rat and DeCastro in one fell swoop.

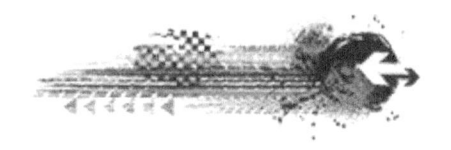

Axel found Scarlett much later.

After church and plans were put into place. After a long conference call with Rider and Grinder over at the Renegade Souls, hiring their infamous tracker to find DeCastro, he hooked up Scarlett's hand, bringing her out from behind the bar.

"Is this where you drag me behind you again? I can walk at your side, you know." She grumbled.

He should feel like shit after the past few hours, and he did.

He didn't like knowing they had someone disloyal under his roof for so long. But having Scarlett's hand in his, hearing how she bitched, like she hated him taking her anywhere—she didn't—he let some of his tension evaporate. Then, taking the stairs, she skipped after him with a running commentary.

"I was working, Axel. I can't be going off with you for afternoon trysts."

He stopped outside of her room. "Trysts? Really, baby? You're too cute."

"Yes, I know. So what's with the dragging me up here?"

"If I wanted to fuck you, I'd fuck you. You know you're weak and wet for me."

"Ugh," she play punched him. "Just because I love you, Axel Tucker doesn't mean I'm weak for you."

"I said weak and wet," he smirked and unlocked her door, ushering her in before him. "Start packing your things."

"Packing?" she parroted, turning in a fast rush to face him, blinking her confusion. Would her beauty ever stop sucker-punching him in the gut? Would he ever feel worthy of her loving him? Probably not, but he was not a fool to hand it back. A man with no morals knew when he was onto a good thing, and Scarlett had landed in his life by fate and by choice, she was everything good in this world.

She was sweet. And kind. She loved the biker life, thank God. And she'd fit in with the MC like she'd been born with leather boots around her delicate ankles. She swore worse than Devil sometimes, and his treasurer littered every sentence with f-bombs.

But he also knew she had a stubborn streak worse than his.

Axel could handle her perfectly, and how to do that was to tell her shit was happening, giving no room for argument or discussion.

Not for the essential things.

And this was one of those.

"You're moving into my house. Today, if you can pack your stuff fast."

He watched the news register on her face, saw it land as her cheeks grew pink and her eyes glistened. He expected a fight, to exchange some heated words about how it was too fast to live together.

He'd held himself back from locking her in his basement for months, keeping her close, so he always knew she was okay. So why else would he suffer that shitty mattress in his club bedroom to be near her?

There was no argument, and Axel's air was pushed out of his torso when the smaller imp hurled herself into his body, all arms and elbows digging in at awkward angles. Those elbows could be registered as a lethal weapon, but he hung on to her, catching her quickly, not letting her go. Never.

"I'm moving into your house because you're so stuck on me, Axel Tucker." She boasted.

"About to change my mind if you sass me again."

"No, you're not." She clung like a limpet, her legs banding around his waist. She brought her nose close to his, and that's when he heard the emotion in her sugary voice. "I love you so much, but I'll miss living here. Can we still stay over sometimes?"

"Yes, we can fuck up here."

"So romantic." She rolled her pretty eyes.

"I'll romance your fucking brains out with your jeans around your ankles and your screams buried in a pillow if you don't start packing your stuff, wildcat."

Her all-over body shudder did things to Axel, derailed his productivity if he allowed it to, but he wanted her in his house, to get her moved in finally. For a man who'd wanted no emotional entanglements, he sure as shit had done a one-eighty when she appeared on the scene. He'd all but bagged and tagged her on sight.

And not a regret was had at all.

He dropped a passionate kiss to her lips, forcing his tongue inside until Scarlett softened in his arms and moaned. Only then did she draw back, playing with his hair and doing a lot of not packing.

Fuck it. He'd carry her home and have a prospect box up her shit later.

"Do you think Roux will mind me living with you?"

"Baby, she's threatened to kick my ass all week if I didn't fix it with you. I think she'll be fine. And even if she wasn't, you're still moving in."

"So bossy."

"Get used to it," he smirked, then dropped her to her feet, smacking her ass. "Now get to it. Ten minutes or I redden your ass."

Her smile blistered him, and while he stood idly in her bedroom, watching as she flittered from corner to corner, tipping things out on the bed, he was overcome with a rushing wave of gratefulness.

He didn't know who to thank for Scarlett.

He didn't deserve someone as sweet as she was, that much he knew.

When she swept by him, Axel inhaled her scent, something subtle and clean, like laundry. He hooked an arm around her waist and pressed their bodies together, back to chest. That overwhelming sensation hit him all over again.

What if she'd tried to steal from someone else's truck? What if she'd never stopped in Utah? The variables were against him, and he couldn't think of never meeting her, not when she made him feel like a titan.

His girl to love and to protect.

And to fight with.

Their living together fights would bring the house down.

"So fucking happy you're moving in, wildcat."

"Me too." She stroked his forearm, leaning her weight into him. "I love you, you know."

"Love you back. And I'll make you happy, so fucking happy." It was his vow, and Axel never lied to those he gave a shit about.

"You already do."

"Gonna make you happy and help you have all those missed experiences. We'll travel and watch all the shitty 90s movies you want."

Turning in his arms, he was rewarded with her nuzzling her face in his chest before she looked at him. "Well, if I wasn't convinced to move in with you before, I am now," she teased, and earned a whack on her ass. As he'd known, she loved it.

"I picked the right old man to rob that day," she gloated, burying her nose in his chest.

What had he done? The redheaded brat would drive him to drink.

Ah, fuck. Who was he kidding? He'd welcome any chaos she brought because you didn't let go when the right thing came along.

For the right one, you took them hostage and made them yours forever.

Axel
SIX MONTHS LATER

"How's that pot looking now, Axel?" asked Butcher with a shit-eating grin all over his mug. The man was drinking coffee Axel bought after leaving the annex he'd built, so his daughter and her family had a place to stay when they came to town. And the asshole thought it was wise to mouth off to him. "Oh, this is the kettle asking, by the way."

The little shit.

"You were sitting on that one a while, huh?"

"You know it," he went on, grinning. "The times you busted my chops for falling for Roux."

"She was a kid."

"Hardly, but here you are with your young, young girl. What's the age difference, Axel? Forty-three years?"

"Oh, fuck off," he half laughed, walking around the kitchen, grabbing meat from the fridge to grill. He left the packages on the sink.

"You gotta give the Souls boy his due, Axe. He waited a long damn time to rub your nose in it." said Chains.

"You knocked him out when you knew Roux was having a baby. Now you're siding with him."

"Chains likes me now."

"Don't push it, man." Replied Chains, smacking Butcher on the shoulder as he collected beers to take outside, where their women were gathered for the cookout. Through the window, Scarlett sent him a dazzling smile that showed him his woman was happy in their life together.

He'd made sure of it these past six months.

Axel never took his finger off their pulse, no matter what other business kept him occupied. And a lot of shit had needed Axel's attention in the last half year. There was nothing like his businesses being attacked to focus a man into doing what needed doing, dirtying his hands. To even ask another MC for their expert tracker's help. But with all that, dealing with DeCastro's bullshit insanity and finally ending his tyranny, nothing swayed Axel's focus on his woman and their growing relationship.

He was an old fossil who could learn new tricks. Who knew, huh?

How else would he know what love languages meant now? Thanks to his woman being vocal and not hiding shit from him, he knew how to take care of her needs.

When he strolled out into the backyard, his grandson attacked him around the legs; he swung Crew up into his arms, accepting the excited kiss on the cheek before setting him down again to chase after his sister.

When he gazed at Scarlett, he found her already watching him. Smiling. Even when she was pissed off at him, he still saw her love shining back, and that was often because neither of them had miraculously changed just because they loved each other to distraction.

As he approached with slow steps, her arms were already raised for him to bend down so she could loop them around his neck. Wearing a pair of white cut-off shorts and a top so fucking indecent to his eyes, he wanted to maul her on the floor; he lingered a kiss on her forehead.

Just this morning, before the sun crested, he'd kissed every inch of her bronzed skin. Now he dropped his lips behind her ear, inhaling her sweetness.

"You're looking extra sneaky today, Axel Tucker. Are you up to bad things?" she asked as he tucked a small red strand of hair behind her ear.

"Yes," he answered as she sank into his body and made bliss pour through his bloodstream. Before she could get into the questions, as he knew she would, he hooked up her hand. "Gonna take you somewhere. We won't be gone long." He then shouted over the beat of the music to let the family know they were going out.

The bike ride didn't take long, and Scarlett looked excited yet unconvinced when she saw he'd brought her to one of her favorite hiking spots. Usually, when they had time, they'd come up here, mainly to fuck in nature because his girl was hornier when she could scream underneath the stars.

"Erm, Axel. I'm not wearing the right shoes for hiking, and we have family at home. Not to mention the burgers. Don't make me miss Chains' famous burgers."

"They're only famous in his warped mind."

"They're delicious, and I want two."

"Wildcat, stop your bitching. You can have two burgers when we get home. We're not going far." Muttering, she slid her hand into his and followed along up to the grassy brink, which overlooked the whole of Laketon. Down below, he could see half of his companies, but they didn't matter at that moment.

Only Scarlett did.

"You know I love you."

"Oh, no. Are you dying? Did the doctor call?"

"Jesus, woman." He half-laughed. "You've been watching too much shit on TV. I tell you I love you, and you jump to me dying?"

"Well. It seems ominous you bring me out here to our favorite make-out place."

"We fuck here, wildcat."

She blushed. "Yeah, that too. So what's going on, Axel?"

"I love you, you little brat."

"I love you, too."

Axel knew that. She told him every day. Showed him that love in hundreds of ways.

He didn't know he wanted an old lady until she was right in front of him, digging her claws underneath his skin, making him different in every positive way a woman could alter a man's basic structure. Scarlett had fast become someone he trusted implicitly. She was level-headed, intelligent, and a great sounding board when he only needed an ear to talk through tough decisions. She was good at seeing things unbiasedly and gave him reliable advice.

She also hogged the covers and kicked the hell out of his legs in her sleep.

Made him eat healthy three times a week.

Also forced him to go for a physical to check his old man's heart was in good working order, her words.

She was still a pain in his ass, and he wanted to strangle her at least once a day, and she was also the love of his existence. Hands down, he'd kill for her.

"Let me be your husband, Scarlett."

The silence almost put a growl in his throat, but he waited while he watched her eyes fill with tears, and when Axel couldn't wait a second longer because he'd expected her to flatten him by jumping into his arms, he rolled his fingers around her throat. "You're marrying me, Scarlett. That's it. You don't get a choice about it."

Fuck. Romantic, he was not.

But she knew that already.

He wanted his woman weak and willing, the way she made him feel. He wanted it more than his breath.

"You make me fucking insane."

"Then be insane, Axel. Be insane for me."

A lone tear tracked down her cheek, and then she jumped into his arms, peppering him like a wild thing with kisses all over his face.

"You're supposed to wait until I say yes."

"You were taking too long, so I decided for you."

"So bossy." More kisses. "So handsome." She was sweetness itself, and he basked in her attentive kisses before he captured her mouth and found her tongue. "My husband. I think I just died and went to heaven."

"Afraid to tell you, sweetheart, you're hooked to me now, so it's the other destination we'll be going to."

This caused her to laugh. She thought he was lying, but he wasn't. Axel had always been destined to go to the burning place. And there was no way he'd be without her in the next life.

Because, as always, shit never went to plan where his Scarlett was concerned. The ring he'd bought sat in his pocket. He'd slide the diamond on her finger in a minute.

Just as soon as he was through doing what they did when they were up here.

Cupping her face, he told her. "I'm gonna kiss you, Scarlett, until you can't breathe. And then I'll drop to my knees and lick up all the mess my kiss has made."

He then started with a kiss for the woman who tried to steal from him and gave Axel everything he never knew he wanted.

It was a good exchange, he reckoned.

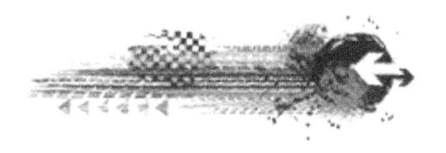

Scarlett
TEN MONTHS LATER

Like most couples, they'd talked forever ago about serious topics.

Axel didn't want more kids, and Scarlett was ambivalent about the whole motherhood thing, so it didn't matter either way. She loved Coco and Crew and always begged Roux to let them babysit for the weekend. That was enough for her.

She never thought she'd be gazing at a pregnancy test stick and seeing the positive outcome.

That night, dressed in the sexiest summer dress, all floaty with thin straps, the one that always got Axel revved up when he saw her wearing it, she started the pasta for dinner. She was stirring the garlic cream sauce at the stove when he came through the garage door, tossing his leather jacket on the coat hooks before heading to her.

A kiss landed on her shoulder. An arm slid around her waist, and as predicted, he stroked the dress's fabric along her waist. "Mm, hey, baby, it smells good in here."

"Some of my DVDs came in the mail today. I thought we'd have a night in front of the TV."

"I can do that; I'm beat. Do I have time for a shower before dinner?"

He did. But she'd burst apart like glitter if she had to wait for another second.

Scarlett wasn't nervous, not after sitting on the news for a few hours alone. She didn't hide anything from Axel. That's why most of their fights were legendary, followed by the best make-up this side of Utah. She wasn't afraid to talk to him about anything, even scary things like having a baby when they decided not to have kids.

Their life was full and rich as it was.

And better than ever.

Even Scarlett could understand how a baby would change things drastically.

"I need to talk to you first, baby."

"Oh, yeah?" he said, eyebrow raised. He hooked out a kitchen chair and parked his ass. Scarlett brought him a beer from the fridge and rested her hip against the sink. "I need a beer for this? *Fuck*. Did you beat up the neighbor kid again?"

Despite the seriousness churning up inside her, she chuckled. "I *hardly* beat up a seven-year-old kid."

"You forcibly took his bike off him, Scarlett. I had to face his dad when he came to the door."

"I was justified, as you know. If the little punk had stopped trying to ram the bike into Crew, I would have left his punk-ass alone. But I got shit done, and he leaves the kids alone now."

"Big tough wildcat."

"You know it. Anyway. I need to tell you something, and I don't want you to hit the ceiling because I'm hungry, and it's pasta night. Besides, when you think about it, this is all your fault, Axel Tucker."

"Fuck me," he sighed like a gale coming through their kitchen.

Axel didn't let the grass grow at all in getting them married. He had her to a celebrant as soon as the engagement ring was on her finger. Luckily, she hadn't wanted a big shindig wedding. It was just their friends and family. Not hers. Fortunately, she'd never heard from them since, except for a birthday card arriving from her mother, which she didn't reply to. They'd burned those parent bridges long ago, and Scarlett was deliriously happy with her life.

"Okay, spit it out. Whatever is my fault."

"Remember, we love each other very much. Actually, you're crazy about me. So you can't lock me in the basement."

"You'd only scream and holler and disturb football Sunday."

Yeah, she would. She hated being away from Axel.

Especially in the recent past, that had been necessary because of what happened with Reno and Ruin's eldest brother. And she'd pined like a Labrador puppy on those nights without Axel.

They were joined at the hip.

Happy idiots in love.

And that happy idiot staring at her had well and truly knocked her up.

"Scarlett, if you've killed someone, just tell me so I can deal with it," he said so seriously she fell fathoms deep in love with him all over again. He'd do that without question; she knew that. And now she was too far away, so she slid onto his lap sideways, her arms looped around his neck.

He smelled of the outside and motor oil. A blended mix of something alluring she loved to smell on his clothes.

"Remember how we talked about not having kids? Well, you got me pregnant." It came out in a rush. She knew not to expect jubilation in his eyes. That's not how Axel worked. He weighed up everything he heard before reacting. It was what made him a great MC president. But more than that, a wonderful husband.

They'd figure this out together like they did everything.

"You're pregnant?"

"Yes. Your damn sperm got arrogant and infiltrated me. Like I said, this is all your fault, Axel. I can hardly be blamed for something you did."

Oh, yeah. She'd toss her beloved man under the fertile bus.

Stroking fingertips along his throat, she waited, their eyes locked.

"You're pregnant, and it's my fault?" and then. "Scarlett, you were there every time for the fucking." His tone was even, but she could tell he wasn't angry. His hands dropped to Scarlett's hips, and whether he knew he was doing it, he squeezed her.

She waited out his thought process, giving him time to think.

Because despite the surprise, Scarlett wasn't unhappy about it. Once she pictured a dark-haired baby with Axel's eye color, she could have exploded with joy.

"Damn," he sighed eventually, running his hands up along her ribs, "I get inside you, and all I think about is coming in you. Filling you until it runs down your thighs."

Swoon, he painted the sexiest picture with words. And it was all true.

"It is my fault."

"I told you." she shoulder-checked him. Then grew sober. "What do you think? I'm good with it if you are."

"I think we'll be elbow deep in shitty diapers in a few months, baby."

Scarlett exhaled. "Just like that?"

Then Axel smiled, and her world steadied again. He leaned in and captured her lips for an all-teasing, over-too-soon kiss. "Sweetheart, we were both there for the fucking. We do enough of it and hardly remember to use condoms. The way you lock onto my cock, it was bound to happen, eventually."

"Oh my God, Axel," she gasped, burying her face in his chest. Axel scratched his fingers through her hair and kissed her again when she lifted her face.

"Can't say I'm not surprised, wildcat, or even if this is the right time, but it's happened, and anything you and me make together is not wrong. I fucking love you more than my life, and I'll love a baby we made. It can't be any wilder than Roux was, so that's a bonus."

"And you're much older now, so you'll know what to do." She praised with a teasing grin.

He lifted a cocky brow and turned her stomach to syrup. "You want me to show you how old I am on the kitchen floor?"

That's how their marriage was. They were open, honest, and faced whatever came their way head-on and together.

Dinner was late because Axel had things to prove. On the kitchen floor. And then in a shared shower. Scarlett didn't mind going hungry, not when she was curled up on her husband's lap that night, discussing what a well-behaved child they would have.

And then, eight months later, Atlas was born.

And twenty years after that, like his daddy, he was a bad boy, untamed as the ocean and with a big, big heart.

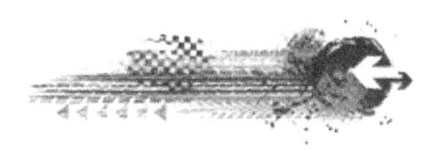

Atlas Tucker
TWENTY-FIVE YEARS OLD

There was nothing unusual about that night as Atlas went on his regular collections around the Diablos bookies. The club had branched out into gambling about ten years back, and as soon as Atlas patched in, he'd been tasked with keeping it in hand, making sure the cops didn't get a sniff of it. Or if they did, ensuring they were paid their bribe to turn a blind eye.

The club was still in the import business, more lucrative than ever, but the bookies were all his, and he worked hard to bring a profit to the MC. His bookies took bets on every sport, from college to the big leagues.

It wasn't late, just past seven p.m., but the December Utah skyline was already shady as he stepped out from the back of the bakery after collecting the nightly takings from the bookie in the back room. When he heard the feminine sound, he was tucking the bagged money into his pocket. It was one of two things; he reckoned. Either a woman was having a good time against an alley wall, or she was in a bitchy catfight.

He'd seen how women fight. Fuck, they fought dirty. Give him a nice knife fight any day.

Nosy, he took a left to have a look, nothing wrong with a little voyeuristic peek, but something alerted Atlas that it wasn't a quick outside bang he heard when the heavy breathing became a tortured, muffled cry. And then another.

His feet picked up speed, and that's when he saw a woman being harassed by two men.

It was more than pestering, spotting a scrape on her cheek and the messy way the wool coat was half hanging off her shoulder as if they'd tried to rip it off her.

"Aww, come on, pretty-pretty, let's have a good time, you'll like it." one said, his voice slurring as he tried to paw at the woman who attempted to step around them, but his friend blocked her path.

"The stuck-up bitch thinks she's too good for us, bro."

The fucking youth of today were as intelligent as a bag of arugula. They could be Atlas' age; still, he'd be worlds apart from those jokers.

For one, he'd never attack a woman.

And for two, it just pissed him off seeing his gender act like entitled fucking pricks.

His presence was announced as soon as he shifted his heavy-soled boots and stepped into the alleyway. All three froze, and the woman's eyes expanded with fear, probably thinking a third bro was joining the party.

Then the two animals turned on him while keeping the woman trapped.

"What's going on here, then?" he didn't expect an answer, but Atlas felt he'd have to dumb shit down and use small words for those two yokels to understand what would happen.

His blood hummed like a song, and he flexed his ringed fingers as he sauntered toward them.

"Mind your fucking business. Fuck off, bro." one spat.

Atlas grinned and sent a look at the woman. Average height, stunning build, all curves, and long legs in the tight ski pants underneath the expensive coat. A discarded purse slumped at her feet. One sweep of his eyes took in every detail of the scene.

"Pleasant friends you have, lady."

"They-they're not my friends. I want to go. Please help me,"

"Do yourself a favor, bro, and fuck off." The other one said, producing a flick knife from his pocket, brandishing it like Atlas would take it as a threat.

Nah. That was his starting pistol, and he grinned again.

Atlas kept a tight rein on himself most of the time, a force of habit now. The discipline of the MC had taught him to harness the bubbling temper within and to use it sparingly. So he reckoned witnessing a woman about to get attacked was as good a reason as he could think of to let his inner psycho out to play.

His mom would be pleased. She was a big advocate of men standing up and doing the right thing.

Rolling his neck, he let it all unfold as if he could see seconds into the future and how it would go down. Then, he moved faster than either man, grabbing the wrist of the one holding the flick knife. One nasty snap and the bone crunched beneath Atlas' fingers.

The man howled in agony, but Atlas kept twisting that arm until he folded like a deck of cards down to the icy floor. He stabilized that man by putting his boot on his neck. He went right on howling, but Atlas was deaf to his agony.

Then he sent his stare to his bro. It was one way in, one way out. He was now the trapped animal.

Atlas smirked and hoped the guy lunged at him. But the guy proved how gutless he was by standing like a statue.

"Aw, you don't wanna dance, *bro*?" he taunted in an even tone. "You only have the big manly balls to harass a woman, huh?"

"It was nothing."

"Doesn't look like nothing to her. Bet all she was doing was walking on the street minding her own damn business when you two fools thought it would be fun to get your pickles wet, whichever way you got it."

"Nah, bro, it wasn't like that. Just having fun."

"They-they were following me," she hiccupped.

Atlas clicked his tongue. "You're adding to the charges."

"You ain't no cop." The guy spat, weighing up the odds of rushing past Atlas. Atlas ground his foot into the piece of meat on the floor, kicking him to keep his trap shut.

"No, you're right. I'm not. I'm worse. I'm the guy about to break your fucking face." Atlas unzipped his leather jacket and showed the cut he was wearing. The white Diablo Disciples MC patch was revealed. And though it was dark, Atlas was sure he witnessed the douchebag rapist-wannabe turning pale.

"Look, all's good, yeah? Didn't mean to…"

"Didn't mean to what? Hassle a woman who didn't want your attention?"

The red mist grew redder over his vision. He could claim insanity for beating them both to a pulp, giving the mouthy asshole two stab wounds to his abdomen as a parting gift, but there was nothing insane about Atlas.

He always knew what he did. And why.

As he exhaled and looked down at the bloodied messes on the floor, he pulled a bandana from his back pocket and wiped off his hands.

He supposed seeing him go Tasmanian devil had scared the woman more because she shrank back against the wall when he approached her with slow steps. He bent at the waist and retrieved her purse, he handed over the heavy bag, and she clasped it like a shield.

"Do you have someone you can call?" he asked.

She shook her head frantically, tears streaking down her cheeks. One cheek now had a nasty scrape, and he felt his insides shift with the crazy thought of tending to the wound like a crazed white knight. Ha.

"They broke my phone while trying to call a car." She stuttered over every word. Fear still latched around the woman.

"You're okay now," he told her, getting a good first look at her, not recognizing her face. And he knew everyone in Laketon, making it his business to know. "You're new in town?"

"Visiting. Going home tomorrow."

"Sorry you had a shitty end to your trip." He shrugged and reached for his phone; the person on the other end answered after three rings. "I need a clean-up on Hyper Street, back alley behind the bakery. I saw two idiots trying to force themselves on a woman."

"You're shitting me, yeah? God's sake, Tucker, I don't have time for your games tonight. Have you killed them?"

Atlas chuckled. Such a nervous nelly for a crooked cop. Atlas assured him they were alive, but might need medical attention. The cop sighed and said he'd send a squad car. It was nice to pay the proper criminals.

He turned to the woman who was watching him like a frightened doe.

"I'm not gonna hurt you. You're okay now." He walked off, but a touch on his arm, although wearing thick leather, sent electricity to his fingers.

"Please, I don't want to be alone."

Atlas sighed again. "Okay, you can come with me. My mom will clean you up and find you a ride wherever you want to go."

"Your mom?"

"Yeah, we all have 'em. I was heading to a family dinner."

And that's how Atlas took a stranger home to dinner.

No wonder his Pops and mom looked at him like he'd grown celery out the top of his head when he walked through the door with the beat-up woman on his arm. He was always prepared to see them in a clinch when he came home. No exception now. His mom was curled in his dad's arms. Thankfully, he'd missed them making out. He liked how they were still in love and wanted to get it on, but he didn't need more childhood trauma from witnessing his dad putting the moves on her.

"What's going on, Son?"

He explained with a few details.

"You get the scene cleaned up?"

"Yep."

"Good."

Scarlett Tucker was about to spring into mom action. He saw it happening as sympathy washed over her gentle face. She was a small framed woman, but fuck, she walloped a mean punch if needed, and she was the biggest protector of them all.

But before that happened.

"Valentina!" His older sister Roux nearly deafened him by screaming. She was staring at the woman clinging to his arm. "What are you doing here? What the hell are you doing with Texas' daughter, Atlas?"

He'd forgotten Roux was in town.

"Ah, fuck." Cursed Axel, like his father and Prez, expected trouble through the door. His stare said a lot, and Atlas only grinned in reply. His dad was a cautious man, always had been, not like Atlas. Axel Tucker wanted his last year as the Diablos President to be uneventful. Guess he wasn't getting his wish.

Wait. What was that?

Looking at the woman, who appeared visibly relieved at seeing his sister, he asked. "You're Texas' daughter?" she nodded, but he still needed confirmation. "From the Renegade Souls?"

"Yes," her voice was delicately sweet.

And that's when he grinned.

Unwittingly, he'd saved another MC princess.

He fucking loved it when he was owed favors.

<u>Up next is Ruin's story.</u>

Renegade Souls MC Romance Saga Series:
Dirty Salvation
Preacher Man
Tracking Luxe
Hades Novella
Filthy Love
Finally Winter
Mistletoe and Outlaws Novella
Resurfaced Passion
Intimately Faithful Novella
Indecent Lies
Law Maker Novella
Savage Outlaw
Renegade Souls MC Collection Boxset 1-3
Prince Charming
Forever Zara Novella
Veiled Amor
Renegade Souls MC Collection Boxset 4-6
Blazing Hope
Darling Psycho

Taboo Love Duet:
It Was Love
It Was Always Love
Taboo Love Collection

Forever Love Companion

From Manhattan Series:
Manhattan Sugar
Manhattan Bet
Manhattan Storm
Manhattan Secret
Manhattan Heart
Manhattan Target
Manhattan Tormentor
Manhattan Muse
Manhattan Protector

Naughty Irish Series:
Naughty Irish Liar

Diablo Disciples MC:

Chains

Reno

Website: www.VTheiaBooks.com
Author Facebook: www.facebook.com/VTheia
Readers Group: Vs Biker Babes

Be the first to know when V. Theia's next book is available. Follow her on <u>Bookbub</u> to get an alert whenever she has a new release.

Made in United States
Cleveland, OH
11 March 2025